Shortcut To The Grave

Ever Chace Chronicles
Book 6

SUSAN HARRIS

SHORTCUT TO THE GRAVE

Summary: Melanie might have taken a shortcut to the grave, but she took to her second life with an ease that surprised everyone. Everything in her life seems to have finally slotted into place—well, apart from a certain sexy-as-sin warlock. The frustrating part is she knows he feels the same, but all the obstacles keep their fire at a frustrating simmer, when she wants things to light up for good.

ISBN: 978-1-63422-428-4 (paperback)
ISBN: 978-1-63422-383-6 (e-book)
Cover Design by: Marya Heidel
Typography by: Courtney Spencer
Editing by: Kelly Risser

Cover Art
© Romolo Tavani/Fotolia

This book can only be dedicated to one person;
The real-life Melanie Newton.
The main reason why book Melanie is so badass and amazing
is because I had the best inspiration to work with.
You inspire me every single day
and
I am so lucky to call you my friend.
(Even if you are to blame for my Funko addition.)

PROLOGUE

T he music pulsed from the club below, the vibrations from the hip-hop track shaking the foundation of the building so hard that up here, on the roof, the vampire felt his toes tingle from the strength of it. The party had carried on for hours, and now, as dawn rapidly approached, it would continue throughout the day.

There wasn't a supernatural creature that danced and fornicated in the abandoned building who cared what time it was. Perhaps, they didn't even know. The building that had once been an apartment complex now lay empty, providing the perfect place for the lower classes of the supernatural community to come and sample the delights that awaited them.

The vampire put his hands up in the air and shuffled in time with the beat, his blood on fire. It had been almost a decade since he had felt such a rush as the high he was on right now. These thrills had escaped him since the night that he became a vampire, having been turned by a vampire who thought he could pay off his drug debts working as a bit of muscle for the older vampire.

Just because you became a vampire didn't mean that your vices were magically erased. The hunger, the craving to not feel at all stayed with you, however you were unable to fulfil that desire. Blood was nutrition, it kept you alive, so to speak. But nothing could compare to the rush of blood to the head that came when you snorted a line of coke or flooded your veins with heroin.

1

The Viking had changed all that. He had found a way to create a drug that could get any supe high as a fucking kite. And the vampire was buzzing. He'd drunk, and he'd fucked, his way through the night and danced like the good ole days when he had raved with the best of them.

He could feel morning approach even as the effects of the drug began to wear off. The bitterness that haunted him began to creep back into his mind. One single tablet and he was hooked. There was no turning back from White Rabbit, his new and improved brand of high.

Feeling the first hint of the sun rising in the distance, the vampire looked over the city of Cork and marvelled at how beautiful it appeared from up here. Continuing to dance, he stepped up onto the ledge of the building, and as the first pangs of despair that always happened when coming down from a high began to shimmer in his body, the vampire knew he was freer now than ever, now that he had found the White Rabbit.

The sun's rays struck a match against his skin, and he slowly caught alight. He hesitated until his entire body was aflame with an orange glow. Then, with his skin burning and his body dying, he stepped off the ledge of the four-story building, freefalling through the air.

Even as his flesh burnt and his bones charred, the vampire did not utter a scream or any expression of the obvious agony that he was feeling.

Instead he went to his death with a smile on his face even as he smacked into the concrete floor that awaited him.

CHAPTER ONE

MELANIE

"Vampire girl, he's coming your way."

Melanie rolled her eyes at the sound of Donnie's voice in her earpiece, but still readied herself to grab the perp who had the team running all over supernatural central for most of the night.

The Clurichaun, a distant cousin of the leprechauns, had been fired from a local pub located on the fringes of supernatural central. He had gotten drunk, fallen asleep, and allowed revellers to drink the pub dry. The Clurichaun had not taken his firing well and used magic to turn all the alcohol bad. According to the owner of the pub, he caused a mass brawl to ensue, wrecking the joint.

And considering that for the last three months things had been creepily quiet on the supernatural crime spree front, Melanie and her team working for P.I.T, the Paranormal Investigations Team, had all but volunteered to go after the mischievous Clurichaun to pry themselves away from the sheer boredom that had plagued them.

You would think being told that Ever was a Valkyrie and her father, Odin, planned to usher in the famous Ragnorok would have made things a tad more exciting than normal. Sadly, that was not the case.

Yeah, Melanie had been training her ass off with Kenzie and Erika, under the watchful eye of her sire, Caitlyn. She'd become stronger, faster, meaner. Concentrating on bettering herself took her mind off the one person who never strayed far from it, even if he hadn't so much as sent her a solitary text over the last 90 days to let her know how he was doing, just to reassure her that he was okay.

Not that I'm bitter or anything.

Melanie inhaled a breath to focus on the task at hand and not on the warlock who was off trying to rid himself of an addiction. She didn't need it, considering she was dead, but it allowed her to catch a hint of the Clurichaun's scent as he came closer to where she hid in the shadows. He smelled of wheat and barley, and it tickled her nose.

"Melanie, he's on you in three, two-"

Melanie dropped to her knees and snapped out her arm, and the Clurichaun ran smack into it. It was almost comical how the little creature did a full rotation, up and over, before landing on his back with a groan. Rising to her full height, Melanie reached into the back pocket of her black jeans and snapped the magical cuffs around the wrists of the Clurichaun. He looked up at her with emerald green eyes, hazed over from the copious amounts of alcohol he had consumed, and grinned.

"Hello, gorgeous!"

Donnie chuckled as he came up beside her. Melanie glanced up as she heard a whoosh, watching as Kenzie stepped off the roof above and landed with catlike grace on the path beside them. Melanie could hear the beat of Kenzie's very human heart, but she was far from human. She was blood kissed; ageless due to the fact that she had drunk the blood of the first vampire, Cain, for many a year. She appeared to be about seventeen years old, yet in a couple of months, the young woman would turn twenty-eight.

Dressed head to toe in black, with a wicked looking scythe strapped to her back, Kenzie was a mirror image of Melanie's sire Caitlyn, who just so happened to be a very distant relative of Kenzie's. Some people had trouble telling them apart, well, those who couldn't hear the beat of Kenzie's heart that is. For them, the newly coloured ends of Kenzie's raven black hair were a clear giveaway to who stood in front of them.

However, it took a foolish man to mistake that either woman was any less dangerous than the other. They had both been forged under the streets of Paris, in different ways, and held a darkness inside them that might never leave.

And aren't you the same? Does the darkness of death not come back to haunt you? Aren't you the one who wakes with a silent scream caught in your throat as you remember the feel of the blade sliding in and out of your flesh?

Lifting her eyes, Melanie gave Donnie a sheepish smile as his own frown greeted her. Sometimes, she forgot that Donnie could read everyone's mind. Working with Caitlyn, Melanie had practiced shielding her thoughts from him as part of her training. She had promised to come to him and Caitlyn if her nightmares became too much. But how could she bother Caitlyn with her haunted thoughts when her sire's screams still woke her during the day, even when the monster who inflicted such scars was dead. As was hers.

But that did not seem to reassure her when the icy fear locked her spine when she was alone at night. It puzzled her that she had nightmares, considering she was absolutely delighted with her second life. The missing piece that she had felt throughout her human life had been found when she was made a vampire.

She had lost nothing with her shortcut to the grave, in comparison to Caitlyn who had lost everything when she became a vampire. How could she reconcile her nightmares when she didn't deserve the right to feel like that?

"You good?"

Donnie's concerned voice dragged her back from her thoughts, and she smiled in response. Thankfully, Kenzie seemed oblivious to Melanie's inner turmoil. The former assassin clapped her on the shoulder, her grin wide and carefree.

"Course she is, Donnie. Perp is on the ground, and there are still a few hours left before daylight. Let's get this idiot back to the station, and we can get a few hours of training in."

Melanie groaned, wishing that her friend was a little bit more normal and wanted to go dancing or anything other than training. Kenzie's grin deepened as she brushed the green-tipped strands of hair off her shoulders, and Donnie reached down and plucked the Clurichaun off the ground.

"Erika said to take the night off. She's off doing something with Loki. Rest up. Watch a movie."

Melanie felt like she needed to clear her head, just stroll around for a while, but if she said she wanted to be alone, Kenzie and Donnie would worry about her and feel the need to stick to her and save her from her melancholy. Caitlyn would understand the need for some solitude; she had more than once walked around the city alongside her without uttering a word.

But both Kenzie and Donnie were social creatures, but growing up in a family where she was overlooked most of the time, Melanie felt comfortable being by herself. Trying to muster up the courage to ask for the time to herself, Donnie nudged Kenzie's shoulder.

"Let's take, Mr. Drunkard back to the station, Kenz. Melanie, didn't Caitlyn ask you to stop by Ricky's and make sure everything was okay?"

God, she could have kissed him...but she wouldn't because

he was like her dad or brother or whatever his mating to Caitlyn had made him.

Donnie chuckled and shook his head as he held her gaze for a minute and said, "Get indoors before morning."

"Yes, *mom!*" Melanie retorted with a mock salute as Donnie nudged Kenzie to move on. They strode away with their prisoner in tow.

"You gotta spoil all my fun!"

"Kenzie, take a night off. Your brand of fun tends to lead to bloodshed."

"Exactly!"

Melanie smiled to herself as her friends and housemates rounded the corner and went out of earshot. There had been a lot of adjustments in the last year, and Kenzie probably had the biggest adjustment besides Caitlyn. The young woman went from having no family or friends to being engulfed in our big and nosey family.

Sometimes, when she thought that no one is looking, Melanie saw Kenzie look around at one of their now weekly gatherings, and blink back tears as if she couldn't believe that she was surrounded by all of this love and acceptance. Melanie knew what she was thinking because it's what she thought too.

Shaking off her thoughts of melancholy, Melanie shoved her hands into her pockets and began to walk toward Ricky's house. She should have known that Donnie would know where she went every couple of nights. It made her feel better, checking on Ricky's house while he was off getting better.

She would never get the image out of her head of Ricky backed into a corner, blaming her for his drug use as his powers threatened to overpower him. He hadn't meant it – Melanie had tasted the lie on her tongue–another perk of her new life. It just pained her so much to see someone she lo– ...someone she cared so much for, hurting so much.

And his son, that beautiful carbon copy of his father who

had just lost his mother and landed on Ricky's doorstep. Melanie hoped that during his recovery, Ricky and Zach could form a bond. She knew deep in her heart that Ricky would give everything he had to be the best he could possibly be for his son.

She pulled her leather jacket snugly around her, for comfort more than anything, considering she was dead, and the cold didn't bother her now. Melanie pulled her headphones from her pocket and popped them into her ears, letting her mind drift as her playlist shuffled through random tracks.

Striding around Cork at night had become one of her favourite past times. There was something so magical about walking around while half the world was asleep, the night sky so dark and vast above her. Once, she would have been terrified to venture too far on her own, knowing that monsters, both human and supernatural, tended to hunt by night.

Now, she was one of the monsters and could hold her own. Even though Melanie had died because of Stephen Donnelly and his need to be become supernatural and stop himself from dying, she was conflicted about how to feel about him in the end. Had he not been the catalyst that had given her the life she had always wanted?

As Drake gave way to a Lindsey Sterling song, one of Caitlyn's favourites, Melanie realized she had walked far quicker than she expected. She had wandered far from the city centre, past Kent train station, and now came to the small secluded bungalow where Ricky had his quant little house.

Normally, on nights when she walked by to simply check on the house in his absence, it was shrouded in darkness, empty and free from the charming man that made her ache. But now, a faint light emitted from the front of the house, a shadow passing in front of the kitchen window before the light winked out.

If her heart could beat, then Melanie was sure it would be racing. It was probably nothing and her imagination was running away with her. However, if someone had broken in and was up to no good, then she would certainly kick some ass.

Pulling her earbuds out, she pressed pause on her phone and contemplated firing off a quick text to Donnie for backup. The other vampire would be here in a flash, and they could both go in together. Melanie shook her head, telling herself that she was indeed an agent of P.I.T and could handle one little perp all by herself.

Thankfully she had a spare key that Derek had given her when he realized she was stopping by Ricky's on a regular basis.

"No point the two of us checking on the place," Derek had told her with a grin before handing her the key.

Slipping it into the lock, she turned the knob slowly, grimacing as the door creaked when she pushed it open. The same scents that always hit her smack bang in the gut whenever she walked in hit her now, leather and motorcycle oil, and now, a faint layer of cat from Zach.

Her eyes were quick to adjust to the dark, scanning the hallway for any sense of movement and listening for the slightest hint of sound. Moving into the cross section of the house where it veered off toward the bedroom or into the living room, Melanie took a step into the living room, cursing herself as she heard the steady heartbeat a second too late, as a gun cocked and rested against her temple.

"You picked the wrong goddamn house to step up to."

Oh, that voice as smooth as honey, one she had craved to hear for the last 90 days, washed over her and she shivered. Smiling to herself, she sighed, rolling her eyes at him even though he couldn't see her do it.

"Look at you, sounding all gangsta and shit. Kanye would be well impressed."

"Lanie? Damn, I nearly shot you!"

Melanie waited as Ricky flicked on the lights and she could drink in the sight of him, her eyes latching onto his emerald ones. She huffed out a breath of relief when she saw that his eyes were clear and alert. Scanning her gaze over him, she took in his mussed black hair, the dark stubble on his chin and finely trimmed beard that seemed to caress his full lips. He wore long shorts to his knees and a vest top.

Ricky had always appeared hot as sin to her, but his arms seemed to have more definition, and he had a new tattoo on his forearm that wasn't in English. Ricky smirked as she roamed her eyes over him and she felt her face heat, even though it was impossible for her to do so.

"What are you doing here, Lanie?"

His tone was tight and clipped as if he had done something wrong and been caught out, but she ignored it. Now that she could catch his scent and see with her own eyes that he was sober, she could not hold his reaction against him because she had intruded on his space.

Stepping further into the room, Melanie leaned against the arm of one of the chairs and tucked her hair behind her ears. "I came to check on the place, make sure everything was alright. Had you bothered to send a text or call, then I'd have known not to bother stopping by because you were home. You are home, right?"

Ricky rubbed the back of his head as he glanced down at the wooden floor. "Yeah, I am. I just didn't tell the rest of them yet. I needed time to get myself and the little man settled back in."

"How long have you been back?"

"A week."

"Oh."

Melanie couldn't hide the disappointment in her voice as she considered he had been home for a week and hadn't thought to text her. And he knew that he had hurt her because he closed the door, leaving it slightly ajar before he slumped down on the sofa.

"I'm sorry I didn't text you or call. I ...I ...damn...I was not in a good place for a while, and the counsellor thought it best that I spend time sorting myself out before contacting anyone. There were so many goddamn times I picked up my phone and typed a message and then erased it."

Ricky sounded so sincere that she couldn't feel angry at him in the slightest anymore.

"It's okay. You had to do what was right for you. You had to get better. That's all that's important. Are you?"

Ricky quirked a brow. "Am I what?"

"Better?" Melanie asked, wanting him to be so.

"One day at a time. That's what they teach you. To focus on today. Up to now, I've been doing better. I still wanna get high. I still crave it, and that's okay. What matters is that I won't do anything about it."

Melanie smiled and when Ricky returned her grin, her stomach did somersaults.

"Why not let us know that you guys were back? I know that Caitlyn would only be too happy to take Zach off your hands for a while. We were all very worried about you, Ricky. We still are."

Ricky scrubbed his hands down his face. "I know ye are. But Zach had to get enrolled in school. Plus, I had legal stuff to sort out with Fionn. Sadie hadn't even fucking bothered to list me as his dad on his birth cert. I had to do some weird DNA test with Zach to get proof before I could even get his medical records. She left such a goddamn mess after her and..."

Ricky broke off as a spark of blue flame came to life on his fingers. Leaning back in the chair, he closed his eyes. Melanie watched him, and she could almost feel him count to ten in his head while he inhaled and exhaled to relax.

When the flames vanished, Ricky lifted his head and his eyes to meet hers, a sad expression on his face.

"One day at a time, right?" Melanie said, pushing as much cheer into her voice as possible.

"Yeah…I guess."

Melanie's phone chimed with a warning that daylight was fast approaching, and she needed to get home fairly sharpish. Standing up, with Ricky following suit, she gave him a quick hug, stepping free of the embrace before signs and signals could get all mixed up.

"I'm really glad you're home, Ricky."

The warlock grinned as he walked her out to the door, holding it open for her as she stepped out onto the moonlight.

"Lanie?"

"Yeah."

Ricky rubbed the back of his neck again. "Don't tell the guys that I'm back yet… if you don't mind. Zach starts school in the morning, and I just wanna make sure the kid is settled before he gets overwhelmed by all his aunties and uncles."

Melanie considered that perhaps it was Ricky who was afraid of being overwhelmed by the team, tasting the half-truth in his words, but she kept that to herself for now. She nodded and told him to make sure he took pictures of Zach in the morning.

Melanie could feel the weight of his gaze on her as she walked away, and she told herself not to look back. But when she did, when she gave in to her compulsion, Ricky was still standing in the doorway watching her go.

CHAPTER TWO

RICKY

Watching her walk away, Ricky fought against the urge to call her back, to spill the beans of the extent of what had happened to him while he had been off to rehab. Or to finish what he started before his mind had been fogged by drugs and magic. Yet, Ricky held back, because while the last three months had not been a picnic for him, he had put his friends through the ringer, and he owed it them to prove that he had redeemed himself.

As Melanie's silhouette vanished in the distance, Ricky closed the front door and strode into the kitchen. With a mere hour or two before Zach would be up and about, there was really no point in trying to go back to sleep. Flicking on the switch on the kettle, Ricky opened the cabinet door above the cooker, his eyes falling on the half bottle of whiskey.

Drink it.

It will calm your nerves.

No one will know.

Reaching up, he gripped the jar of coffee next to the booze, pulling his arm back and closing the cupboard door. Smiling at the small victory, Ricky mixed up his coffee and waited for the kettle to boil. Draven told him that testing himself in such a way was reckless, that he walked a very thin line with his feeble attempts to prove to himself that he could abstain.

To Draven, he was reckless; but to Ricky, every single time he said no when the demons in his mind encouraged him to indulge, it was as if he had fought and won the smallest of battles. He needed that.

One of the counsellors at Havana told him he could still drink, but in moderation. Every single part of his life would need to be done in moderation now, for fear of relapse. Ricky had never done anything in his life in moderation, but he was willing to try.

The kettle boiled, and Ricky poured the boiling water into his mug and stirred, not flinching at the way his magic stirred at the heat of the mug when he lifted it to his lips and drank deep. Glancing down at the ring on his finger, Ricky fiddled with it as he drank his coffee, knowing he no longer needed the damn thing, but he kept it where it was as a crutch, just in case he lost control again.

Making his way into the sitting room, Ricky sank down on the couch and leaned back, the mug still gripped in his hands. He tried to reassure himself that his friends would be happy to see him. He was the one who had cut off contact while he was in rehab to concentrate on getting himself well and bond with his son.

Draven, true to his word, had stayed for the first month with Ricky, his mom and Zach in the onsite cabin that his friends had paid for, and man, had he earned his keep. Draven did more in that first month for Ricky than he could ever have imagined, and there was no way he could ever repay him.

Crooked smile tugging at his lips, Ricky reminisced about the first day Draven had introduced his method of get Ricky clean and sober, and Ricky's initial reaction to it. Now, he felt restless if he didn't follow Draven's fitness regime.

A knock sounded at the door before it flung open, Ricky barely had time to cover his eyes before the curtains were yanked open, and he was blinded by the sun. Draven stood in front of said window, his face grim and his arms folded firmly across his chest. He was dressed in what Ricky suspected was running gear, and Ricky was so not interested in being his running partner.

"No, just hell no."

"Both the body and mind must be strong to overcome what is to follow."

Burying himself under the covers, Ricky scowled at Draven. "My body is good. I pass my fitness tests for the department every goddamn year. I don't need all that bullshi-"

"Richard Moore." Ricky darted upright at the sound of his mother's voice, and he knew by her tone that arguing was futile.

"Richard Moore, you get out of that bed right now, and you do as Draven tells you to. We did not put our lives on hold for you to sit back and not listen to the advice given to you. I raised you better. Now get up."

"Yes, Ma'am." Ricky could not argue at her logic, so he shooed them from the room and dressed in the clothes and running shoes that Draven set down on the bed for him. Ricky nodded to his mother as he strode out the door of the cabin and breathed in the crisp morning air. Draven was stretching when Ricky strode out and indicated for Ricky to copy him.

Of course, Ricky felt extremely stupid, stretching out his limbs, and he grumbled while doing so. Draven shot him a look that had him closing his mouth and staying silent. It was the least he could do after all.

Draven spoke in a soft tone that prickled on Ricky's nerves. "You have induction at nine, and they will explain how the next three months will go. They have classes you can go to and occupy your mind. Group activities you are encouraged to attend. Each evening, you are free to return here for time with your family."

Ricky rolled his eyes, but Draven continued.

"Every morning, you will rise at dawn and join me in a run. After

*a week or two, we will began training your mind to calmness and work
on some practical ways of self-defence where you are not solely depen-
dent on your magic."*

And then Draven took off in a slow jog, not waiting for Ricky to
follow but knowing that he would.

And he had, every single morning for two weeks. Slowly,
Ricky began to enjoy the routine of it, could feel his body
growing strong and the fog in his mind clearing. Sometimes, he
went out for a run himself after dinner, music pumping in his
ears, especially if he'd had a bad day during one of his mandated
therapy sessions.

Telling a stranger all about himself and what had driven him
to take the white rabbit from Tadgh had not come easy to him,
and Ricky had more than once vented his anger. But, to the
therapist's detriment, he never pushed Ricky too hard, as he
believed Ricky would have to trust him before they would make
any progress at all.

Even when, after a painful lesson in magic with Draven, and
an argument with his son over something so stupid he couldn't
remember how it started, Ricky had gone for a run and ended
up in a bar. He sat, sweat soaking his skin, a finger of whiskey in
front of him. He stared at the drink for about an hour, shaking
his head as the man behind the bar offered him something else
to take the edge off.

Ricky had sat there for an age longer before he shot off a text
and asked Draven to come and get him, because he did not
know if he could leave the bar by himself. Draven replied
stating he had been in the carpark waiting for Ricky's text and
would wait until he had the strength to leave of his own
volition.

It took him another hour of battling with his mind before
Ricky strode out that door and got his ass into the car. Draven
never said a word but nodded his approval. The next morning,
Ricky was outside stretching before Draven emerged from the

cabin.

After that night, Ricky had made a conscious decision to be present in all of his rehab related stuff, not just physically like he had been, but mentally.

He learned so much about himself that it surprised him. He now understood where his triggers stemmed from: Sadie, his Da, his own need to try and rebel against everything his father wanted him to be. He voiced his fears over Zach and not being able to be a good father to him.

He spilled his guts about his feelings of inadequacy within the team, that he was the weakest link. He even told his therapist about his feelings for Melanie, and how he had resented her for being so much better at being a supernatural then he was. It cut him like a knife to voice it.

Ricky used to think that those who needed therapy were weak, but the energy it took out of him every single session, and the exhaustion that overwhelmed him, proved he had been wrong all along. It took a shitload of strength to seek help when you needed it.

"Ricky?" A small voice dragged him from his thoughts, and he turned to face his son. Glasses perched on the bridge of his nose, Zach was a mirror image of Ricky, down to the black hair and green eyes. Because the boy needed glasses, his own people saw him as defective. It was the only reason Fionn had handed custody of Zach to Ricky–to protect him. The shifters did not value what they saw as weakness.

"Hey lil' man, you all excited for school?"

"No."

The tone was one Ricky was familiar with, since it came out of his own mouth more times than not. He regarded his son with a smile.

"You liked the school when we went to visit last week right? They are gonna teach you how to use your magic as well as be a cat. The teachers are really nice. You promised to try for at least two weeks... remember?"

The boy nodded. "You said you'd teach me to play the guitar if I promised to try my hardest."

"And I couldn't ask for anything more. Today's Friday you know, so no school tomorrow. You can stay up a little later, and we can watch a movie."

The boy's eyes lit up. "Can we watch Black Panther?"

"Again?" Ricky asked not bothering to mask his amusement. He could recite the film word by word by now, considering this could possibly be the hundredth time they watched it together. Ricky would do anything to bond naturally with his son, and if he had to watch a movie over and over again, then he would do it.

Zach nodded eagerly, and Ricky chuckled, rising to his feet and ruffling his son's hair, making sure to do so behind the ears and earning a purr from the small boy.

"Then it's a deal. So, go pick out something to wear. Wash and dress and...?"

"Brush my teeth." Zach groaned.

"Exactly. Now, off you go. Do you need any help?"

The boy strode off ignoring him, and Ricky rolled his eyes behind his son's retreating back. Ricky waited until the door closed behind Zach before he went to his own room and dressed. He itched to go for a run and clear his head, but that could wait until after Zach was safe in school. Then, Ricky would be alone with all that was on his mind.

And his resolve would be truly tested.

Dressed in jeans and a t-shirt, Ricky made his way back to the kitchen and poured some of Zach's favourite cereal in a bowl. Opening the fridge, he took out the lunch he had made last night for Zach and put it into his Black Panther schoolbag. The child was a little obsessed, and Ricky was trying his darndest not to spoil him rotten, but considering he'd missed out in the first five years of his life, the boy could be a little spoiled.

"When do we get to see the vampires again?"

That question was one of the most asked questions by his son. Another one of the little guy's obsessions was vampires, especially Caitlyn, and he had been asking to see them since they arrived back in Cork last week. Up until now, Ricky hadn't felt he could face Caitlyn, Donnie, Derek and especially Melanie. Even Sarge, because that man had been more of a father to him in the years he had known him, and Ricky had let him down.

Ricky pointed to the bowl of cereal, waited until Zach had begun to chew the brightly coloured grains before he said, "I'm heading into the station today to talk to my boss about going back to work. How about I ask Caitlyn if we can stop by, maybe Sunday evening, to see her on the way to Grandma's house?"

The boy nodded eagerly as he ate his breakfast. It had taken the full three months to fall into this pattern of some ease, plus countless arguments, countless nights where Ricky lay awake and doubted himself. His mother, bless her, tried not to interfere, allowing Ricky to be the parent he so desperately wanted to be. Zach had ignored him for the most part, only curling up to him when there was music or movies involved. Ricky had grown frustrated, not knowing what the hell to do.

One night, deep in the Armagh countryside, over a coffee, his mother had told him that Zach had lost so much and been shunned by everyone who he knew growing up. It would take time to trust Ricky, because he probably feared Ricky would leave him as well.

And Ricky even had one of his questions answered where Sadie was concerned, and the burning hatred tainting his mind lessened after a conversation with Zach.

"Momma told me you sang like an angel."

The statement came out of the blue, one rare sunny afternoon as Zach played outside and Ricky strummed his guitar and sang a tune. He'd stumbled over the chords at the statement, setting the guitar down as Zach crawled into his lap, and Ricky thought his heart would burst.

"Your mom liked to sit and listen to me play while she read her books." It was the hardest thing Ricky had done, speak of Sadie without malice or resentment in his tone. But Zach would not grow up with a father who spoke ill of his mother.

"Momma told me stuff before she died."

His words were muttered against his chest, so Ricky placed his fingers on the boy's chin and lifted his eyes to meet Ricky's.

"Do you want to tell me?"

"I don't want to make you sad. Momma said she made you sad and could not make you happy again."

Ricky's heart almost broke as the child explained it so clearly, his innocence such a wonderous thing.

"You can always talk to me about your mom. Even if you think it will make me sad."

Zach crinkled his nose, pushed his glasses up his nose but said nothing else.

Ricky gently said to him, "Did your mom tell you about why we were no longer friends?"

With a small nod, Zach replied, "Momma said she had done a very bad, silly thing and hurt your feelings. She said she was not hon... hon..."

"Honest?"

"Yeah, she was not honest with you, and it made you not like her very much. But she told me that you would love me because I was the berry best parts of each of you. Is that true?"

Biting back the grin that twitched his lips at the mispronunciation, Ricky thanked Sadie silently, who, in her own way, had owned up to her mistakes, and now, Ricky had to take ownership of his own.

"Your mom did some silly things, but so did I. I treated her very badly, and I'm sorry that meant I didn't get to know you sooner. But I loved your mom very much, and she was right. You are the best parts of us both."

"I miss her." Zach sniffed.

"I know you do, buddy, and that's okay. You can talk to me anytime about your mom, okay?"

"Okay."

And from then on, at least Ricky knew that Sadie hadn't shoved the blame all the way in his direction. He respected the hell out of her for it.

Glancing down at his boy, Ricky had to nearly force him to brush his teeth and out the door so that they would not be late. Arriving at the school gates, Ricky ignored all the admiring glances in his direction as Zach slipped his hand into Ricky's, his nails digging into his dad's skin.

Ricky crouched down, so he was face to face with Zach. "You got this, bud."

"If you say so."

Ricky got back to his feet and ushered Zach into his class. Frozen to the spot, he clung to Ricky's leg, and it took a lot of persuasion to pry him from that position. In the end, it wasn't Ricky or the teacher, but another boy who asked Zach if he wanted to join their band. Zach was gone without even a goodbye.

Like father, like son, eh?

Ricky lingered outside in the halls until he was shooed away by the teacher with a smile on her face.

When he walked out and into the sun, he slipped on his shades and strode down the path until a figure leaning against a car stopped him in his tracks.

Of course Derek would have known the moment Ricky arrived back in Cork. His friend was a handsome bastard, his eyes watching Ricky like only a wolf could. His face was a mask of indifference, yet Ricky could see the tension coiled in his closest friend's body.

"You look good."

"I feel good," Ricky replied, shoving his hands into his pocket. "Did Melanie tell you I was back?"

"No…. your mam did."

"Figures."

They stared at each other for a while, neither knowing what to say. In the end, Ricky bit the bullet and ran a hand over the nape of his neck.

"I was planning on coming by the station later. Few things I needed to do first and collect Zach at midday."

Derek still said nothing, and Ricky blew out a frustrated breath. "What do you want from me, D?"

"I just want to know my friend is alright. That he's not hiding anything else from his team and family."

The anger and fear in his tone was a hundred percent warranted. And Ricky made to laugh it off, but swallowed back his go to method of deflection. Lifting his gaze, Ricky looked into the eyes of a man gone wolf, the amber burning in his friend's brown eyes.

Talking a step closer, Ricky told Derek the mantra he had forced himself to say to the reflection in the mirror every single morning.

"I am an addict. Today I stand at 96 days clean and sober. I own my mistakes and strive to be better than I was yesterday. I am not responsible for how others see me, only for how I present myself to them. I will work to make amends to those I hurt while I was less than myself," Ricky paused, lifting his brows at Derek, a tick in the jaw the only indication that Derek had heard him at all.

"And if anyone has a problem with that, they can go fuck themselves."

Derek engulfed him in a hug and Ricky let him, trying to

ignore the way his heart pounded in his ears as Derek muttered, "Welcome back, partner."

THE TABLE and all its contents ended up on the floor with a crash as Freya roared her frustration, as each tiny step she took sent fresh waves of agony through her spine. From the moment Odin had driven a blade into her back and severed her spinal cord, Freya had been pushing herself to get back on her feet, literally.

Her anger had grown, the bitterness at being helpless ate away at her. The Valkyrie attended to her as was their duty, but she saw it in their eyes when they looked at her, broken and defeated, that they feared she would never be the warrior she was.

Freya knew that was what they thought because it was what she also thought. Healers said that the damage was so extensive, Freya may never gain control of her lower limbs. Ten days later, Freya moved her toes. Two weeks later, she stood for the first time with Danae holding her up like a crutch.

Today, Freya took her fifth step forward in succession before she crumpled to the ground, her scream carrying with the wind.

"Perhaps, now is the time to call Ever and Erika back to Valhalla?"

"I said no."

"But Freya..."

"I ordered you against it, Valkyrie. Do you question my orders?"

"No Ma'am."

Freya braced her arms in front of her and dragged herself up to her feet again slowly. She would heal herself. She would be strong. She would not fail.

For when the time came, and it would, Freya would drive her sword through Odin's heart. She would cripple him, one way or another. For Freya was a keeper of secrets, and the biggest secret had yet to be revealed.

Standing on trembling legs, Freya steadied herself and called forth one of her healers.

"Again." She ordered, and the healer obeyed, sending healing waves up and along Freya's spine.

The burn tingled all the way down to her legs, and Freya, as stubborn as she had always been, defied the odds and took another step forward.

And then the warrior smiled.

CHAPTER THREE

"Focus."

The word came out in a growled order as Ever brushed a stray strand of golden blonde hair from her eyes. Considering she had recently remembered that she was a Valkyrie queen to be and could kick some serious ass, she was more used to giving orders than receiving them, and being ordered about, especially by a male, should have irked her nerves.

But when the male giving her orders was handsome, muscular and shirtless, it was hard to focus in the slightest. He stood in front of her, all 6ft 2in of him, dressed in loose track pants that hung dangerously low on his lean hips. He was barefoot and mouth wateringly delicious.

"Maybe," Ever smirked, yanking off her own sweat laden vest, standing in nothing but a training bra and shorts. "if you weren't standing there, all shirtless and gorgeous, a girl could concentrate."

Derek Doyle gave her a wolfish grin as he began to circle her, his eyes never leaving hers. She mirrored his movements, bracing herself for another attack.

"Focus," was all her mate said, but the order was gone from his tone, and now he was simply playing with his prey.

Three months can change a lot, especially when your megalomaniac father was off licking his wounds somewhere after Erika, Loki and Thor had dented his ancient pride. When Ever decided that she was tired of running, of letting fate decide her happiness. Once she decided to live in the moment, things had gotten a hell of a lot easier, especially for her and Derek.

On the night Erika spilled to the team about her plan to defeat Odin, Derek had laid his heart out on the table, telling her that if she did not want him, he would still stand by her side, protect her with his last breath, Ever knew that she could not be without him, even if it meant that their time together was short.

She chose to push memories of past lives with Derek to the back of her mind, because she, this Ever Chace, loved Derek Doyle with every fibre of her being. This was the life that she wanted. This was the man she wanted as her own.

"So, what do you think, Ever? Do we do this thing together?"

She faced away from him, closing the door before she turned back. Reaching down, she yanked her t-shirt over her head and dropped it to the floor, a rush coming over her as lust flared in his eyes.

Heart beating a tattoo in her chest, she came to stand before him and wrapped her arms around his neck.

"Together, Derek. We do this together."

Derek's mouth was on hers a second later, his hands on her hips holding her firmly in place in case she decided to run again. She wanted his hands on her skin, she wanted his lips on her body. She wanted to imprint herself on his skin so that everyone knew they were one.

She broke from his searing kiss to a press her lips to the chiselled jaw, her hands gently caressing his chest. When Ever used her teeth on the pulse at Derek's neck, he growled, but it was not a warning growl. It sent a shudder through her.

"Ever."

Derek's growl dragged her back from her thoughts, a smug

grin on his face and eyebrow raised. "I know what you're thinking about, but save it for later. Much later."

His words gave a hint of sensual promise, and Ever grinned back at him. "I have no idea what you are talking about. I was merely thinking of how sweaty we already were."

Derek rolled his eyes and chuckled, and then he snapped back to serious Derek and lunged for her so quickly, she had to use all of her speed to dodge his grasp. Ever twisted and with the force of her movement, she caught Derek with an elbow to the stomach, earning a grunt from her mate. He braced his feet and lifted his fists, raising both brows this time in challenge.

This routine had become second nature to them. They trained, they prepared, they solved crimes, and then they went home together, though the later was still the cause of some argument between them. Ever wanted to stay in her home, and Derek wanted his. They were both as stubborn as the other, so they spent alternative nights. Even if they had an argument, they always ended up under the same roof every night.

That was except when Erika needed girl time away from Loki.

Derek took his opportunity, kicking out with his foot, hard enough to jerk her back and earn a return a growl of her own.

"You know that when I face Odin, none of this will matter, right? I will need to use my powers to summon enough lightning to combat his own. I should be practising with Erika. Not that I don't enjoy our little sessions …." She trailed off with a grin as Derek circled her again.

"When *we* face Odin," Derek stressed, his lips turned down in a frown. It was still hard to imagine all of them going up against Odin for her, to help her. "We need to be ready. If whatever powers you have fail, then you must be able to defend yourself."

Ever indicated down to herself. "Um, Hello. Valkyrie here, I know how to fight. And I'm centuries older than you! I should be the one training you!"

"I do love an older woman."

It was Ever's turn to roll her eyes. It would seem that Derek had developed a wicked sense of humour lately as if he was trying to compensate for the much loved, sarcastic warlock that was noticeably absent for the last few months. Derek didn't talk about it, but Ever knew it was killing him that he didn't know that Ricky had been on a downward spiral, and that was primarily down to her.

This time, when Derek punched out a fist, Ever ducked, using some tricks that Erika had taught her. She dodged under his oncoming blow, using her smaller frame as leverage to get close to his body. When she was at his side, Ever hooked her leg around the back of his knee and dragged him down with her as she went to her knees.

Derek hit the ground with a grunt, his body slamming hard against the training mat as Ever straddled his hips, grinned down at him, her hands on her hips in confident pride.

A smile played over his lips before Ever was suddenly pinned under the wolf, not that she was complaining. They were both breathing heavily, Derek's eyes turned amber with lust as he leaned down to press his lips to hers. Her hands drifted into Derek's hair to drag him down closer, and Ever wrapped her legs around his waist, locking him in place.

"Showers." Derek groaned against her lips.

"I would prefer, wolf, if you would stop manhandling my sister for one moment."

A booming voice doused any flames of lust. Ever squirmed out from under Derek and got to her feet. In front of her stood her most beloved brother, Thor. His reddish hair was pulled back into a ponytail, his armour of Asgardian metal was gone and replaced by boots, jeans and a long-sleeved t-shirt. He might look ordinary, if not for the 7ft height and the obvious wave of power that rolled off him.

Erika had told her of Thor's actions against Odin, yet Thor had not come to visit Ever since then, and she feared he was angry with her. Yet, the smile on his face as he ran his eyes full of thunder over her sent her racing toward him.

"*Bróðir*," Ever said in old Norse, jumping into his arms and laughing as he twirled her around, as if she were not the eldest sibling in this embrace. "Brother, it is so good to see you."

"And you, little Valkyrie. I told Loki that I would stop by."

"I'm afraid our brother has been rather distracted by a certain Valkyrie General of late."

A throat cleared behind them, and Ever turned to see Derek pulling a t-shirt on. She was suddenly nervous, introducing Derek to the brother she loved dearly. As if sensing her reluctance, Derek strode forward with the confidence of a wolf and held out his hand to Thor, as if he were a mere mortal and not the god of thunder.

"Derek Doyle. I'm Ever's mate."

"I know who it is that you are, Champion."

A muscle ticked in Derek's jaw, but Thor took his hand eventually. "Do I need to tell you that if you hurt her in any way, I will grind your bones to sand with my hammer?"

"If I ever hurt her, I will gladly give myself over to be ground to sand by your hammer."

They stared at each other for a moment, nerves fluttering in Ever's stomach, but then Thor clasped Derek on the shoulder so hard that Ever feared he had dislocated Derek's shoulder.

"You will do, wolf. You will do."

Thor stepped back and peered down at Ever. "I come bearing news from Odin."

Ever's stomach plummeted, even as Derek entwined his fingers with hers.

"Then whatever you tell us needs to be heard by Erika and

Loki." Ever walked over to where her things were placed on the side while she spared with Derek, sending off a text to tell Erika she needed to get to the station a.s.a.p.

Ever had barely put her phone down when the other Valkyrie appeared in a blink of an eye. Small but fierce, Erika was gorgeous, with sun kissed skin, hair and eyes the colour of whisky and curves to die for. She was also the most feared and ferocious warrior to grace the sands of Valhalla. We weren't surprised when…when Erika had recently learned that she was the daughter of the god of war, Tyr, though she had avoided meeting him so far.

Flashing Ever a grin, Erika stuck out her tongue at Derek before her eyes landed on Thor.

"Daughter of Tyr." Thor gave her the typical Asgardian greeting for Erika's lineage, but Erika flinched under it for a moment before she acknowledged him.

"What do you want, Thor Odinson?"

Ever went back to stand beside Derek once again as she spoke, explaining to Erika that Thor had news from Odin.

"Where is my brother, Valkyrie? I hear he is never far from your side."

"She left me handcuffed to the bed, Thor. I felt very abandoned."

Erika snorted as Loki appeared beside her, pressing his lips to her cheek as she rolled her eyes and blew out a breath. "Yes, Loki, darling," she drawled. "Please tell everyone about your sexcapades. Not embarrassing at all."

"Or nauseating."

"Or inappropriate." Ever chimed in after Thor.

Loki bowed low at the waist, eyes full of mischief and mayhem. "Have you met me before?"

Erika folded her arms across her chest and glared at Thor. "Well, Thunder, come on, what's the skinny on Odin?"

Thor looked blankly at her, as if she had spoken in another language.

"Dude, seriously? You are the guardian of earth, and you don't even know how to speak like the puny humans?" Erika teased.

"Can we concentrate on the matter at hand please?" Derek growled, tension flooding his entire body.

Thor shoved his hands into the pockets of his jeans, a very human gesture. "Odin reached out to me, asking me to come forth and propose a conclave. He wants to sit down and discuss a possible truce, to see if an agreement can be reached to end this war once and for all."

"And use it as an excuse to kill Ever? Nah, not happening." Erika spoke the words Ever was thinking. Why now? Why after all this time was Odin looking for a peaceful resolution?

"He has lost us all." Ever muttered, repeating the words louder as if trying to make sense of it. "His favoured son rose up against him, sided with Valkyries, sided with his family against him. He is the Allfather because he is a father to all of us. If we no longer see him as such, does he not lose some of his power? Odin fears he will have nothing left after Ragnarök because it has finally dawned on him that should he succeed and kill me once and for all, then neither Thor nor Loki will ever forgive him."

"You really think that Odin would withdraw from his claim of power because he is afraid of being lonely?" Loki asked her.

"Can you really be a god if there is no one left to worship you?" asked Ever.

Erika shook her head. "Please do not tell me you are considering this? Please do not tell me that somewhere in that pretty little head of yours that you think that Odin is doing this for any other reason but to kill you?"

"He is still our father."

"I think he lost the father of the year badge when he killed you six times in cold blood."

Ever glared at her best friend, even though she knew she was right. This was something that needed to be thought through in depth. It was worth hearing what Odin proposed, even if it was a rouse to get Ever in place to end her life and take control of Valhalla, and all the power that came with ruling the Valkyries.

"What does he want?" Ever asked Thor even as Erika swore.

"He would like to meet, in a place of your choosing, like we all once did, and see if perhaps he could avoid slaying his only daughter. He said that Loki could weave his tricks so that no magic, no violence would be permitted inside the space while talks took place."

"And when does he want to have said talks?"

"He wishes to spend at least one birthday with his daughter. Official birthday that is."

Ever Chace had been borne in September, yet Ever the daughter of Odin had been borne a long time ago in the month of March on the shores of Valhalla.

"I need some time to think about this."

"What the fuck?" Erika exploded, marching toward Ever. She poked a finger in Ever's face. "You should be telling the asshole to go jump off a cliff! He is manipulating you, Ever. It's my job to tell you so."

"You have made your opinion quite clear, General. Now, back the hell up."

Ever could see war brewing in her friend's eyes, her fists clenching and unclenching. Erika snarled, and instead of backing down, she inched closer to Ever. Ever stood her ground, even as she felt the boys ready to break up the fight.

"I will not watch him kill you again. Especially if you walk the fuck into his sword."

"That is my choice to make, Erika. My goddamn choice."

Ever reached out and cupped her friend's cheek, and the

moment she did, Erika's anger swayed. "If you cannot contain the anger in you long enough for us to finish what we started, then step down. I do not need a general who cannot back my play."

Erika ground her teeth together, spun on her heels, and strode away from them, standing off to the side with her back to them. Ever could see the rise and fall of her shoulders, as she reigned in her temper and probably other emotions that spurred her actions. Ever understood where Erika was coming from, considering it was the Valkyrie's role to protect her. She'd also been the one responsible for killing each manifestation of Derek every single time Ever had been slain.

Ever closed her eyes, inhaling a breath before she blinked them open again. A wave of nausea and dizziness swept over her, and she swayed, reaching out a hand to stop herself from falling. Derek grabbed her before she listed over, and it took a few minutes for the unease to dissipate.

"Are you okay?" Derek asked, concern laced in his tone.

"I'm good. Just low blood sugar. We were sparring before all the surprise."

"Sparring is not what you were doing when I arrived."

Ever grinned at Thor, acknowledging his attempt to defuse the situation before she said to him, "Tell Odin I need to time to consider his offer and speak with my war council to see if we all agree to this conclave. I will give my answer when I have one."

"I will tell him."

Her brother turned to leave, stopping only when Ever called his name. "Come by the house tomorrow night. We can all have dinner and catch up. We will not speak of war for one eve."

Thor flashed her a grin that brought her back to her child-hood. "Will there be mead?"

Ever chortled. "I think we could arrange that."

"Then yes, I will be there."

Thor lifted his hand into the air and Mjölnir flew through

33

the air as if it appeared by magic. It sang as it came into contact with Thor's palm and blue flickers of lightning coursed over her brother's body. With an ear-splitting crack of thunder, Thor was gone, leaving nothing but the remnants of his power lingering behind him.

"And they say I am the dramatic one in the family. Could he not have used the door?"

Loki's joke broke some of the tension in the room, as Erika walked back to stand by Loki, who dutifully wrapped a protective arm around her waist. From the battle raging in her eyes, Ever knew they would have this discussion once again. But Erika motioned her head toward the door to the gym and the person standing in it.

Ricky stood rooted to the spot, his mouth hanging open, his eyes fixed on where Thor had been moments before. He shook his head and lifted his eyes, clear and alert, to glance at them. Shaking out his shock, the warlock forced his lips to kick up into a smile that should have come easy to him.

"If I was not stone-cold sober, then I would think I was still high as a bloody kite."

CHAPTER FOUR

RICKY

After picking Zach up from school and prying information from him about his day, Ricky had dropped the kid off at his grandma's house, much to both their delights. He was reluctant to leave Zach, but Ricky knew it was down to his fear of facing his team at the station. By the time he dragged himself from his mother's, darkness had begun to descend, and his mother all but pushed him out the door.

He'd sat in the carpark for another hour, debating whether he should just try again tomorrow. When he realised that he was procrastinating, Ricky got out of his car and slipped into the station. The halls were quiet, peaceful even, as he strode to the Paranormal Investigations Team's room. But no one was there.

Closing the door behind him, Ricky continued on to the gym, stepping inside before his eyes fell on a hulking mass of a man carrying a mystical hammer and vanishing in a flurry of blue and the roar of thunder.

Erika noticed Ricky first and gave him a small smile as the others in the room all stared in his direction. When he picked his jaw up off the ground, his heart beating hard against his chest, he tried to give them an easy smile, but it felt all wrong as

Ricky said, "If I was not stone-cold sober, then I would think I was still high as a bloody kite."

The joke fell flat, and they stood there awkwardly for a few moments before Ricky turned and walked out of the room, leaving them all standing there to gawp at him.

They don't even know how to act around you.

They can't even look at you anymore.

You don't belong with them anymore.

"Fuck this shit," Ricky mumbled to himself as he shook his head, making a beeline for the side door and the safety of his car. He almost made it, even had his hand on the door handle, when a calm voice said, "And where do you think you are going without so much as a hello."

Ricky blew out a breath, taking a second to calm his racing heart before he dropped his hand from the door and peered up sheepishly at Caitlyn.

"I was planning on doing a runner."

"I am happy to stop that. Donnie will be delighted to see you since you neglected to answer anyone's calls or texts while you were gone."

"Jesus, Caitlyn. Way to guilt a man."

Caitlyn said nothing more, simply stepped in front of him and took him in her arms. Ricky returned her embrace, feeling even more awkward then he already did. Sensing his unease, or maybe she saw it in his head, Caitlyn let go of Ricky. He felt himself blush when Caitlyn, who was just about the most beautiful woman in the world, cupped his cheek.

"You are well, *oui?*"

"Today I am."

"Then that is all we can ask for."

"I would ask for my mate to stop touching my best friend like that or a man could become possessive."

Ricky jerked back at the sound of Donnie's voice, embarrassment tingeing his cheeks even more. His thoughts became a tangle of apologies and regrets, mixed with all the things he wanted to say but couldn't.

"Hey, Ricky, breathe for me, mate. I was only messing." Strong hands landed on his shoulders. Ricky felt his magic stir and blew a breath out his nose, feeling the heat and smelling the smoke in his nostrils.

"You know, I planned to do this one at a time and be cool, calm and collected. Then I saw a frickin' Norse God in our training room and all sense of calm went out the goddamn window!"

Blowing out another breath, Ricky glanced up at Donnie, the vampire who knew inside his head better than anyone else possibly could. Donnie stared at him with those see all eyes of his. Ricky inclined his head, and it was as if he could feel Donnie rummaging around in his head. Donnie squeezed his shoulder, then punched him gently.

"Dude, this place has been hella quiet without you. We need a serious catch up over a pint."

"I don't drink anymore."

Donnie froze, his eyes darting to Caitlyn as if he were a dear caught in headlights.

"I'm only playing ya, Donnie. I still drink... I just have to do things in moderation for now. A catchup over a pint sounds good."

Donnie gave him an ear-splitting grin. "C'mon then. Everyone else will be waiting to see you."

Donnie set off ahead of them, but Caitlyn fell into step with him. "How is the boy?"

Ricky gave Caitlyn the first hint of a genuine smile. "Zach is awesome. He is wicked smart, sometimes a little too serious, and asks when he can visit the pretty vampire way too often. I can't believe he's actually my kid."

"Well, I certainly can. And you and your son are welcome in our home whenever you wish. It would be nice to hear a child's laughter in my home again."

Ricky reached out and put a hand on Caitlyn's arm, stopping her just shy of the squad room. "Cait, I have no clue how to be his dad. I didn't exactly have the best one in my life. I wanted to ask you for help, if I need it. But I am not willing to do anything that will make the demons you carry worse. If I've learned anything in the last three months, it's how your demons can threaten to drag you down to hell with them."

Caitlyn pursed her lips in thought for a moment before she bowed her head, her eyes a sheen of wetness. "My demons will always be there, as I am sure yours will. I am honoured that you ask me of all people for help. I would lay down my life for you and yours. I would very much like to be the cool aunt."

She pushed open the door and held it open for him. Ricky swallowed hard before he steeled his courage and went inside. Derek sat behind his desk, Ever perched on the edge of it. Erika stood off to the side, popping a luminous green bubble. Donnie was seated at his own desk, and Sarge, the backbone of the team, stood at the top of the room, his eyes full of concern as he watched Ricky.

The only two that were missing were Melanie and Kenzie, but he was suddenly glad of it. Ignoring everyone else, Ricky strode up to Sarge, then he waited as his boss ran his gaze over him and said, "Welcome back, Agent Moore."

"Thank you, sir. It's good to be back."

"And are you back?"

"I am if you will have me. I know I royally fucked up. I'm sorry for that. But this team comes only second to my son. I don't think I could get through this without them."

Sarge crinkled his salt and pepper moustache. "That is good to hear, son. You feel overwhelmed again, and you come to one of us. You might feel guilty for hiding what was happening to you, but those agents behind you have spent far too long drowning in their own guilt for not being there for you."

Sarge paused, lifting his gaze to the rest of the team. "The guilt has to go. If you walk on eggshells around one another, then we might as well disband the team right now. Ricky cannot continue with his sobriety if he constantly feels he is being watched by us. We must trust that he will come to us. You will, won't you, son?"

"Yeah, I will."

"And you lot," the bear growled. "did you let your teammate down? Yes, but not as much as he feels he let you down. If you do not have each other's backs, then what the hell are we doing here? You need to decide if we stay as a team, right here, right now. If we move forward then cut the B.S and get on with it."

The entire room lapsed into silence as Erika of all people, pushed off the wall, yanked out his chair, and pointed to it. "Sit your ass down, warlock, before we get another lecture. You're making shit awkward."

Ricky snorted. "Since I'm making shit awkward and everything, should I point out that you need to keep your boyfriend fed? Keeps him from snacking on your neck."

Erika swore and covered her neck, the ghost of a smile on her lips as he sank down into his chair, and everyone laughed. Ricky leaned back, the feeling of unease evaporating as he watched those he considered family getting back to normal. He set his booted feet on the edge of his desk, while Sarge went over details from a most recent crime scene.

"Onlookers said the vampire stepped off the roof as the sun rose with a smile on his face. The building used to be a nightclub, and it seems as if illegal parties were being held in there."

"The victim," Derek continued after Sarge. "Was a nobody, made a vampire 'bout two years ago, and when he didn't have any valuable powers to call his own, it seems like he fell in with the wrong crowd. Vanished off anyone's radar until this morning."

"I did find an ID in his pocket as well as an empty packet

that looks like it had some kind of pill in it." Erika pinned the little baggy onto the board as everyone tried to avoid looking at him, but Ricky knew what was in that bag, the logo on it clear.

"It's White Rabbit," Ricky uttered quietly. "It causes various effects on different supes, but it's supposed to give you the high you just can't get because normal drugs don't affect supes like they do humans. For me, White Rabbit stripped me of my magic and made me feel normal, like myself. It also made me an insensitive asshole, but yeah."

Ricky cleared his throat, and Derek nodded at his statement. "There's a new player in town. Ironically, with everything else going on, he calls himself the Viking. He is the mastermind behind all of this. No one knows what he looks like or who he is. We need to flush him out."

Everyone started to voice their opinion about what should be done, as Ricky set his feet back on the floor and put his face in his hands. He knew the only way of smoking out and squashing the spread of this toxin within the supernatural community, but he did not know if he was strong enough to go down the rabbit hole so soon again.

He blocked out the noise around him and counted to ten in his head as he whispered, "Send me in."

Both Donnie and Derek snapped their heads in his direction. Gathering his courage, Ricky found his voice and repeated his words, "Send me in."

"Hell no!"

A chorus greeted him. Sarge regarded him for a moment and held up his hand to silence them all. He motioned for Ricky to continue.

"Send me in. It's not gonna be hard to let it slip that I went off the rails and got hooked on White Rabbit. I have contacts, deep in the supernatural underworld, who might lead me in the right track. Let the rumour spread that I was fired from P.I.T.

for misuse of the drug policy. Make it look like I went all supervillain on you guys, and I'm alone in the world."

"Ricky, you just got back," Derek said in that serious tone of his. "We are not going to send you undercover by yourself fresh out of rehab."

Ricky folded his arms across his chest and in his best steady voice said, "I appreciate your concerns and acknowledge them." Everyone froze and stared at him like he was from outer space. "But you are talking out your ass. Erika was only fresh out of being kidnapped, and you sent her into a fighting ring."

"Technically, I sent myself, but I get your point."

When no one else uttered a syllable, Ricky held out his hands. "Who else could you send? Everyone knows Derek is too much of a straight arrow to not stand out. Caitlyn is the queen of vampires, and no one would believe she was an addict. Donnie's her plus one, so he's out. The Valkyrie over there would frighten the bejaysus out of everyone. If not me, then who? Kenzie? Not while I have breath in my body. That girl's been through enough."

"I understand your logic, Ricky, really I do," Sarge began, leaning against his own desk as he looked over at Ricky. "But I understand everyone else's concerns also. If we sent you in alone and anything happened to you, no one in this room would ever forgive themselves."

"Send me in with him."

Ricky's head snapped to the door where Melanie and Kenzie stood, having somehow walked in unnoticed. Damn, she looked good, standing there, hair the colour of flames hanging loose down to her shoulders, tight dark jeans moulded to her skin and black boots ready to kick ass. He began to shake his head, but she held up a hand to stop him.

"It wouldn't be hard for people to believe that being a vampire changed me. It has. We just need them to believe I've reverted back to my old hacker days. That I bucked against the rules and pressure put on me by my sire. That I was lured to the dark side by a man. Considering that's how I ended up getting arrested in the first place, we can persuade them that I am blinded by Ricky's charms."

When no one made any attempt to argue with her, Melanie continued, "I still have some hacker friends that I still talk to. I can reach out, see if anything bites."

"Before anyone agrees to anything, I don't need a babysitter."

"I'm not a babysitter. I am a full member of this team, and since not a single one of them is arguing with me, I guess you are outvoted, and we get to be partners. Woohoo."

Ricky glanced at Caitlyn, waiting for her to argue, but his best defence simply shrugged, stating, "Sometimes as parents, we must let our children make their own decisions and be there to support them, no matter the outcome. Melanie knows her own mind."

Ricky got to his feet and walked over to stand in front of Melanie. "You sure about this? Are you sure you want to do this with me? Once we take the first step, we gotta see this through."

"Bring it."

Turning to Sarge, he beckoned the older man forward. "You gotta do this loud and very public. You gotta say stuff you know will invoke a reaction from me. Caitlyn has to disavow Melanie for this to work. You and D, ye gotta let me go. We have to make this real."

Sarge nodded. "Erika will be your point of contact since she can flash in and out without a trace. You get in and out. You come back to us whole. Both of you."

"Absofuckingloutly."

Turning back to Melanie, Ricky said. "I hope you can act, babe. Because shit's about to get real."

Yanking open the door to the squad room, Ricky blew the door off its hinges with a blast of magic. "How fucking dare you! I am a founding member of this team. You can't fire me for no reason."

Sarge inhaled a breath and let loose a growl so loud the whole building vibrated. "I will not have a drug addict on my payroll. I will not jeopardize the health of my team because you have no self-control!"

The words stung, prickling at the insecurities Ricky carried. To emphasize the fact that he lacked control, blue flames engulfed his palms. Ricky let a snarl curl his lips as he backed into the main floor of the Garda station and in full view of those still milling about filling in reports.

Derek stepped in front Sarge as if to protect him and Ricky sneered, "Oh, here he is, the blue-eyed boy who can do no wrong. The perfect soldier. Would you roll over and let him scratch your belly if he fed you treats, Doyle?"

Derek growled, his eyes glowing amber as Donnie and Caitlyn flashed some fang. "And everyone, now here comes the royal family... make sure you bow down and kiss their feet, won't you, because heaven forbid, you make a mistake."

"Leave now, Moore. Before I separate your head from your body."

Ricky moved toward the door, his magic still pulsing in waves around him. "I'll go. I don't want to spend another night stuck with you goody goodies. But I ain't leaving without what's mine. Come on, babe, let's get outta here."

Melanie made to follow him out, Caitlyn grabbing her arm to stop her. Melanie moved like liquid, slipping free of Caitlyn's grasp with ease. Melanie walked over to him, took his hand when he doused his flames, and rested her head on his shoulder.

"You walk out that door, Melanie Newton, and you are no longer under my protection. I will cut you from my line. Stay with us."

"I'm sorry, I can't... I love him."

Derek stalked across the floor, stopping only when Ricky

flung a ball of blue in his direction. "You are going to ruin her life, mate."

Ricky tightened his grip on Melanie's hand. "I'm not your mate, Derek, not after you threw me under the bus. And you heard her, Melanie loves me. What's a guy to do? Next time we see each other, Doyle, you won't have a Valkyrie bitch to protect you."

Derek lunged for Ricky, but Ricky was ready for him. Pushing out his magic, Ricky conjured the illusion that Derek was on fire, the flames hurting Ricky instead of Derek, yet his friend howled in agony. Ricky left them trying to put out the pretend flames that burned Derek as he guided Melanie out of the station and into his car.

And he hoped to the gods that their display was enough to set tongues wagging.

THE VIKING SET down the phone and grinned, delighting in the fact the warlock's world was falling down around him. He would be easier to manipulate, to use against the police force that were beginning to be a pain in his neck.

When his contact called to tell him that Delaney had fired Ricky and Melanie, and his Mel had left with the warlock, the Viking knew he would do anything to win her back. If he had to kill the warlock in order to do so, then so be it.

Melanie would never know, for a junkie overdosing happened every day in this city. While she might be heartbroken to begin with, she'd soon forget she ever had feelings for the addict.

Pressing the button on the intercom, he waited until a gruff voice answered before he spoke again. "Find Ricky Moore and convince him to come play a hand. I want to see if we are being played."

"Yes, boss."

Disconnecting the conversation, the Viking lifted his beer to his lips as he pulled a picture from his pocket. A younger version of himself and Melanie stared back at him. She laughed, while his face was pressed into the curve of her neck. She looked so alive, so full of life, and now she was vampire.

He had made a mistake before, letting her go...

But he was never letting her go again...

CHAPTER
FIVE

Melanie studied Ricky as he leaned his head against the headrest, eyes closed, his fingers toying with the skull ring that doused the extent of his powers but still gave him access to them. They'd stormed out of the station, tires screeching like Bonnie and Clyde, driving in silence for about ten minutes before Ricky yanked the steering wheel to the right and cast them off the road. Melanie let him have his few minutes of calm before they dove into whatever the hell they had chosen to dive into.

"I'm sorry, I can't ... I love him."

If Melanie's heart still beat, it would have sunk into her stomach at the comment, and she was so glad that she could no longer blush. When she was human, she'd had the biggest crush on Ricky, and there was definitely a spark between them even now, but Melanie had had her heart trampled on before, as had Ricky, and they both needed to be sure before anything could happen...well, anything more.

That brief brush of lips moments before he went off to rehab held within it a promise of things to come, and Melanie hoped that both their hearts could survive the fire that might just consume them.

"You're staring at me, Lanie."

Lanie.

When she'd come back as a vampire, Ricky had started to use her full name, a thing he rarely did with any of his friends. He used her full name when trying to put distance between them, and the sound of the nickname reserved only for him sent shivers down her spine.

"Just trying to make sure your head doesn't explode."

Ricky turned his face to grin at her, and it was the most genuine smile that she had seen light up his face in ages. Tension crackled in the air as he cleared his throat and dragged his eyes from hers to stare back out into the dark night.

"I need to make arrangements for Zach. You want me to drop you at Caitlyn's to pick up some stuff?"

"Don't think it would be very convincing to drop me off when Caitlyn has banished me from her line. I can sneak back later before dawn and grab a bag."

"Okay...yeah...okay."

Ricky turned the key in the ignition and drove the car in the direction of his mom's house. The last time the two of them had been there, Ricky had nearly come to magical blows with his brother Killian over stupid comments. Melanie had been the one to defuse the situation, wondering if Ricky and his brother would ever be on good terms. Over the last three months, Melanie had thought about her own family.

For god's sake, they didn't even know she was a vampire. Hadn't called her when she died or anything.

"You okay?"

Ricky must have noticed the tension in her body. She hadn't spoken to a member of her family since she had taken the deal to join P.I.T. and avoid a lengthy prison sentence. It was the best decision she had made.

"I'm good. Just thinking about my family. Makes me feel murdery."

Ricky chuckled and tapped a finger on the wheel in time with the music. "Ya, family can do that to you. You don't talk about them much."

Melanie shrugged, turning her head so that Ricky couldn't see her eyes. "Nothing much to say. I joined up with the right side of the law, and I was no longer wanted. Not that I was before. I wasn't exactly the kind of girl your dad could marry off to foster good relations between crime gangs, and I wasn't the type of girl my mom could go shopping with."

The tapping on the wheel halted as Ricky directed the car into his mother's drive. He pulled the car to a sudden halt, snapping off his seatbelt and inclining his body to face her. "Your dad sounds like a jackass. He'd probably get on with mine...or would have. If they don't see how truly special you are, then that's their fucking problem."

Ricky reached out as if to touch her, something crossed his face, and then he pulled back, getting out of the car with such speed, a vampire had to be impressed.

With a sigh, Melanie followed his lead, getting out of the car and striding toward the door. Ricky didn't wait for an answer, simply opened the door and strode in. Melanie hung back in the foyer, not sure what to do until Diane's voice beckoned her into the kitchen.

Diane looked like a stereotypical mom that you saw in baking commercials, the ones with aprons and flour streaked cheeks. She stood at the kitchen island, a rolling pin in hand. Zach perched high on a stool, watching his grandmother make whatever it was that she was doing. Ricky leaned against the fridge, observing them with a sad smile on his face.

"Melanie!"

The little boy who was so like his dad scrambled from his seat, crawled up her legs and engulfed her in a hug. Her smelled like flour and cat, mixed with a scent that carried a hint of Ricky. The little boy pulled back, pushed his glasses up the bridge of his nose, smearing flour on his lenses as he informed her that they were baking cookies.

"I can see that, Zach-attack. I bet they are going to be yummy."

"I will share mine with you."

"Thanks, Zach." Melanie replied with a grin, as the boy slid from her arms and back to the spot he once was. Melanie felt eyes on her, and when she lifted hers to hold his eyes of emerald green, they seemed to smoulder as they held her gaze.

"What?" she mouthed, but all she got was a lopsided smile that made her insides flutter.

"I'm going to stay at Grandma's tonight, Ricky."

"Are you now?" Ricky asked, lifting an eyebrow at his son. Three months and the little fella still refused to call Ricky 'Dad'. But it seemed like Ricky was handling things well enough as he continued, "And what have we talked about before? We do not demand to do things; we ask politely."

"Can I please stay over at Grandma's tonight?"

"Yes, you may."

The boy nodded, his glasses slipping down his nose again as Killian strode into the room. He ruffled Zach's hair as he walked by, inclining his head to Melanie and then to Ricky as he filled a mug with coffee and then left moments later.

"Mom, I have a favour to ask."

"You know the answer is yes... now use your own advice and ask your son."

Melanie bit back a grin as Ricky rolled his eyes, but did as he was told. He pushed off the fridge and reclined in a kitchen chair, beckoning Zach to him.

"Zach, come here a second."

The boy hesitated, looking to his grandmother before he climbed down the chair and pounced on Ricky. Ricky growled at him softly, Zach returning the growl with a grin.

"Melanie and I have to go do some important police work.

That means I would like you to stay with Grandma for a few days. Is that okay with you?"

"Do you have to go catch some bad guys?"

"Indeed, we do."

Ricky ran his fingers through the boy's hair, Zach purring at the motion. Then, fed up with his dad's fussing, he swatted his hand away. He patted Ricky on the nose twice and then nodded his head.

"Okay. So, does that mean I don't have to go to school?"

Ricky laughed. "Oh no, mister, Grandma will take you to school or…"

"I will."

Killian came back into the kitchen and held his brother's stare for a second before Ricky continued, "Or Uncle Killian will. I will ring you every day to find out how school was. You be good for Grandma and Uncle Killian, buddy. That's all I ask."

"Okay."

Ricky kissed the boy on the top of his head, and Zach scurried away, lights flashing as he changed into a sleek black cat. Killian, to Melanie's shock, began to count to ten as Zach bolted from the kitchen, and when Killian reached ten, he took off after the boy.

Ricky rose from his chair, walked around and embraced his mother. Stepping back, Diane Moore cupped her flour caked hands to her son's cheeks. "You will be careful. I don't want to know what you are up to, but you will be careful." She lifted her eyes to glance at Melanie. "Both of you."

"Yes, Ma'am." Ricky said as he stepped away. "You call me if he gets too out of hand."

"Richard, I raised you, and you turned out good. Hellraiser that you claimed to be. I think I can handle that sweet boy. Now, go and do some police work."

Ricky turned on his heels and went in search of Zach, leaving Melanie alone with Diane. "The best thing that woman did was give birth to Zach," she muttered, knowing full well Melanie would hear her. Louder she said, "Sadie was never right for him. He thought he loved her, but he was never happy. I want my boy to be happy."

Lifting the rolling pin, Diane pointed it at Melanie, a firm yet friendly smile on her face. "I don't wish to speak ill of the dead, but Sadie and Ricky were never a good match. I told him so, and that is why we had a falling out. He never looked at her the way he looks at you. That is how a man should look at a woman."

"There's nothing going on with us." Melanie could taste other people's lies, yet she was almost certain the sweet taste of a lie coated her tongue.

"Let's see if you say that the next time we meet. Richard had a lot of time to think while he was recovering. Now he knows exactly what and who he wants."

Melanie opened her mouth to retort when Ricky came back into the kitchen and beckoned for her to follow him, stopping in the arch of the door. "Mam, Zach..."

"Is being collected by Fionn at two on Saturday for their weekly playdate. I remember. Now shoo... I have cookies to bake."

They were back in the car and reversing out the drive after a few brief goodbyes, Diane arching her brows when Ricky rested a hand on the small of Melanie's back and directed her out the door. His hand felt like a brand along her spine, his fingers hot even through the fabric of her tee.

"You have two choices. Back to mine for a couple of hours, and then you can drop back to your house to get some stuff. Or you can slip out of the car and get back before dawn. We need to start our infiltration tomorrow night, and if the house is being watched, people need to see you leave my house with me and not Caitlyn's."

She peered at the clock on the dash. It was still early enough, yet Melanie considered that perhaps Ricky might need a few minutes to breathe by himself. He looked tired, weary, so Melanie took the first option.

"Sure, I'll head back to Caitlyn's and grab a bag. If someone is watching, then all they will see is me leaving with a bag and headed to your place."

"Okay. I'll go for a run, clear my head. I should be back before you."

Melanie snorted before she could stop herself. "Since when do you run?"

"Blame Draven. For the first month up in Armagh, he'd have me up at the crack of dawn to go for a run. Soon, I was going by myself when I needed to get clarity."

"Did it help?"

"Yeah, it did."

"Good. I'll see you soon."

Melanie slipped from the car the moment Ricky pulled over a short distance from Caitlyn's house. He drove away as soon as she was a safe distance from the house, and Melanie rolled her eyes.

Caitlyn's house was a remarkable work of art that her sire had created, a piece of her in every nook. The monster that had sought to covet Caitlyn as his own tainted the beautiful home and forced the traumatised vampire to stop going into her own bedroom.

When Cain had violated Caitlyn once again by coming into her home, threatening those who had made their way inside her heart, the one she had closed off after the deaths of her family, her beautiful children. Caitlyn had made the decision to start over, in a home that both she and her mate Donnie created.

Of course, Melanie and Kenzie were welcomed as well, Caitlyn eager to keep her niece and Melanie close. To keep them safe.

Melanie slipped inside the front door, felt the presence of

her sire before she saw her, and made her way toward the front room. Melanie couldn't not hide the smile tugging her lips as she took in the sight in front of her.

Donnie sat on the couch, his long muscular legs stretched out in front of him, one arm on the back of the couch and one hand running fingers up and down the arm of the vampire sound asleep in his arms. Caitlyn lay between Donnie's legs, tucked up safety, an aura of contentment echoing from her. Her head rested against his chest, one hand over where his heart had once beat, the other under her own cheek.

Melanie made to remove herself from this private moment, but Donnie jerked his head, motioning for her to sit. Melanie sank down into a chair facing him, the older vampire's eyes not moving from the rugby game that played.

"Do you miss it?"

Donnie didn't even skip a beat, probably reading the question in her mind before she spoke it. "Sometimes. I miss the adrenaline of a game. Chasing the victory and that feeling of winning a game and being cheered is unreal." Back when he was alive, Donnie played for his club and country. He had been about to retire due to head injuries, but before he could, he had died and been reborn as a vampire by Caitlyn.

"But being an agent, the thrill of the chase, and catching an UNSUB, it gives me a purpose, and chasing after Caitlyn for so long gave me enough adrenaline for a lifetime. I ruined my career; I was an asshole for the later part of my career because the end was coming, and I didn't want to go back to being a nobody."

"I get it. I used to feel like that when I was hacking. The feeling of sneaking in and not getting caught was a natural high. I think I was tired of being a nobody, too."

Caitlyn jerked in her sleep, soft mutterings of French flowing from her lips as her eyes darted from left to right in her sleep. Her fingers clutched the material of Donnie's jersey as he whispered to her that she was safe, and he was there. As suddenly as she jerked, Caitlyn slipped back into slumber with a sigh.

"I don't understand. Cain is dead. How can he still haunt her so much?"

Donnie ran a hand over the bristles of hair shaved down to his skull. "Cait, she is afraid to relax. She lived for hundreds of years, terrified that Cain would track her down, and she would lose all over again. She can't squash that fear because he is dead. She fears that sometimes; the dead do not stay dead."

Melanie thought of her own nightmares that had begun to haunt her at night, even thought, Melanie was the happiest she had ever been in her new life. Donnie frowned as she shivered.

"Stephen Donnelly is dead, and you are not. Remember that."

"I'll try."

"Do that," Donnie replied with a grin.

Melanie rose, standing and watching the two vampires who, in the last couple of months since becoming a vampire, had treated her far better than her biological family ever did.

"Did you want to be a dad, I mean…before, when you were alive?"

The words were out before she could stop them, and she noticed Donnie flinch. His eyes darted down to Caitlyn who had gone ridged, obviously awake but keeping her eyes firmly shut.

"When I was alive," Donnie replied, and with every single word he spoke, Melanie tasted the truth in his words. "I didn't know what it was like to have a family. I wouldn't have made a good father to anyone. Sometimes, I wish that Caitlyn and I were human. That the only woman I have ever loved could carry my kid. But life has a funny way of proving that you have exactly what you need. It gave us two fully grown adults as kids. I'm content with my lot."

"Kenzie and me, we are lucky to have you both. And for the record, I think you'd make a brilliant dad. You are to me."

Donnie cleared his throat as Melanie left him to mull over her words.

"Melanie?"

She turned to look at him and saw a sheen of wetness in his eyes as he said, "He might be my best friend, my brother, but if he hurts you, he will have me to deal with. There is a long line of people who would break his legs if he so much as makes you cry."

"I don't know why everyone is throwing about relationship advice when there is nothing going on with me and Ricky."

"Uh huh… whatever you say, *Lanie*." Donnie replied with a chuckle, and Melanie wanted to strangle him.

Throwing her hands up in the air, Melanie left Donnie and Caitlyn to their moment of stillness. She rammed a few clothes and bits and bobs into a bag. Sitting on the edge of her bed for a few minutes, she replayed everyone's comments over in her mind.

Swallowing her fear, Melanie wondered if she was ready to play with fire…and if so, was she about to get burned?

CHAPTER
SIX

RICKY

The run helped him to clear his head and prepare for what the upcoming days might unload on him. Hood up and music thrumming in his ears, Ricky could almost forget why he needed the routine of his feet eating up the pavement as he ran, the burn in his lungs, the stretch of his muscles. He'd have to alter his routine slightly, forsaking early mornings for last minute runs before the sun came up.

Ricky knew he was doing the right thing by going undercover to weed out the person who was dolling out drugs to supernaturals and getting them killed. The part that plagued him was why had he not dobbed Tadgh in as his dealer. The intern was still working with P.I.T, and the warlock with an affinity for chemistry was their best lead. So, why had he kept Tadgh's secret?

Because you want drugs.

Why out your source?

Junkie, junkie, junkie...

No! Ricky scolded himself for his thoughts, knowing he had kept Tadgh's secret so that the warlock could feed information back to the person he was creating White Rabbit for. If they had trouble weeding out the dealers and the kingpin, then Ricky would make his presence very well known.

For now, he would allow himself to revel in the fact that Melanie would be sleeping under the same roof as him. Ricky was certain that Melanie had no idea what they would have to do in preparation for this undercover mission. He would do his best to throw her out of her comfort zone, to make her realize the promises he made to her meant that he wanted to be a better man for her, that he spoke the god's honest truth, and she did not need her truth-seeker ability to know that.

Washed and dressed in shorts and a t-shirt, Ricky sank down into his chair in the living room, the soft hum of music playing, a lamp the only light in the room. His blood sang with anticipation as he tried to focus on the book he was reading and not on the turn of a key in the door, the sound of Melanie letting her bag fall to the floor and the timid patter of her boots coming down the hall.

Ricky kept his eyes on the page in front of him, but he couldn't see the words, aware of Melanie's intense gaze on him. He peered over his shoulder, a smug smile tugging at his lips as she watched him.

"If only Kenzie could see you now. She follows this Instagram page where people post pictures of hot dudes reading."

"So, you think I'm hot?" Ricky asked, his grin deepening as Melanie bristled.

"Kenzie certainly does."

"Kenzie's not the one I'm interested in."

Melanie's eyes widened even as she rolled her lush green eyes at him. Ricky fought back the urge to stride right on over and kiss Melanie so hard that she would be in no doubt of his intentions. But he would be patient. He would get this right.

He closed the book, set it aside, and motioned for her to sit. He almost chuckled as Melanie sat as far away from him as possible, as if she needed the distance. Not that she would get much, sleeping under his roof.

"Make yourself at home. The windows in the bedroom and my en-suite bath have sun proof glass so you'll be safe. I stopped and got some bottled blood on the way home. I put half in the fridge, left half out…didn't know whether you drank it chilled or not."

"Thanks. This is weird right? You feel weird about this too?"

Ricky leaned forward and rested his chin in his hands, amusement at her unease building inside him as he said honestly, "Nope. This is the least weird I've felt in a long time. Just relax, Lanie."

Sinking back in her chair, Melanie folded her arms across her chest as Ricky began to speak, very matter of fact. "Now, we need to build up the pretence that you and I are a couple. Did Caitlyn or Donnie speak to you about …" Ricky broke off, rubbing the back of his neck. "Certain things before you left?"

If Melanie had blood coursing through her veins, then Ricky was sure she'd have blushed a shade of crimson. Pushing the hair from her face, she scoffed. "I know about the birds and the bees, thanks."

"But did they explain what would be expected from me if I was actually dating you?"

Melanie's silence and deer eyed expression made her even more adorable as Ricky said in as monotone as voice as he could, "Vampires who are dating non-vampires are just as territorial. They leave their mark and want to wear the scent of their lover on their skin so that other supes will know that their significant other is not available."

Melanie opened her mouth, letting it snap shut as Ricky continued, "Vampires often take a live lover so they can drink right from the source. Any vampire that comes within sniffing distance will know that our scents are mingled together."

Brow furred; Melanie glared at him as if he was making this

up even though she could taste the truth in his words. She was the one, freshly made a vampire, who had been inches away from sinking her teeth into his neck, claiming that he was hers and damn, he wanted to be claimed like that by her again.

"Lanie, you're going to have to drink from me."

Melanie was up and out of her seat before he'd finished his sentence. "Um, nope...that's not gonna happen...I've never...I can't."

Ricky got up and stood in front of her, his hand grasping hers, so she was forced to look at him. Melanie clenched her jaw, forcing her lips closed, but Ricky sensed her pretty little fangs had slipped free of their own accord.

"I'm not going to force you to drink from me, no matter how much I want you to. You'll have to drink some of my blood one way or the other, because no one will believe that we are together if you don't drink from me. You will sleep in my bed, wear my clothes so my scent will linger on your skin. I'll take the couch. There's also something else."

Ricky let go of her hand and lifted his own to cup her cheek, letting his thumb trace over her bottom lip. Much as he expected, Melanie jerked back from his touch, her fingers touching where his thumb had been moments ago.

"Not a sinner will believe us if you can't stand to be touched by me."

"I ...it's not that...I..."

"We can work on that. Now, just go and get some sleep. We will have time tomorrow before we have to make our first appearance as villains."

Melanie glowered as he grinned. "You're looking forward to playing the bad guy, aren't you?"

"It's good to be bad sometimes."

Melanie barked out a laugh, and it eased some of the tension in her as she sauntered by him. Ricky leaned back, listening to her milling about in his room, muttering to herself. He closed his eyes and thought of her, red hair loose and resting on his pillow, curled up in a bed that no other woman had ever slept in. Ricky had left a long loose tee for her to wear, and he curled his fists to fight the urge to go and see what she looked like in it.

"It's stupid, you know."

Having not even heard her come back in, Ricky slowly opened his eyes and drank in the sight of her. Dressed in a battered Captain America tee that came down just below her knees, Ricky roamed his eyes over her long, lean legs and up to the tangle of flame red hair that hung loose down her shoulders. His pulse quickened, and he knew that Melanie could hear the pounding of his heart.

"What's stupid?" Ricky replied, his voice husky as he tried to clear it.

"You sleeping out here. I mean...doesn't it make sense, from what you said, that sleeping in the same bed would imprint our scents on each other?"

This made Ricky's heart beat even faster, and his mouth ran dry. This was more than he could hope for, sleeping the day away beside her, even if she only did it because it helped the case.

"I'd never force you to do something you didn't want to."

"And if I said I wanted to."

"Then a man could get ideas." Ricky teased with a grin.

Melanie threw her hands up in the air. "Fine, whatever. Do what you want. Freeze your ass off out here for all I care." Storming off, Melanie closed the bedroom door with an audible snick, then after a pause, she opened it again.

Ricky gave her a few minutes to settle into bed, *his bed*, fighting back the urge to race after her. Slowly, he flicked off the light, padded down the hall, and pushed open his bedroom door.

His breath hitched, reality far better than any fantasy that he could imagined. Curled up on the far side of the bed, snuggled under the duvet, her back to him, Melanie Newton looked like she belonged in his bed. Like an idiot, he stood there for an age until the vampire in his bed growled at him.

"Come in or get out. You're letting the light in."

"Yes, bossy boots."

A snort sounded from under the covers as Ricky grinned, closing the bedroom door. Making his way over to the bed, he slipped under the covers, letting out a sigh and closing his eyes. He wanted to reach out and touch her, pull her close to him and never let her go. But he couldn't, not just yet. Ricky willed himself to sleep, however, he found having a sexy red head next to him made it hard to sleep.

Melanie didn't seem to have the same problems as he did, her breathing, the automatic thing most vampires did, their intake of breath not a necessity, just a simple reflex left over from when they had been alive, the air that went into their bodies of no use to them or anyone else, suddenly stopped and she lay there not moving an inch.

Turning on his side, his hands resting under his head, he drank in the sight of her, thinking back to all the way in which he had hurt her. He teased her, wanting to keep her near but at a safe distance. He blamed her for his lack of control on his magic and sending him down a dark path. He lashed out at the one person he was pretty sure he was in love with, who he'd always been in love with from the first moment they'd bantered after she'd joined the team.

Sarge introduced the newest member of the team, a timid nerdy looking girl who seemed to be terrified of her own shadow. Ricky had met her once before, waiting for Sarge to offer her a chance to work off her sentence with the team and not let her talents be wasted in prison.

The only human on the team, Meanie Newton appeared terrified by the bulking mass of Donnie, the intensity of Caitlyn and the brooding presence of Derek. Even with just the bare minimum of supes in the room, the girl was having a hard time trying to stay chill. Ricky wasn't in the mood to babysit her, especially with all the shit in his head, but damn it if he didn't have a hero complex.

Sitting down on the edge of her desk, Melanie's fingers stopped their frantic typing as she peered up at him over those large rimmed glasses with frightened green eyes. Ricky reached over and pushed her glasses back up her nose. A blush seeped into her skin, and he flashed her a grin.

"Pretend they are all wearing teddy bear costumes."

"I'm sorry...what?"

"Being around this grouchy bunch can be intimidating, even for me. When I feel overwhelmed, I like to picture them dressed as teddy bears. Apart from Sarge, because he actually is a bear."

His joke had its intended affect as Melanie laughed, the sound sending a flutter through his stomach he tried to quash down. Melanie clasped a hand over her mouth even as Ricky whispered, "You're picturing it now, aren't you?"

"You are terrible!" Melanie chided him, obviously more at ease now that the tension left her shoulders.

"Terribly handsome, right?" He said with a wink, and she rolled her eyes.

"Humble, with just a hint of Kanye."

The squad room laughed at her statement as Ricky shrugged his shoulders. Derek clapped him on the shoulder. "She's got you made, Ricky. Stop flirting and let's go, we got a case."

Ricky smiled at the tech girl. "Later, Lanie."

"My name's Melanie."

"I like Lanie better...it's like we already have pet names for each other."

Melanie hissed at him, and Ricky decided to play a little harder, enjoying feeling like his old self, even just for a minute or two.

"I do like a girl with a bit of fire in her, Lanie, babe." He clicked his fingers, a spark of blue flame lingering for a minute before it was gone.

Melanie was still glaring at him when Derek dragged him from the room.

A strangled cry dragged him from the edges of sleep. Melanie was lying on her back, her hands clawing at her stomach.

"Please, please don't kill me," she begged, tears streaming down her face. "You don't have to do this. Please, Stephen, please."

Ricky had no idea what to do. He knew she'd been having nightmares, anyone who was tortured and murdered would, and just like he had back then, he felt helpless.

"Lanie, Lanie…wake up, babe…it's okay."

She hadn't wanted to sleep alone. That was why she'd asked him to come sleep beside her. Shoving down a growl of frustration, Ricky reached out and pulled Melanie to his chest, holding her arms so she couldn't hurt herself even as she dug her nails into his skin. He hummed a tune as he rocked her back and forth, but still she did not wake.

Trapped in her own nightmare, Melanie lashed out, slapping him in the jaw so hard his teeth rattled. Yet, he refused to let her go. He held onto her as if they were each other's life raft, and he could stop her from drowning.

Eventually, Melanie stopped the fight within her mind, and she clung to him, wrapping her arms around him. Goddamn, she even snuggled into his chest. He eased them down, pulled the covers over them, and waited for her to wake herself.

As if she sensed him, Melanie's eyes fluttered open, her sleepy gaze meeting his.

"Ricky? What happened?"

Ricky ran a hand over her hair. "You had a nightmare, Lanie. Go back to sleep, I got you."

She reached up, touching the spot where she'd smacked him. When he winced, she snapped upright, switching on the light. Her eyes widened with shock and disgust at herself.

"Hey, it's okay. Derek has clocked me worse when we've sparred."

"I don't...I didn't...I hurt you."

"You were hurting yourself. Better me than you." He sighed as she pulled out of his grasp, embarrassed by her lack of control. As if she just realized their positions, her head snapped up to look at him.

They sat there, for several heartbeats, as neither of them knowing whether or not to lean in and add fuel to the fire that was between them. It was Ricky who decided to be the sensible one, to wait until the time was right. Nightmare-induced sex was not what he wanted, even if he craved Melanie more than he'd ever craved drugs.

"Picture him dressed as a teddy bear."

"I'm sorry, what?"

Ricky tucked a strand of hair behind her ear. "I watched you sleeping, and I remembered your first day at work. You were afraid of Donnie and Derek, even more so of Caitlyn. I could feel it and so could they. I came over to you, and I said–"

"You told me to picture them all dressed up as teddy bears... and then you flirted with me."

"I haven't really stopped since."

Melanie gave him a small smile, and he greedily drank it in. "I couldn't look at them for days without imagining them as bears."

"Then I accomplished my goal. Use it for Donnelly. Picture him dressed up as bloody Big Bird if you have to. Or talk to me, Lanie. Don't ever stop talking to me."

Fingers playing in the ends of her hair, Melanie looked at him with amusement. "You know, it's kinda creepy, hearing some guy say he watched you sleeping."

"But I'm not just some guy, am I, Lanie?"

She mulled over his question, opened her mouth to speak,

but chose not to, chewing on her bottom lip so much that Ricky wanted to replace her teeth with his own.

Melanie looked down to the spot where she had slept, and then glared at Ricky, at war with her own thoughts. As if she made her decision, Melanie lowered herself back down and rested her head on his chest, above his heart. No doubt she felt the beat of it, hammering against his chest, the spike in his pulse.

Yet, she didn't say a thing as Ricky reached out and turned off the light. There, shrouded in darkness, Melanie didn't so much as utter a word as he shifted, lowering his head down on the pillow, his arm wrapping around her waist, the other tracing down her hair.

For an age after Sadie, Ricky was a *bed um and leave um* kinda guy. He hadn't wanted the intimacy or being like this, vulnerable with another person, because of a deep-rooted fear that he would fall and be hurt again.

"Goodnight, Ricky."

"G'night, Lanie."

Melanie was asleep within seconds, and Ricky breathed in the apple scent of her shampoo and imagined what it would be like to fall asleep every single day with her in his arms.

And for the first time in a long time, Ricky fell asleep with a smile on his face.

CHAPTER SEVEN

MELANIE

Waking up in a tangle of delicious warlock was something Melanie had fantasized about ever since she'd first laid eyes on the so-called bad boy of P.I.T. Now, as she drowsily dragged herself from slumber, she realized that sometime during the night, Ricky had twisted so that she lay with her back to him, his arms wrapped tightly around her. His breath was warm against her neck, his lips mere inches from her throat.

She tried to squirm out of his grasp, stopping when she realized all it was achieving was putting her rather close to a part of Ricky that was standing to attention. A giggle slipped free of her lips before she could stop it, the sound enough to rouse Ricky from his slumber.

Melanie could have sworn she felt the press of his lips to the side of her throat as he murmured against her skin. "Morning."

"Morning. Could you let me go, please?"

Ricky definitely pressed his lips to the side of her throat this time. "And if I said I didn't want to?"

"Ricky..."

"Damn, that sounds sexy. Say my name again while you're in my bed. I wanna remember this."

"Are you still asleep?" Melanie asked him because she really needed him to be awake right now.

"If I wasn't awake, you'd be asking a lot less questions and wearing considerably less clothes."

"Ricky...I..."

Melanie yelped as she found herself under the weight of a grinning Ricky, as he ducked his head and pressed his lips quickly against hers. He was up and out of the bed before Melanie had time to react. She spluttered in surprise, not knowing what the hell was going on.

"I'm gonna take a quick shower. We have lots to do before we head out, and Erika will be stopping by for updates."

The grinning warlock strode off into the bathroom, devesting himself of his clothes and leaving them in his wake as Melanie groaned, placing a hand over her forehead. It seemed whatever restraint Ricky had been leaning on was gone, and he was done playing around.

It made her angry, this hot and cold routine and, along with her embarrassment over her nightmares, her temper boiled over as she flung back the covers, stormed into the en suite, and stood in the steam-filled room with her hands on her hips.

"What the hell was that? You can't just wake up and kiss me and then run off before I have a chance to say anything. I mean, what are we doing here, Ricky? I don't do well with hints. You're an adult, well you're supposed to be anyways. Speak your fucking mind!"

Her voice rose at the end of her rant, and then she realized that beyond the shower door, Ricky was naked, all dripping with water. Slapping her hand over her eyes, she backed away, smacking into something hard and marble to the touch.

"Lanie, unless you plan on joining me, can we have this conversation when either I'm less naked or you're even more so."

Shaking her head, Melanie managed to flee from the bathroom before she took Ricky up on his offer. Sitting on the edge of his bed, she waited as the shower turned off. A few minutes later, Ricky strode out, wearing nothing but a towel around his waist and a smug grin of male satisfaction.

"Have you decided if you're gonna bite me or not?" His words were blunt, teasing with just a hunt of seriousness.

"I most certainly will not. What the hell is up with you? Are you …?"

"Am I high? Is that what you were going to say?" Ricky snarled as if he were the vampire and not her. "What? You think I can't be straight forward without being high as a kite? Maybe I'm just sick of wanting you and not having you. Maybe I'm not going to deny what I want anymore. Now, even if you don't want to drink my blood, you still have to bite me. I need fresh bite marks before we head out."

Melanie got up and shoved him hard, but he refused to be moved. "That is not what I meant, and you know it. You push me away and then you reel me back in and then you wake this morning like the most natural thing in the world is to kiss me."

"It is."

"I'm sorry, what?"

Ricky's lips curved into a wicked smile, and Melanie could not take her eyes off his mouth. "It is. Last night, sleeping beside you, I realized I was done pretending there was nothing between us. I told you, many times, that I wanted to give you time to fit into your vampire skin. I gave you time. I told you I wanted to be a man who was worthy of you. I am goddamn now. Yes, I'm an adult. I'm not hinting …I'm telling you now, Lanie. You and me, it's inevitable."

Melanie shoved him again, because she could do nothing else against the weight of the truth she tasted in his words. "And do I have any say in this?"

Ricky's eyes twinkled with mischief. "You had your say when

you pinned me up against the station wall and told every single member of the team of your intentions. 'Mine,' you said."

"It was my first day back."

"Why didn't I see you claiming Donnie or Derek as yours?"

Anger fuelled her embarrassment even as Ricky reminded her of what he had said to snap her back from a haze of blood-lust. "I remember telling you that you could have a bite if you wanted, but the first time you sank your teeth into me, I really wanted to be inside you."

"Ricky... I..."

Ricky gave her no time to argue, capturing her mouth in his, a hand snaking around to the back of her neck to deepen the kiss. While she succumbed to the feel of his lips on hers, his tongue swept across her bottom lip. The sensation of his teeth tugging on her lips made Melanie keep her hands clenched by her side.

He walked her backwards, her legs hitting the side of the bed before she fell backward and away from Ricky. She was suddenly very conscious that the only thing between them was a fluffy towel, a t-shirt, and her underwear.

Ricky's face was flush, his chest heaving as he leaned down close enough to kiss her, but stopping before closing the final distance. "No more hints. No more subtle. No more dancing around us."

Melanie steeled her resolve as she reached out her hand to tug the towel away, but a voice from outside snapped them back to reality.

"By the gods, please don't make me endure this. Get your asses out here so we can go back to pretending that you weren't just about to bump and grind."

Melanie groaned at the sound of Erika's voice, even as Ricky quickly kissed her again on the lips. "To be continued."

Melanie stared at the ceiling, trying to calm the storm that was raging inside her as Ricky dressed, begging herself to not so much as speak. When Ricky was gone, she quickly dressed in black jeans and boots, riffling through Ricky's t-shirt drawer until she found a band tee and pulled it on over her head. It was loose, so she pulled the fabric ends together and knotted them. Running her fingers through her hair, Melanie strode out and into the kitchen, halting when she saw that Erika was not alone.

The man sitting next to Erika, his hand possessively cupping the back of her neck, was more than just a man. He smiled knowingly at Melanie, quirking a brow, his eyes like constellations as they twinkled with mischief. Loki, prince of Asgard and Erika's boyfriend or consort or whatever, might appear unassuming in a tailored suit, but Melanie recognised a dangerous man when she saw one.

"We are sorry to interrupt your fun, but we wanted to let you know we will be at Slither tonight as back up. We will be hidden from all but you, so worry not."

"I was going to say, just remember you guys are supposed to be all over each other, but I don't think that's gonna be problem," Erika said with a smirk.

Ricky leaned against the countertop, ignoring Erika as he pointed to the fridge. "Grab some blood, babe, you look a little pale."

Erika laughed as Melanie glared at him. "Sure you don't want us to leave so you can take a bite outta him, vampire girl? Or maybe you want him to take a bite outta you?"

Melanie hissed at the Valkyrie, opening her mouth to blurt out some snappy comment when all the came out was, "You shut up."

"Oh fierce."

Loki leaned in and whispered in Erika's ear, the Valkyrie rolling her eyes before the Norse legend vanished. Erika tossing a wink in Melanie's direction before she disappeared too.

"Is that my t-shirt?" Ricky said before he took another gulp of his coffee.

"Yup." Melanie opened the fridge and took out a bottle of blood. She was intensely aware of Ricky watching her as she popped the lid of the bottle and swallowed. When it was drained, she wiped her mouth and licked her lips. Expecting him to be repulsed by her casually drinking blood, he surprised her by walking over and pecking her lips quickly as if he sensed her discomfort.

"You gotta stop doing that!"

"What?"

"Kissing me!"

Ricky shrugged. "You ready to go to Slither?"

"I'm trying to have a serious conversation with you!"

"And I'm trying to subtly avoid it. Would it help if we made out again?"

Ricky didn't wait for her answer, simply grabbed a croissant, bit into it and said, "Our lift is waiting. C'mon, Lanie."

The blacked out taxi cab lingered outside the gate as Melanie stomped out, sliding in when Ricky held open the door. He scooted in beside her. Melanie grinned at the driver.

"Trying to earn a few extra euros?"

"Make sure you tip well." Derek returned her grin as Ricky tapped the back of the seat.

"Onward, Jeeves."

Derek chuckled, shaking his head. He watched as Ricky reached over and took Melanie's hand in his. She made to pull away, when he said, "Ah, ah …you are supposed to be so in love with me that you went all good girl gone bad. Hold my goddamn hand."

Melanie let out a sigh of frustration, trying to ignore Ricky as he traced her palm with the pad of his thumb. Derek watched them, his eyes filled with amusement, and ignored the glare Melanie shot in his direction.

"According to my C.I., Slither's boss, Viper, claims to have his scales in every part of the criminal underworld. He owns

Slither, and I think he's your best bet at weeding out this Viking character."

"Has news spread of my fall from grace?"

"Well," Derek began, and you could almost feel the disgust in his voice. "Chester called Caitlyn as soon as the sun went down asking of it was true that Melanie had taken off with the warlock. It's caused quite a stir among the masses."

"Good."

That was all Ricky said before ignoring Derek to lean his head back, his hand still in hers. Melanie thought he looked peaceful with his eyes shut, as if he were mediating. Derek pulled the car down the side lane by Slither, a dingy backend bar that looked as appealing as a trip to the dentist.

Derek switched off the engine, turned around in his seat, and waited until Ricky opened his eyes to look back at him.

"Have you a plan?" Derek asked.

"Yeah, I have a plan."

"Is it a good plan?" growled Derek.

Ricky shrugged, grinning at his best friend and partner. "Meh, I have a plan."

"I don't have a good feeling about this."

"That's because you're a control freak and have to sit on the side-lines while Lanie and I have all the fun."

Derek opened his mouth to retort but snapped it shut again, his jaw clicking with an audible sound that only widened the grin on Ricky's face. Melanie watched him, her eyes roaming over his handsome features, the stubble curving around lips that were as sharp as they were sensuous. He'd puzzled her this morning, catching her off guard with open affection, much like he was doing now, even in front of Derek.

But, was it all a ruse to make her at ease with his touch and his kisses, because of the mission? Once this was all over, and Melanie was used to being this close to him, would she be left with nothing more than a hunger for him, even fiercer than her hunger for blood?

As if he sensed her eyes on him, Ricky's lids fluttered open. From the look in his eyes, a hunger of his own, she knew that what he had said about not pretending there was nothing between them was true.

"Rethinking that decision not to bite me?"

Derek barked out a cough up front as Melanie slapped at Ricky with no force of malice behind it.

"I know what you're doing."

Ricky arched a brow in response, something all the members of the team seemed to excel in.

"And what is that, babe?"

Melanie tried to ignore the heat as Ricky circled the soft skin on her hand with his thumb. "You are kissing me, touching me so that we look that part of the couple who can't keep their hands off each other. You want to keep the façade of our cover story. You are shocking me now so that I won't flinch and give the game away when we have to pretend."

Ricky daggered her with his gaze, his smile dipping as his voice lowered, husky and dangerous. "I'm touching you because I want to. I'm kissing you because I want to. If Erika hadn't interrupted us, then we'd have done something I've been fantasizing about since you gave me attitude with those gigantic glasses perched on your nose and your cheeks flamed with embarrassment."

The sickly-sweet taste coated her tongue, and Melanie was totally glad that she could no longer blush. Ricky leaned in so that his breath tickled her ear as he whispered, "I hope you still have those glasses somewhere, because I'm looking forward to showing you exactly what I've been dreaming of for the last three years."

Melanie clasped a hand over Ricky's mouth, stopping him

from saying anything else in front of Derek, who was trying, very unsuccessfully, to not look in their direction.

Derek pulled the car to a halt not far from Slither, snapping off his seatbelt and turning to face them.

"If anything looks like it's about to go sideways, you get the hell out of dodge."

His dark brown eyes were directed at Melanie, and she nodded. "Yes, sir."

A snort sounded from Ricky as he made to slide from the car, popping open the door as he muttered. "Yes, Dad."

Ricky was out the door a second later, and Melanie hated that she already missed the feel of his hand in hers. Making to follow the frustrating warlock out, Derek yanked the door shut and locked it.

"You think for a second that he cannot deal with being in there, you simply get him to Erika, and he is out of there. No undercover job is worth his sobriety. We cannot lose him. I won't lose either of you."

"If I didn't think I could keep him safe, I'd never have offered to be his partner."

"When it comes to those we love, we can often be blind to their faults."

Melanie scoffed. "Speaking from experience?"

"Absolutely. Ever ran because she didn't want to deal with our impending battle. I chased after her and left you and Ricky to land yourselves in the mess you ended up in."

Everyone was sharing secrets tonight, the truth of it weighing heavy on Melanie as she licked her lips. "Ricky did what he did because he wants to handle things by himself. He wants to be as strong and as brave as those he surrounds himself with. None of us are to blame for it."

Scooting her way across the seat, Melanie gave Derek a small smile. "And I was never blind to his faults. I knew he came with baggage, and I still fell for him. Even now, it scares me that he can have this effect on me."

Derek reached out and gave Melanie's shoulder a squeeze. "Just remember that you have that effect on him as well. Sadie... Sadie was never right for him. He never looked at her the way he looks at you."

Melanie said nothing more; he was the second person in so many days who had said such words to her. She was done with this embarrassing conversation already, and Derek knew it.

"Watch your backs and stay safe. Intel is all we need for tonight. Have some fun if you can," Derek said with a grin.

A sharp rap came on the window as Melanie sighed and slipped from the car. Reaching into her pocket, she whipped out a tenner and tossed it in Derek's direction. With a wink, Melanie grinned at the wolf. "Keep the change."

Closing the door to his chuckle of laughter, Melanie stepped up beside Ricky who watched her with open curiosity.

"What'd he say?"

Melanie tapped her nose. "None of your business. Now, let's go and show the world just how badass we are."

Ricky ensnarled her by the waist and pressed his lips to hers in a possessive act that set her body on fire. He pulled his lips from hers and she followed his mouth, wanting more, *needing more.*

Smugness washed over his features, causing Melanie to roll her eyes. Ricky extended his arm, waiting a second before Melanie linked her arm into his. She relished in the feel of his body so close to hers. They held each other's gaze for second more before Ricky moved them forward. No more words had to be spoken. They both knew that a match had been lit within them, and it would either smoulder or consume them.

CHAPTER
EIGHT

RICKY

R icky wasn't sure of the exact moment he decided to throw caution out the window where Melanie was concerned, but damn, he was enjoying himself. What had started out as just a casual way to steel her reactions against him, quickly turned into a blatant play of seduction. Already, Melanie was pushing back, playing with him.

"Take that smug look off your face," Melanie bit out, yet there wasn't a trace of venom in her tone.

"Why wouldn't I be smug? I have the most beautiful vampire in my arms. There is not a supe alive or dead that would think I had lured you to the dark side if I wasn't so utterly smug about it."

"Then stop playing games. We have a job to do."

Ricky angled his body so that they faced one another again, letting a slow smile tug up the corners of his lips as Melanie glared at him. Her red hair was silky smooth, and he itched to reach out and run his fingers through it. Melanie chewed on her bottom lip, a nervous habit that she must not realize she did. Unable to douse the urge to touch her hair, Ricky reached out and tucked a stray behind her ear, relishing in the shudder that coursed through her as he did.

"Why are you glaring at me?"

"I'm hoping you'll spontaneously combust."

"Been there," Ricky snorted in reply. "Done that. Not really interested in doing it again."

Memories of losing control of his magic and burning down *The Crown of Midnight* hotel sprang into his mind, and the magic that coiled inside him like a viper ready to snap to attention and unleash its true power on the world caused him to shiver. In order to get Erika to safety, he'd risked his life and ended up on the path that led to his addiction.

"You ready to head in?" Ricky blew a breath out, trying to push away memories of failure and embarrassment.

"Sure." That was the only reply he got from his vampire girl. Even as he expected her to slip out of his grasp, she leaned forward and pressed her lips to the curve of his jaw, dragging a rumble from his chest.

"Now who's playing games?" Ricky teased as he reached down to intertwine his fingers into hers.

"Not me. Just showing you that you're affected by me as well. This goes both ways."

"It certainly does," Ricky replied with a smile in his voice.

Hand in hand, they strode to the entrance of Slither, and if Melanie was surprised that there was no security at the door, she didn't show it, using her free hand to gently brush her hair from her shoulder. The entrance to Slither wasn't much, and you'd miss it if you didn't know where to go. Hidden between two a donut shop and a coffee shop, Slither appeared to lead to perhaps an apartment above the businesses. Just like a lot of specialized clubs within Supernatural Quarter, Slither masked its appearance until you stepped over the threshold.

Once inside, they were hindered by another door. Ricky reached out and knocked three times, then two, and then four times before the door opened to nothing but darkness.

"How did you know that?"

Ricky moved inside the now opened door, lowering his voice as he answered Melanie's question. "When Sadie did what she did, I went off the rails and came here a lot because it's the last place D would think to look for me. Not a lot of places would serve me after D showed up with that scowl of his."

Melanie smiled, and Ricky's heart did a little skip. Damn, he really did have it bad.

The moment the door closed behind them, a faint luminous green light illuminated the way. Ricky placed a hand on the small of Melanie's back and directed her into the dark, following the strips of light along the floor. The pulse of music vibrated beneath their feet, but nothing except a wall stood in front of them.

Ricky reached out with his hand, feeling the thrum of magic. The magic in him rejoiced, wanting for him to reach out and take control of it. His fingers danced over it, the invisible thread of power that Melanie seemed oblivious to. The power called to him as if trying to seduce him, but it was Melanie's voice that snapped him back to reality.

"Am I missing something?"

Ricky blinked a few times and shook his head. "Do you trust me?"

"Sure."

Chuckling at the uncertainty in her tone, Ricky slipped his arm around her waist and stepped forward, moving Melanie with him. Magic washed over him, drenching his skin and tensing his muscles for just a brief moment before they stepped into the club, and Melanie staggered up against him.

Ricky dropped his hands to her hips, steadying her, and himself in the process. Melanie looked at him, tipping up her chin, her lips pulled by her teeth. Trying to shake off the lure of the magic, Ricky leaned down and kissed her in full view of the room. When she didn't immediately kiss him back, Ricky swept his tongue over her lips and got the reaction he wanted.

Melanie growled, her mouth opening so that Ricky could sink them deeper into the kiss. The kiss was careful, even if it was filled with pent up passion, as Melanie tried to restrain herself. As Ricky ran his tongue over the spot where her fangs would spring from, Melanie staggered back, her eyes flashing red in anger or in lust, Ricky wasn't sure.

Careful to keep up the façade, Ricky grinned and put two fingers to where Melanie's lips had been moments ago. Her nostrils flared as Ricky crooked his finger and headed over to the bar.

Slither hadn't changed in the four years since he'd been here. Snake print wallpaper adorned the walls, reflecting against the green backlight. The small room was circular in shape, the dancefloor lowered by three steps leading down to an area that was packed with gyrating bodies. Ricky swallowed hard as he remembered that he'd once been so drunk in here that he'd basically gotten down and dirty in the corner of the dancefloor, not caring who saw him.

The mirrored ceiling was voyeuristic, reflecting the images of those who revelled on the dancefloor for all to watch. Suddenly, Ricky wanted to get Melanie out of here; she was too pure for a cesspit like this. He wanted her far from it. Panic flared inside him, and he felt his fingers twinge with a familiar surge of heat.

As if sensing that he was about to lose his shit, Melanie coiled her body up against his, and for a minute, he lost all thought. The magic receded at her touch. Flashing her a grateful smile, one which she returned, Ricky was reminded about how terribly he had treated her.

"I'm sorry," he mumbled, earning a surprised frown from Melanie.

"For what?" For a minute, as she expelled a breath she didn't need, Ricky could almost imagine that they were back to being just Ricky and Lanie, before a monster had killed her and before he'd fucked up.

Leaning in closer, his words a whisper in the din of noise. "For being an asshole. For the way I treated you while I was... well, while I was high. For not doing what I wanted to and asking you out on a date. I want to wine and dine you, make you laugh at my stupid jokes and treat you like you deserve to be treated."

Continuing after he cleared his throat, Ricky said, "I spent a lot of time thinking you deserved better than anything I had to offer. We didn't have the chance to start out right, and it's all my fault."

"Ricky," Melanie started; however, he gave her no chance to speak as he pulled away from her, his hand falling to the small of her back again as he lifted two fingers and the bartender slithered over.

The bartender, whose eyes were yellow and slitted, was also the owner of this bargain basement establishment. He studied Ricky as his head tilted, forked tongue flickering out.

"Been a minute, Moore," the snake shifter hissed.

"Sure has, Viper. Now how bout you get me and the lady a drink."

Viper's eyes darted to Melanie, who rolled her eyes at his attention. He continued to stare at her as if trying to trace her, only stopping when Ricky clicked his fingers in front of the snake's eyes and flames erupted. "Eyes on me, Viper, or I will burn this shithole to the ground."

Viper wasn't swayed much by Ricky's threats, instead he hissed at Melanie. "Is your hair naturally red?"

Without skipping a beat, Melanie smirked. "No. I soak it in the blood of my enemies every night. Do snakes bleed red?"

Viper hissed, stepping back as Ricky chuckled, and dragged Melanie closer to him. "She has you there, Viper."

The snake inclined his head. "I like her."

Ricky snarled at Viper. "Mine."

Inclining his head once more, he took their drink order, and Ricky could feel Melanie's eyes on him. He looked at her, his eyes narrowed. "What?"

"Mine?"

"Was I lying?" He grinned, handing Melanie her drink that had just been set down in front of them before taking his own. He lifted it to his lips, inhaling the scent but lowered it before taking a sip, much to Melanie's curiosity.

"First drink since rehab. I'm a little nervous." Ricky explained, feeling heat in his face and neck.

"Everything in moderation, right?" Melanie teased, lifting her own drink to her lips and taking a sip. She kept her eyes on him as he followed her lead, feeling the comforting burn of the whiskey as it made its way down his throat.

"Now, that wasn't so bad was it?" Her tone was light, encouraging, and Ricky wondered what he had done to deserve a girl like her.

He kissed her quickly, ignoring the stares from the criminal underworld as he led Melanie to a table overlooking the dancefloor. He angled his body so that she stood in front of him, one hand on her hip, her head leaning back to rest on his chest. He wished they were anywhere but here, so he could take her in his arms and simply be.

"You're tense as hell, Ricky."

"I've got my vampire girl in my arms, and my thoughts are on anything but solving this case." He gritted out, smiling when Melanie snorted.

"Half lies, Ricky."

"But half the truth as well."

Wanting to change the narrative, and spying their supposed backup, Ricky nudged Melanie. Her eyes followed the direction in which his went, eyes bulging in surprise at what they found.

Loki and Erika were locked in a passionate embrace, and

although her back was to them, her whiskey coloured hair unmistakable even in this harsh light. Her legs were around his waist, and his hands were embedded in her hair. The god of mischief sensed their eyes, and without missing a beat, he lifted his head to grin at them before turning back to his Valkyrie.

Ricky glanced down at Melanie and wiggled his brow. Melanie smacked him and ground out. "Don't even think about it."

Ricky made to answer but was jolted by a shoulder so hard that he let go of Melanie and braced for further attack. Two vampires, one small and pudgy, one tall and wispy, snarled at him. The smaller of the two reached out and made to shove him, but Melanie caught his hand and snarled.

"Don't."

"We don't like cops in here." The vampire ground out, winching as Melanie twisted his wrist.

Ricky reached out and placed a hand on Melanie's shoulder. "In case you haven't heard, I'm no longer a cop. Got the sack today. Fucking idiots. Now, back off before my girl here snaps you like a twig."

"Is it true…" the taller one began, and Ricky didn't have to be a vampire to smell the nervousness in him. "Is it true that you're one of Caitlyn Hardi's vampire?"

Melanie flashed some fang, and damn if Ricky didn't find it incredibly sexy.

"I was. Now I'm only aligned to myself." She lifted her head in Ricky's direction. "And him."

Ricky lowered his head and pressed his lips to the curve of Melanie's neck. She twisted the vampire's wrist again; Ricky heard the bones snap as the vampire yowled in pain and staggered back. Tall vamp made to step up, but Ricky called forth his own magic and flicked a small blue flame at his feet. Ricky enjoyed watching the vampire flail about as he tried to out the flame.

Grinning, Ricky wrapped his arms around Melanie's waist, and she rested her hands over his. He swayed their bodies slightly in time with the music, closing his eyes as if he could pretend that this was permanent, because if he had his way, Melanie would never leave his house ever again.

"Look."

His eyes sprang open, his gaze following hers to where a drug deal was going on in the corner, not far from where Erika and Loki had finally detangled from one another and watched with hawk eyes.

"There's a rabbit on the package," Melanie whispered, and Ricky could feel his whole-body freeze.

This is it.

This is your chance.

You can be you again. You can be more without your magic.

She would love you more if you were not so broken.

Swallowing down his insecurities, Ricky could only watch as the supe rammed the tablets into his mouth and swallowed. The shame of Ricky's addiction weighed heavily on him as he, just for a moment, felt envious of the man.

The drug taker shuddered, his eyes glazing over as his facial expression changed to one of contentment. He lifted his arms up in the air, and the music changed to a deep metal track that had the shifter punching the air.

"He won't stay euphoric for long. The drug is working its way into his bloodstream. It will either take away the call of his magic, or send him into a rapid decent where the man is not in control but the animal."

Ricky hadn't expected to tell Melanie all of that, but the vampire in his arms listened intently before she asked, "Is that what it felt like for you?"

Keeping his eyes on the shifter whose fur began to sprout on his arms and face, Ricky sighed, "My magic was gone. The weight of it was gone. It left just me, and I found that I was blaming the magic for everything in my head. The drugs didn't work. They made everything worse. I still hated myself."

Ricky felt Melanie flinch in his arms, knew she was tasting the truth in his words, but neither of them could continue when the shifter's eyes rolled back into his head, and he collapsed onto the dancefloor. People screamed, rushing away, the music dying off as the shifter convulsed, his back bowing as the transformation from man to animal continued.

Yellow patches of fur sprouted as clothing ripped, flesh split and bones broke. The dancefloor cleared, many supes fleeing in anticipation of what was to come next. Now naked, fur continued to cover the naked man's torso as massive paws replaced hands, claws as sharp as any dagger scraped the ground leaving an imprint.

A mane of hair surrounded the man's face, his body shaking from the force of the change. With one final roar of agony, a monstrous lion got to his feet, nothing human remaining in its eyes of brown with orange flecks. Shifters were known to be larger than the size of a normal animal, and this lion was no exception. It stood taller than Ricky, its body mass the same as a small SUV, its paws bigger than Ricky's head.

One of the shifter's friends made to step up and try and calm him down, but his friend was not in front of him now. The lion had swiped him forward and pounced, crunching down on the bones in the man's neck before anyone could stop him. Blood soaked the lion's fur, and the body of his former friend twitched once, twice before it stilled. The lion continued to tear the flesh from the bones.

"I think I'm going to be sick," Melanie said, and she gagged. She and Ricky both knew she couldn't be sick, not really.

The lion's eyes snapped in their direction at the sound of Melanie's voice, and Ricky shoved her behind him, lifting his hand and sparking the flames in his palm.

"Lanie, don't run. Back away slowly and get out of here."

"I'm not leaving without you."

"Dammit woman, even vampires wouldn't survive being eaten by a lion," he snarled, fearful for her life.

"I'm pretty sure warlocks taste nicer than vampires with all that warm blood and all."

Well, she had a point there.

The lion roared, rattling the building, blood dripping from its teeth. It took a shaky step forward and collapsed. The body began to tremble again, until flesh replaced fur and bones rebroke, forming a naked man lying on the floor, not moving at all.

Ricky darted down the steps, ignoring Melanie's gasp. He dropped to his knees, placed his fingers to the pulse on the man's neck. It was too late; the shifter was dead. Grinding his teeth together, Ricky lifted his eyes and saw the dealer, pale as death, staring at the dead shifter. He met Ricky's eyes before darting out the door.

Erika was up and after him barely a second later, Loki draining his drink before casually walking out after his Valkyrie. A hand on Ricky's shoulder drew his eyes from the shifter. One glance was all he allowed himself, the punch of softness in Melanie's eyes too much for him to bear.

Peering down at the dead shifter, Ricky watched as the man's features blurred, replaced by his own. Ricky's eyes stared back at him, drained of life and taken by the drugs that he still craved, even after watching the lion shifter eat his friend and die.

CHAPTER NINE

RICKY

"We need to go before P.I.T. arrives."

Melanie squeezed on his shoulder, stepping back as Ricky rose. Needing to feel like he was still alive, his emotions somewhat adrift, Ricky pulled Melanie into his arms. She came without a fight, wrapping her arms around his waist and resting her head on his chest.

"You okay?" she asked with a hushed tone, fearful of those who has stayed to watch the horror unfold.

"I am now."

Sirens wailed outside, and Ricky reluctantly let go of Melanie and caught her hand, all but dragging her from the scene. Instead of heading out the way they came, Ricky ushered her behind the bar and pushed open a door with a "Staff only" sign. Bypassing the small office that was in front of them, Ricky felt around the wall and pressed down on the lever to the secret emergency exit he'd used once or twice before when escaping from this place.

Stepping out into the alley, the cold night air caused him to tremble, but Ricky was sure it was a mixture of the frigid temperatures and a little bit of shock. Straightening his jacket, he cleared his throat and glanced around the alleyway, wondering what to do next. Cop Ricky would take off after the drug dealer, but newly reformed criminal Ricky wouldn't be bothered to go after the lowlife, he'd be protecting his own ass.

As if sensing his confliction, Melanie nudged him with her shoulder. They were alone in the alley, but while they were trying to maintain a cover, Ricky knew they needed out of the alley a.s.a.p.

"Which way did they go?"

Melanie stood with her hands on her hips, frowning with concentration. "Well, based on the direction of the wind, the broken sticks in the corner, and the disturbance of the dirt, I'd guess they went left."

Ricky couldn't hide the surprise from widening his eyes as he turned to look at Melanie. What the hell had she been learning while he was away?

"You could really figure it all out from that?" he asked, and if he was not mistaken, there was twinkle in her eyes.

"No, doofus, they sent me a text…. see?" Melanie grinned as she held out her phone to show him the text from Erika.

Knowing he was affected by the dead shifter in the club, Melanie was teasing him, trying to make him laugh so he would forget exactly what was racing through his mind.

"Smartass. C'mon, let's catch up with them."

Ricky took off in a slow jog, knowing Melanie would be able to keep pace with him with her vampire speed. They barely made it around the corner when Erika stalked out of the shadows, the biggest grin on her face. Loki leaned against the wall, watching her much like a hunter studies its prey.

The dealer whimpered as Erika clutched the collar of his shirt and brought him under the glare of the streetlight. Blood seeped from the dealer's nose and forehead. Ricky shook his head even as the Valkyrie grinned some more.

"Why is he bleeding?" Melanie asked.

"Because he's an idiot?" Erika replied, batting her lashes

innocently even as Ricky chuckled, knowing full well that Erika had revelled in inflicting pain on the scum.

Melanie snorted. "I didn't know that idiocy caused people to just start spontaneously bleeding from the nose."

Erika shrugged. "It's a new phenomenon."

Ricky shook his head, ignoring the banter between the two women and strode over to the dealer, who ducked his head so as not to have to look at him in the eyes. Ricky held out his hand under the man's nose, letting his magic spark in his hand. That was enough to get the man's attention.

"I don't know nothing."

"Chill, Jon Snow, I just wanna know where you got your product. Maybe get me an intro. I'm interested in a business venture."

The man vigorously shook his head from side to side, his eyes fearful and panicked as he spat out. "He'll kill me if I say a word. I'm just a dealer, the lowest in the operation. I don't even know his name."

Ricky played with the flicker of sparks on his palm, turning them over and along the skin of his fingers. "But you can send word up the chain. Will you tell the Viking that Ricky Moore wants a meet?"

"Sure…sure…anything you want, boss."

Quenching the magic in his palm, Ricky drew back, motioning for Erika to let the man go. With a sigh, Erika unclenched her fist, and the dealer made to run. Ricky stepped into his path.

"Double-cross me, mate, and I'll send her after you. If you think she's good with her fists, wait until you see what she can do with a knife. She will cut you in so many ways and make it look like art."

The man paled as Erika took a step forward. "Boo."

He bolted from the alley, and Erika cackled, all while her immortal lover watched in amusement. When the man turned the corner, heading away from the growing number of police on the crime scene, Ricky strode forward out of the line of sight, Melanie and Erika following suit.

Ricky passed by Loki, a man he had little conversation with before. Loki was a bundle of magical energy that Ricky could feel even from the short distance away. He arched a brow at Loki, grinned and pointed back at Erika. "Your girlfriend's a little psycho."

"Thank you. She is just my kind of crazy."

Ricky chuckled as Erika elbowed Loki in the ribs, but the Norse legend looked unaffected.

"What do we do now?" Melanie asked, folding her arms across her chest.

"I don't know about you, Newton, but I'm going home to finish what we started in the club." Erika smirked, and Melanie glared at her. "Maybe if you two just got it over with then the waves of sexual energy coming from you both wouldn't set the rest of us off."

Loki came up behind her, his hand going around her throat as he winked and they vanished, leaving Ricky all alone with a very worried looking vampire.

"She's lying, right? I mean, she's teasing, right?"

Ricky kept his expression blank as Melanie clamped a hand over her mouth. He shrugged and was unable to stop himself from laughing as she reached out to smack him. Quick as he could, he ensnared her wrist and growled, "You wanna spank me, babe. I'm down for that."

Melanie froze, her eyes going wide, and with little strength, tried to pull back her hand. It was all the invitation he needed. Twirling them so that she was up against the wall, Ricky pressed his body up against hers, his heart hammering in his chest as he reached out and lifted her by the hips, so she had no choice but to wrap her legs around his waist.

In the shadow of the alley, Ricky pressed his lips to the curve of her jaw, and Melanie's arms snaked around his neck, her fingers tugging on the strands of his hair. Kissing his way along her jaw and up the curve of her neck, Ricky used his teeth to tug at her ear, and Melanie reacted by digging her nails into his scalp.

When he placed his open mouth to the curve of her neck and bit down gently where her pulse once had been, Melanie jerked in his arms and moaned, lowering her own mouth to the pulse at his neck. His blood rushed with anticipation. He felt the barest brush of her fangs, and his hips moved of their own accord.

"If we could have a moment, please?"

A cool, collected voice caused Melanie to yelp and push at Ricky's shoulders until he let her go, his fiery vampire hiding sheepishly behind him. Being caught by Caitlyn Hardi while making out in darkened alleyways was nearly as bad as getting caught watching porn by your mother.

Donnie stood by his mate's side, looking as uncomfortable by what they had almost walked up on as Melanie did. Caitlyn folded her arms across her chest, her own expression schooled from years of acting like an ice queen in order to keep her heart safe after an ocean of tragedy had crashed down over her life.

"Mortified, mortified, mortified." Melanie chanted over and over again behind him, but Ricky couldn't help but laugh while he straightened his clothing.

"Sure. It's not like you interrupted anything interesting that was about to happen."

"I think we all have a clear idea of what was about to happen, Ricky. No need to elaborate."

"Oh my god," Melanie said against his back. "I want to die."

Donnie barked out a strangled laugh. "Too late for that, little sister. You're already dead."

Caitlyn lifted a hand, but the slight smirk that tugged her lips was enough to know that she wasn't angry or anything, she was simply trying to embarrass Melanie. Catching her eyes, those gunmetal greys of Caitlyn's, Ricky was nearly floored when she gave him a hurried wink as she asked, "Care to tell us what happened?"

"I'd rather not." Melanie croaked under her breath, not catching Caitlyn's meaning. Donnie coughed, turning away as his shoulders shook. Ricky had to bite his lip to stop from laughing even as Caitlyn pretended to glower at Melanie.

"I was referring to what happened in the club, ma petite vampire. I'd rather stay away from fornicating in alleyways."

Ricky snapped his gaze to Donnie and said with a grin, "You're missing out."

"We fornicate enough, bro, believe me."

"A shifter took some White Rabbit," Melanie rushed out, stepping out from behind Ricky, her eyes still on the ground as if she were ashamed of being caught with him.

You mean nothing to her.

Why would she care about a junkie?

She'll lose interest once the appeal wears off.

"He changed into a lion and proceeded to have his friend for dinner. The human wasn't there anymore just the animal." As Melanie continued, the voices in his head taunted him. Donnie turned back to face Ricky, who had zoned out until Donnie came to stand beside him. Steering Ricky away from the woman, Donnie spun him. He had little choice but to look up at the former rugby player.

"You really believe that, don't ya? You think that once Melanie gets what she wants, she would drop you? You really are stupid if you think you mean nothing to her."

"Donnie, I love you, my brother, but stay the fuck out of my head. I'm not good enough for her. We both know that. Do you honestly think you are good enough for Caitlyn?"

Ricky hit a nerve, and his friend snarled. But Donnie would not be swayed but Ricky's diversion tactics.

"You really can't see it, huh? The way she looks at you isn't the same way she looks at other guys."

Ricky dared to roam his eyes toward Melanie, his pulse quickening when he spied that her eyes were on him. She gave him a coy smile, nodding as Caitlyn said something, but she never took her eyes from him.

Maybe, just maybe, she could be his.

"There it is. There is the Ricky Moore mentality that you need. Forget the last three months. She won't wait forever."

"Shouldn't you be warning me off her?" Ricky queried; his brow raised.

Donnie clasped him on the shoulder. "Make no mistake, bro, you hurt her, and there is a long line who will want a word with you. But none of us will stand in your way if ye make each other happy."

"What are you two muttering about?" Melanie broke in, causing Donnie to grin.

"Just having a friendly word."

"Yeah, well, go have it somewhere else."

Donnie chortled, nudging Melanie's chin with his knuckles as he strode back to Caitlyn, leaned in and whispered something that had the regal vampire shaking her head with a smile on her face.

"It's still strange to see her smile so easily, isn't it?"

Melanie spoke the words he was thinking, because being happy was difficult for Caitlyn. Everyone on the team had wanted for Caitlyn to be happy, to finally breathe so to speak now that her maker, Cain was dust on the wind. Caitlyn had been slowly becoming who she always was meant to be, even if it had taken centuries to do so.

"I believe it's even harder for her to believe that she can be happy."

Melanie tucked her hair behind her ears. "I'm so embarrassed!"

"By getting caught making out in an alley or by getting caught making out with me?"

Melanie glared at him, folding her arms across her chest and pushing up her breasts, as Ricky dropped his gaze to them. "Are you for real? I was embarrassed because my kinda parents found me moaning in an alleyway. If you think that I was embarrassed because it was you, then you need your head examined."

Ricky held up his hand in surrender. "I'm an idiot. Forgive me?" Pouting his lips, he batted his eyes at her, sending her into a burst of laughter that made his stomach flip.

"You are an idiot. Come on. I could do with something to eat."

Ricky wiggled his brows suggestively, and Melanie rolled her eyes and walked backward out of the alley.

"You have a filthy mind, mister, and I am not going to enable it."

"Keep taunting me, babe. See how naked it gets you."

Melanie grinned, a slow and sexy smile that was only for Ricky. "That's not very threatening, *babe*. I think you'd use any excuse to see me naked."

Ricky shrugged, holding out his hands in mock deference, completely captivated by the girl–no woman–in front of him. Donnie was right, he needed to take his head out of his ass and see where this thing with Lanie was going; they both deserved to know.

Melanie continued to walk backward, sashaying as she did. For every step forward he took, she took one back until she reached the mouth of the alley. Ricky quickened his pace, reaching for her when she chortled, stepping back further and collided with a couple who was passing by.

"Oh god, I'm sorry–" Melanie's words broke off as her eyes widened, surprise washing over her face as she stared open mouthed at the couple she'd backed into.

Ricky came up beside her and wrapped an arm around her waist, feeling the tension in Melanie as she continued to stare at the couple. There was nothing out of the ordinary about them that Ricky could pinpoint. It was obvious the female was a supe, but the dark-haired man was the one who had Melanie's full attention.

Tall and lean, he was obviously human, mortality showed in his features, though most of them were masked by a goatee the same colour as his hair. His hair was tied back in a ponytail, braided at the top into fine lengths that Ricky had seen somewhere before but couldn't place.

"Hey, I'm sorry. We were messing about and my girlfriend wasn't watching where she was going. My apologies."

The man didn't even look at Ricky; his eyes were predatory as they roamed over Melanie. Ricky was fit to deck the guy for daring to look at his girl like that.

"Of all the people to run into me, I never expected it to be Ms. Melanie Newton. Damn, Mel, you look good. Death becomes you."

The stranger spoke to Melanie with an over familiar tone that frayed on Ricky's nerves. His voice was sweet as honey, his smile as smug as his demeanour.

Melanie shook her head in disbelief, blinking a few times before she found her voice and said, "I didn't know you were back in Cork."

The woman stuck to the stranger's side clucked her tongue impatiently, but she was silenced by a glare from her partner. His head came back to face Melanie, his hands tracing the goatee curved around his lips.

Melanie's hand gripped the side of Ricky's tee, her discomfort obvious even as Ricky said, "As I said, we're sorry for bumping into you. Now if you'll excuse us, we must be going."

"Mel, please don't tell me that after three years, you don't even have two words for me? I thought we meant more to each other than that."

The man reached out to run his knuckles down Melanie's cheek, but Ricky grabbed his hand before he could lay a hand on Melanie. The dark-haired man simply shrugged off Ricky's grasp and continued to stare at Melanie.

He was seriously started to piss Ricky off.

"C'mon, Mel. Did dying douse the fire in your soul? Haven't you missed me?"

Something snapped in Melanie, and Ricky reacted as she sprang forward, grabbing her by the waist and holding her back. The burn in his arms caused him to hiss out a breath as Melanie struggled against him in earnest.

"Lanie, you're hurting me," Ricky said softly, and Melanie froze, settling into his arms and turning to glare at the man in front of her.

"I wish you'd never come back. You set me up!" Melanie snarled out.

"If they told you that, then they lied, babe."

Stabbing her finger toward the man, Melanie scowled. "You don't get to call me that. You lost that right when you let me get arrested, and you ran away. I'd have rotted in jail because of you."

The man roamed his eyes over Melanie once again, and she snarled. "Looks like things worked out for you in the end, Mel. I am truly sorry for what happened. I didn't know that he was a cop. If I had, I'd have killed the snitch."

"You may be back in my city, but you stay the hell away from me, Greg DeShane. I want nothing to do with you."

"You so sure about that, Mel? If I don't matter to you, then why are so angry, babe? Maybe you missed me after all?"

He thought he would be less affected by her in person, yet he found he still craved her as much as he had when they'd been together. She was more now, even more fiery than she'd been as his hacker sharing his bed. He still wanted her, even if she was now a vampire and part of a society he detested.

He hated seeing the warlock's hands on his woman, the way he'd claimed her with his words, and how she angled her body to his. The warlock had called her his girlfriend, but he'd kill him for that.

As her eyes of pale green flashed red with bloodlust, Greg DeShane rolled up his sleeves and grinned at the vampire in front of him. Her eyes were full of hatred and disgust for him, the man she once claimed to love.

He could still win her back, still persuade her that she was better off with him.

If not, he'd simply kill her....

Nothing would get in the way of his mission...

Not even the woman who still held his heart captive.

The supernatural race would be wiped out, leaving Melanie as the last vampire standing ...if she came back to him.

CHAPTER TEN

MELANIE

"I don't know about this, Greg. I mean we could really get into trouble for it."

Greg laughed off her reluctance, pressing his lips to the top of her head before he picked up his bottle of Landshark and took a slug. Melanie pushed her glasses up the bridge of her nose and chewed on her bottom lip as Greg reclined in his chair in their tiny little apartment.

"How are we going to change the world if we are afraid to try?" he asked her, his voice cool and sultry, lowered to a husky tone as it always did when he tried to convince her to do something she didn't want to do.

"You're asking me to hack a police data base and track down the names and addresses of the members of the Paranormal Investigations Team? Why?"

Greg shook his head and set his beer down on the table, before resting his feet up on it. "That's a need to know, Mel. I'm trying to protect you. Don't I always protect you?"

He did, damn it. Greg always protected her, telling her he loved her, and Melanie loved him too. At the start, she did anything within her power to make sure he stayed with her. She wasn't the best looking, she wasn't even the smartest, but her skills with a computer had put her on Greg DeShane's radar, his good looks and charm tangling her in his web, and now she was powerless to struggle her way out.

"I won't do anything that could get someone killed, Greg, you know that."

Greg held up three fingers. "Scouts honour. You trust me, don't you?"

Melanie bobbed her head, a bitter taste on her mouth even as she could not vocalize the lie. With every passing day, she trusted him less and less. The more unsavoury characters knocked on their door, every time Greg shut her out of private phone calls and decided it would be best if she stayed at home when he went out to meet contacts, her trust in him wavered until it had Melanie planning a way to escape.

Greg's phone chimed. He stood, chugging down the remains of his beer before he pulled Melanie upright and kissed her. She tried to fake her response and remember the romantic man who had swept her off her feet in an internet chatroom. He had been so kind, caring for her when she felt alone in the world.

Greg had been the prince who had come to rescue her from her golden tower, freeing her from the prison of neglect her parents inflicted on her. Except, she'd traded one prison for another.

Backing away, Greg eyed her suspiciously, handing her an earpiece as he threw on his jacket.

"Get the names, Mel. Tell me where they live, and then it will be over. We will have enough money to start over wherever you want. A house in suburban America? Doesn't that sound like heaven."

Melanie nodded, shoving her thick rimmed glasses up her nose again. She plonked down on the ground again, folding her legs and tapping on the keys of her laptop with intense speed.

"That's my girl."

Greg strode out the door with utter confidence that she would do as he asked. So far, all they'd done was hack into people's bank accounts who had too much money. They'd leaked intel on a prominent politician who had a taste for underage boys. And, they shut down a power grid so protesters could hang their banners under the cover of darkness.

Melanie had a sneaking suspicion that this next act of rebellion was something she couldn't live with. It barely took her ten minutes to hack into the Garda database and get a list of active agents within P.I.T.

Tomas Delaney
Derek Doyle
Caitlyn Hardi
Donnie O'Carroll
Richard Moore
Fionn McHale
Carter Mills

"Mel, do you have the names?" Greg's voice rang through the earpiece.

"Their firewall is taking longer than expected to break through. I'll need a few more minutes."

"You aren't lying to me are you, Mel?"

"Of course not!" she exclaimed. "If you think you can do better, feel free to try."

There was a pause as Greg hesitated, and Melanie knew that if he had someone else who could do what she did, then he'd probably walk away.

But wasn't she pushing him out the door? She certainly would once he discovered what she was about to do.

Sending the anonymous email, Melanie crossed her fingers, hoping that the P.I.T. team would take her email seriously, or else she was a dead girl walking. Greg's bosses wouldn't take her duplicity well.

"Carter Mills, shifter. Resides at 102 Oak Drive, Ballincollig. Lives alone. Currently not on active duty due to an injury received in the field. Should be vulnerable."

"Good girl. See you soon, babe."

Melanie yanked the earpiece out of her ear and tossed it aside. Switching screens on her laptop, she watched Greg's phone blink *onscreen, moving toward the house he thought held one of the agents sent to hunt their group down. She also hacked one of P.I. T.'s phones and saw that the team had already gotten to Carter's house and lay in waiting for the criminals.*

Greg would be pissed when he found out that Carter Mills was killed in action two weeks ago, and his house was empty because of it. He'd be gunning for her, but she was a masterful hacker. Her new passport and I.D. were burning a hole in her pocket.

Melanie could not take her eyes off the screen as Greg's phone blinked at Carter's house. Forcing herself to snap the laptop shut, she took a hammer to it, breaking the tech into tiny little pieces. Removing her sim card from her phone, Melanie snapped it in two.

Rushing into the bedroom, she grabbed her stashed backpack, slinging it over her shoulder before she pulled a duffel filled with cash from her personal stash. Setting a baseball cap on her head, Melanie didn't spare the apartment a second glance as she strode over to the door and yanked it open.

Staggering back with a yelp, Melanie came face-to-face with an angry wolf, his eyes amber, his vest spelling out exactly where he worked, and Melanie's shoulders sagged.

A million thoughts ran through her mind: Had she masked her IP address? Had she been too cocky when she slipped behind the firewall and left a digital footprint? She was always so careful; what the hell had happened?

Melanie dropped the duffel, let her backpack slip off her shoulder and lifted her eyes for a second to the wolf before she dropped her gaze again.

"You got my email, then?"

"Turn around and face the wall, Ms. Newton. Hold your hands out in front of you."

Melanie did as she was told, didn't even argue when she was never mirandized. She didn't so much as flinch as handcuffs snapped shut on her wrists, and she was steered out of the apartment and placed in the back of a police car.

The wolf sat beside her, not speaking for a few minutes until he said, "You know he hung you out to dry? He blamed you, claimed you were the mastermind behind it all."

"Whhatt?"

"Before he shot one of the vampires, he rattled off your address and told us you were the top dog, the one pulling the leash. No offense, but you look like you should be in college, not hacking a government database."

To her embarrassment, tears welled, falling in earnest. The wolf handed her a tissue, and she smiled at him gratefully.

"Wanna know what I think?"

"Sure, Agent Doyle. Sure."

The wolf smirked when Melanie said his name, but didn't question how she knew it.

"I think he used you. I think he filled your head with words of love and rebellion, and you fell for it, hook, line and sinker."

Melanie snorted. "Don't sugar-coat it, Agent Doyle."

"And the moment when it stopped being fun, when you took off the rose-coloured glasses, you wanted no part of it, and this was your only way out."

Melanie shrugged. "Well, I was planning on leaving the country, but you kinda ruined that plan."

"Sorry. You know we only want the truth. My boss will be fair with you if you're just honest."

"Uh huh, sure." Melanie leaned her head back against the headrest and closed her eyes. "Just wake me when we get there."

She pretended to sleep, and Agent Doyle let her. But even though Melanie had betrayed Greg, his lies were like a stab through the chest. He'd blamed her for all of this, and now... now she would rot in prison just like him. At least that was some consolation.

Later she'd found out that Greg had slipped free from the police after shooting one of the vampire's in the chest. He taken her escape money and disappeared. And now he was back, but Melanie was no longer the girl she had been back then.

The shock of seeing Greg in the flesh again was done, and all Melanie felt was anger, especially as Greg seemed to think that nothing had changed in the almost four years since she had been arrested and given the chance of redemption.

Melanie felt the warlock tense beside her, and one look at the dark expression on his face, the heat that emulated from him, was enough to focus on him rather than Greg. Ricky looked like he was willing to burn Greg from the inside out and would wear a smile doing so.

"Hey, I'm good. Reign in the macho caveman stance, and let's go home."

Ricky's lips curled into a smile, even as his eyes still were focused on Greg. "Home?"

Melanie rolled her eyes, thanking him silently for still teasing her and reminding her why she had fallen for him.

"Sure, sure."

Ricky slung his arm around her shoulder, pulling her close. To Greg, he drawled. "You're lucky that I'm on a promise or I'd have knocked your teeth out."

The girl at Greg's side, someone Melanie detested with all of her cold, dead heart, coiled herself around Greg much like a leech on his skin. Her hair was a mousey brown, and she would have been considered pretty, if it wasn't for the constant scowl on her face. Once upon a time, Jaime Cross had been her best friend, or the closest thing Melanie had to one. But when they had met Greg, Jaime had slowly pulled away from Melanie, because Greg had chosen Melanie over her.

As a siren, Jaime was not happy with that.

"Melanie, nice to see you are finally dating on your level."

"Jaime, nice to see that you are clearly punching above your weight. How are you liking my leftovers?"

Jaime opened her mouth, the scent of magic filling the air. Ricky, who had once been under the trawl of a succubus, lifted his hand, and his own magic burst into being.

"So much as try and use your magic against us, and I'll make you wish you were dead."

Jaime clamped her mouth shut, terrified of the flames that lingered in Ricky's palm. Greg clicked his fingers at Jaime, and she huffed, pursing her lips but doing as she was ordered to do.

"Mel, I'm so glad we ran into each other," Greg drawled, and ice clung to Melanie's spine as she tasted the truth in his words. "Maybe, once the shock has worn off, we could meet up, have a coffee and catch up?"

"Um, no chance."

"I think you'll change your mind." Greg glanced down at his arm, Melanie followed the path in which Greg's eyes travelled and bile crept into her throat. Ricky was oblivious to the exchange as Melanie took in the tattoo that was etched into Greg's skin, a tattoo of the symbol for the show, *Vikings*.

All the pieces suddenly slotted into place; the drugs with White Rabbit, Greg's nickname in the chat group in which they had met and now, the goddamn tattoo. She'd been an idiot to not consider it before. The bastard who had taken her on his trip into criminality, was the kingpin behind the drugs enterprise that had hooked Ricky on White Rabbit. It was all Greg!

Greg smirked the minute he realized she had figured it out and had the audacity to wink at her. Melanie lurched forward, pointing her finger in his face.

"Did you know?" she snarled, getting right into his personal space. "Did you know who he was to me when you sold him the White Rabbit?"

Greg continued to grin, but his face went blank. "I have no idea what you are talking about."

Lies, lies, lies...

Melanie smiled and flashed a bit of fang, a wave of satisfaction washing over her, giving her a sense of bravado. "Things have changed in the last three years, Greg. I'm not the same naive girl anymore. I'm a vampire who kicks ass and takes names. I'm the child of a vampire queen with powers of my own. I can tell you're lying, and I can smell the fear on both of you."

"Mel, come on."

"Don't," Melanie said holding up her hand to stop him from yammering on. "I don't want to hear it. I can't stomach the sight of ye right now, but Ricky wants to do business with you so here we are."

Greg inclined his head. "I understand. Had I known you'd have reacted like this, Mel, I'd have given you fair warning I was back." Taking a card from his pocket, Greg made to hand it to Melanie, but Ricky snatched it from him before she had to take it.

"I'll speak with you soon, Mr. Moore."

Steering Jaime away, Greg left, walking down to the end of the street before he peered over his shoulder to find her glaring after him. Mistaking her gaze for one of intrigue, Greg grinned, that breath-taking smile that had once captured her heart. Now, it only instilled fear and an abundance of rage.

Greg had lured them into this...lured Ricky into his addiction. If he hadn't been trying to draw her out, would he have even targeted Ricky. Was this all her fault?

Ricky rested a hand on her shoulder and damn her, but she flinched, guilt seeping into her bones as she peered up at him. Ricky didn't say a thing, waiting for her to take the lead and tell him what was going on in her head. When she didn't speak, simply because she couldn't trust the words that would come out of her mouth, Ricky shattered the silence.

"So, that's the prick who sold you out?"

"Pretty much."

"And he's the one responsible for White Rabbit?"

"Yeah."

Ricky stalked around to face her, cupping her face in his hands. "You know it's not on you? My addiction. If it wasn't

White Rabbit, it would have been something else. I was spiralling long before I popped those pills."

"Yeah," Melanie croaked out, emotion thick in her voice. "When I died, and you had to use magic to find me."

"Nah, Lanie. I was spiralling a lot longer than that. I used it as an excuse, but it was never about you. It was always about me."

Even though she tasted the truth in his words, Melanie didn't want to believe him, she wanted to wallow in her own self-pity and darkness. Reaching up, she lifted Ricky's hands from her face.

"Let's just go. I want to wash this night off my skin."

Melanie rushed out of the alley, feeling the blaze of Ricky's anger as he stalked after her. Holding out her hand, she hailed a taxi, wishing Derek would show up and debrief them so that she could avoid another conversation with Ricky.

Jumping into the backseat, Ricky smoothly slipped in beside her, barked an address at the driver and tried to catch her eye but Melanie fixed her gaze firmly out the window as she watched Cork pass by in a blur of lights and night.

As they pulled up outside Ricky's house, Melanie was out the door and into the house before Ricky handed the driver his fare. Devesting herself of her clothing, she stormed into the bathroom and locked the door firmly behind her. Turning on the shower, she ducked under the spray as she heard Ricky try and open the door.

"Try and hide from me, Lanie. Just try and block me out. It won't work. I've had a taste, and I need more. We aren't done, not by a long shot."

Melanie let her head fall back against the cold tile, the water cascading down her skin as she heard Ricky mutter a curse, but leave her alone. The door to his bedroom closed softly as he left, and Melanie hoped he could not hear her as tears broke free. She sobbed until she could sob no more.

Turning off the shower, Melanie stepped out and took her time drying off. Dawn was approaching, it called to her as she took one of Ricky's hair ties and pulled her damp hair off her face. The long tee she'd worn the night before was neatly folded on the sink, where it hadn't been before. Melanie tried the door, but it was still bolted. He'd used magic. Of course he had.

Unlocking the door, she walked out into the bedroom to find Ricky already laying under the covers, a bottle of blood on her side of the bed. His eyes were closed, his torso bare, his own hair loose around his neck. He looked good enough to bite.

Instead of indulging in her wants, Melanie slowly walked around and drained the bottle of blood in seconds, not realizing how much her emotions had frayed on her hunger. Ricky hadn't so much as moved an inch as Melanie peered over her shoulder at him, the only sign that he sensed her watching him was the rush of heartbeats that quickened his pulse.

Sliding under the covers, Melanie didn't hesitate to scoot over to him, curling up into his side. Ricky reached under her head, so that she rested in the crook of his arm. With a sigh, Melanie closed her eyes, inhaling the scent of him, oil and leather, and wished she could stay like this, in his arms for the rest of their lives.

But she'd be content with today...

CHAPTER
ELEVEN

MELANIE

There was an eerie moment of silence after Ricky's statement, each of the team digesting the implication that someone they worked with, someone they had welcomed as part of their team, had been deceiving them all this time. Derek was the first to react, slamming his hand down on the table so hard Melanie jumped.

Something dragged her gaze to Caitlyn, whose face had donned a mask of deadly calm, as was her tone when she said, "Tadgh. Anna's assistant Tadgh. The very same Tadgh that is currently, at this moment, on a date with my niece?"

Ricky ducked his head as he scrubbed his hand over the stubble on his chin. "Yeah, I wanted to use it. But now, if DeShane knows we are not looking to deal with him, there's no point in keeping it to myself. You might as well arrest and interrogate him."

"I'll rip his head clean from his shoulders," Caitlyn snarled, heading for the door and only stopping when Donnie surged forward and snagged her around the waist.

"Kenzie can handle herself. We will tell her when she is back with us. You march in there, all badass and shit, and she won't thank you for it. Sit her down and talk to her. Let Kenzie make up her own mind."

Melanie could almost see the cogs turning in Caitlyn's mind as she stilled in Donnie grasp, listened to his words and then settled into him by leaning her head back against his broad chest.

"*Mon amour*, thank you. I should not have let my emotions steer me."

"Believe me, I wanna kick the little git's ass as much as you, but Kenzie, she can handle him by herself."

Everyone waited as Donnie kissed the side of Caitlyn's neck, and they returned to their seats, with Caitlyn allowing Donnie to pull Caitlyn into his lap. Melanie smiled, always delighted to see them like this when once there was a possibility that too much darkness would prevent them from finding happiness. It gave her hope that happiness was possible for her, too.

Her eyes wandered to Ricky, and she found him looking straight at her. He grinned, a sight that had once made her human heart flutter and her stomach do somersaults.

"Call DeShane. Set a meeting. We can send you guys in, and if thing go south, arrest him. We need to get White Rabbit off the streets, and if we take out his chemist, effectively cut the head off the snake, then we might be able to wipe out his organization."

"I'll meet DeShane by myself," Ricky stated, his tone firm like he would not change his mind.

"Like hell you will," Melanie blurted. "And let him think he's intimidated me? Let him feel even the slightest victory over me. I want to be the one to slap the bracelets on him. I want him to know that I beat him."

"I won't let him hurt you, Lanie."

"Neither will I," Melanie declared, the resolve in her voice surprising even her. She was never afraid to speak her mind with the team, even when she had been terribly human and intimidated by the overwhelming power of the supernaturals she worked with, they had always listened to her opinion and taken it on board.

"Okay then," Ricky said.

Melanie looked at him suspiciously, her lips pursing as she regarded him. "You're not going to argue? You're not going to tell me I can't go?"

Ricky shrugged, trying to appear nonchalant as he lifted his mug to his lips, drawling out his answer. "The last time I tried that shit, you ended up dead. If you wanna back me up on this, then have at it. I'm good with that. Doesn't mean I won't fry the bastard if he looks at you wrong."

Before Melanie could answer, Derek tossed Ricky a burner phone. Ricky caught it, plucked the card Greg had given him out of his pocket and dialled the number. Ricky didn't even have to put it on speaker, since the rest of the team all had supernatural hearing.

"Yes."

That voice. That smug, confident tone that caused Melanie to shudder and had Ricky glancing in her direction.

"It's Ricky. When can we meet?"

"How's my Mel today?"

Steam, real goddamn steam came out of Ricky's ears, and he had to move the phone away as he calmed himself down.

"My Lanie is good. She hasn't been your Mel in a long time. You had your chance DeShane, and you fucking blew it. Don't bother pulling that crap with me. Either you wanna do business or you don't."

There was a pregnant pause before Greg sighed impatiently. "Tomorrow night. I'm hosting a poker night. Warehouse down by Western Road. You'll feel the glamour once you're near."

"I'll be there." Ricky made to hang up when Greg called his name.

"Bring Melanie. You don't, and the deal's off."

Ricky chuckled. "Melanie will be where she is supposed to be. By my side. I see her value, her worth. Shame you couldn't or it might have been me wearing a shade of green. See you tomorrow night."

Ricky hung up the phone and tossed the burner on the table. "Dickhead."

"And you just goaded him. Flaunted me in front of him. Made him mad. I know him. He won't like it."

"I don't give two monkeys what he likes or doesn't. He tried to use you against me, but I was having none of it."

Erika popped back in that moment, halting the argument that was brewing, and Melanie was thankful because she was not even sure why she was angry at Ricky. His words were meant to stand up for her, not dismiss her. Then why did she feel anger bubbling up in her chest?

Melanie turned her head away, looking to the Valkyrie who she trained with most weeks, a strange expression marring her utterly stunning features.

As if sensing Melanie's eyes on her, Erika lifted her head, and Melanie was wondering what had put that look in her friend's eyes.

"You okay?" Melanie queried.

Erika plastered a smile on her face. "Sure. Hundred per cent. Everything's fine."

Bitterness coasted Melanie's tongue, and her face contorted as the taste hit the back of her throat. Erika held her gaze as if in warning, but it was not Melanie's place to call her out on her obvious lies.

"You ready to go, boyband?" Erika smirked at Derek who growled, hating the nickname Erika kept calling him, even though whatever centuries old grudge the Valkyrie had with her queen's champion and mate had evaporated once Erika had snared Loki.

SHORTCUT TO THE GRAVE

"I really wish you'd stop calling me that," Derek muttered as he stood and walked over to her.

She grinned, waved, reaching out to grab Derek before she left. He was visibly pale. Seems the werewolf still didn't like being flashed around the place.

Ricky cleared his throat, glanced down at his hands as he said, "You gals mind giving Donnie and me a second. Please."

Caitlyn rose with a grace that Melanie had always been envious of and strode from the room without a second thought. Melanie looked from Ricky to Donnie before following Caitlyn out the door. She was standing in the doorway to Zach's bedroom, and Melanie left her to it, going to sit down on the couch. A moment later, Caitlyn came in and reclined in one of the armchairs.

Melanie tried not to listen, blaming it on her vampire hearing, but she was simply nosy. Caitlyn had closed her eyes and moved not an inch.

"Here. Take this and hold onto it just in case," Ricky said.

"In case what, buddy?"

"In case something happens to me. It's my will. It's only to be opened if I die. Hopefully, you won't need to open it until I'm an old man, but still…."

Melanie heard no more as the kitchen door closed with a snick. She hissed as if she could feel the magic preventing her from listening. Did Ricky think Greg would kill him? She wasn't about to let that happen.

"He is just doing what he feels he needs to do. Becoming a parent changes your outlook on life."

Emotion clogged Melanie's throat at Caitlyn's words, because while Caitlyn would always be a mother, she was robbed of the chance to see her children grow, to be all that they were meant to be. Sometimes, Melanie wondered how Caitlyn got up every morning and functioned.

She leaned forward, resting her chin in her hands.

"Vengeance drove me for centuries. The only reason I never stepped under the sun was my need for vengeance. Then it was my job, righting the wrongs and helping those like me. And then on my darkest of days, when I was not strong enough to function, as you put it, I had Donnie to keep me going."

Melanie tucked her legs underneath her, watching the small smile tug on Caitlyn's lips as she spoke of Donnie. Caitlyn caught her looking, and her smile deepened.

"How are things going with Ricky?"

"Infuriatingly."

Caitlyn chuckled, a husky sound. "That, *ma petite* vampire, is not at all surprising. Does he make you happy?"

"Sometimes." Melanie ventured, knowing that every word she spoke was the honest to god truth. "Other times he just frustrates me."

"I understand," Caitlyn replied, a coy smile tugging her lips as the kitchen door opened and the men emerged. Donnie, looking mildly uncomfortable, strode over to reach out his hand for Caitlyn, who took it without question.

They all bade each other farewell, leaving Melanie and Ricky alone. She stared at the floor so that she wouldn't glare at Ricky. "You're not going to die."

"One day I will."

"Stop." She growled, shaking her head from side to side.

"Stop what? Telling the truth. Lanie, I'm not immortal. I *will* die. I will grow old and die. Or I might end up killed on the job. I have Zach now. I have you. I needed to make sure someone knew my wishes."

"Please don't talk like that. Please don't talk like that when we are…" Her voice trailed off as the words stuck in her throat.

Ricky crouched down, taking her hands in his. "When we are what, Lanie?" Her warlock all but purred her name. When Melanie refused to say the words, Ricky flashed her a crooked smile.

"Well, I was just hoping that you'd... I was hoping that you'd fall in love with me?"

"Oh, Ricky." Melanie sighed, rolling her eyes even as she felt the smile on her lips. He leaned forward, pressing his lips to hers, and she felt the heat of him in that kiss. He was fire inside, coursing with magic, and when he kissed her, it was if he struck a match inside her, making her feel alive.

Reaching out, Melanie allowed herself to run her fingers through his hair, shorter than it had been when they had met, but long enough to be silky smooth under her touch. He continued to kiss her, biting down on her lower lip when he wanted her to open up her mouth for him. Then his tongue was worshipping her mouth, tasting and devouring her until she was dizzy with the taste and scent of him.

Ricky slowed the kiss, and Melanie thought he was going to drive her insane as he moved his luscious lips to kiss her cheek, her jaw, the curve of her neck. Pulling back, he grinned at her before he reached into his pocket and took out a small pen knife.

"Whatever you plan to do with that, it's a no from me."

Ricky grinned and wiggled his brows. "I want to wear your marks on my skin when we go to face DeShane tomorrow night. I knew I'd have to coax you; I knew you'd fight me. I also know you haven't drunk from a human before, and that fucking turns me on like you wouldn't imagine."

Melanie tried to argue, to escape, but Ricky simply captured her in his arms and switched their positions so he was seated, and she was firmly planted in his lap. The evidence of how turned on he really was there for Melanie to feel for herself.

Flicking out the knife, Ricky turned her palm over, pressing the metal into her flesh. Melanie hissed, trying to yank her hand back, wondering what the hell Ricky was up to. When blood welled, Ricky set the knife down and lifted her hand, his tongue licking out and catching the blood as the wound began to heal.

Oh, dear gods she was burning up. Hunger like no other snarled in her stomach, and her fangs descended as Ricky traced his tongue across her palm again. Her eyes darted to his lips, smeared by her own blood, and she was powerless to stop herself.

Lunging forward, she shoved Ricky down on the couch and straddled him, capturing his mouth with hers. Her tongue swept across his lips, the taste of blood loosening a growl in her chest as Ricky's hands went to her hips. She was sloppy with her fangs, not used to kissing with them, and nicked Ricky's tongue.

The moment she swallowed down the taste of him, his blood, the magic in it, her back arched, and she ripped her lips from his, trying with all her might to fight against her nature. Melanie could hear the racing of his heart; she could see the pulse hammering at the side of his neck. The hunger called for more; it had had a taste and was not sated yet.

"Off," Melanie ordered, her voice not sounding like her own as she tugged on the edge of Ricky's t-shirt.

Her warlock was only too happy to comply, whipping off the t-shirt in record speed. His hands went to her abdomen, yanking her own tee up and off, leaving her straddling him in just her bra and jeans.

Sitting back, Melanie tried to regain control of herself, but Ricky was having none of it. His palms went back to her abdomen, slowly working their way up, cupping the underside of her breasts, his thumbs slowly, torturously rubbed against her nipples through her bra. Hot, wet lips pressed against the flesh of her breast and Melanie leaned into him, a low moan escaping her lips.

One hand snaked around to unclasp her bra, and then Ricky took her right breast in his mouth, and she jerked, his other hand massaging her neglected breast. Her mind fogged as Ricky devoured her breast as he had her mouth, leaving her hot and bothered and very, very hungry.

"Ricky, please..."

Lifting his mouth from her breast, he gave her a wicked grin that had her shivering, even though he was burning her up. "Stop what, babe. You want my mouth somewhere else?"

Images raced through her head as her hips moved of their own accord, rubbing against his erection through the fabric of their jeans. It was Ricky's turn to hiss out a breath, his hands going straight to pop the buttons on her jeans. Slowly, deliberately, he pulled her jeans down over the curve of her ass even as she sat back so her could pull them off.

The hunger punched into her gut, wild and vicious. She wanted nothing but Ricky's blood in her mouth, his hot delicious blood flowing down her throat. She wasn't sure she could ever stop.

Staggering to her feet, Ricky stood seconds after her, stripping off his own jeans and standing in all his glorious nakedness. Before, Ricky had been drop-dead gorgeous, but all his running had toned him and given him muscles and a very sexy v that dipped on his hips.

He stalked toward her, and Melanie held up a hand to stop him, needing a minute to centre herself. If she was being truth full, she was looking for a way out, because she wasn't sure Ricky would survive if she couldn't control herself.

Ricky dropped to his knees, yanked down her panties and pressed his mouth at the juncture of her thigh. It snapped whatever control she had. With as growl, Melanie yanked Ricky up, and ignoring the grin on his lips, pushed him back down on the couch and straddled him, taking his cock in her hands. He jerked, groaning as her fingers wrapped around him.

Adjusting her lower half, Melanie lowered herself slowly, feeling the head of Ricky's cock at her core before she sank down onto him. They both moaned; Melanie's walls clenching around the rigidness and size of Ricky as he bucked his hips once, twice, his hands on her hips.

They began to move together, and Melanie leaned down and kissed him. Ricky slid in and out of her as she rode him, his hands on her hips tightening as she ripped her mouth from his and hissed through her fangs. Ricky quickened the pace, his heart racing, the chords in his neck straining as they both neared release.

Melanie felt the heat of his hands on her hips like a brand, and struggled to stop the orgasm that was threatening to overwhelm her.

"Not yet, babe. Don't let go yet."

Slowing the torturous slide of his cock, Ricky tore his gaze from her, giving her a biteable view of his neck, and Melanie snarled, shaking her head, rising up and slamming back down hard enough to almost drag them both over the edge.

"Please, Lanie. Baby, I need you to be inside me too. *Please.*"

The please came out in a breathy moan as Melanie watched Ricky struggle for control. The hunger in her surged, and she was either powerless to stop it, or hell, she just wanted to bite him. Hand on his throat, Melanie yanked him to her, placed her mouth over his pulse and when Ricky's entire body shuddered, she growled and sank her fangs into his neck.

As Melanie drank, her first swallow of Ricky's blood working down her throat, she felt his cock tense inside her. While she drank deeper from his vein, they orgasmed together, riding the aftershocks. She sank her fangs in deeper and continued to drink.

She couldn't stop herself.

CHAPTER TWELVE

RICKY

There was no holding on, no finesse or feats of sexual prowess. The moment Melanie sank her fangs into his neck and drank, Ricky came hard and fast, grunting as Melanie's sex clenched around his cock, milking him as much as her mouth was drinking down his blood.

His brain was fogged, his body sated, his cock still twitching as Melanie rode her orgasm. Her sole focus was on his blood, and, after a few minutes, when he was able to think clearly again, Ricky realized that Melanie was having a little trouble stopping.

Spots darkened his eyes as Ricky reached out and slid his fingers into Melanie's hair, giving it a little tug to try and get her attention. An animalistic growl answered him, Melanie's hand latching around his throat, preventing him from moving an inch, the sheer strength in her grasp astounding.

"Lanie, babe. Enough."

"No." Came back a growl, and Ricky knew that his Lanie was still in there.

He rotated his hips, and she hissed. Beginning to feel untethered, Ricky smiled softly.

"Babe, if you want us to spend the day in bed, then you're

gonna have to keep me conscious. Please, Lanie, it's starting to hurt."

As if those were the magic words, Melanie ripped her fangs from his neck, his blood dribbling from her fangs and staining her lips. She hadn't been tidy. Rubbing her mouth with the back of her hand, she stared wide-eyed down at him, scrambling off his body and scooting back to the far end of the couch.

Ricky made to follow after her, the room spinning as he sat up to quickly. Arm braced at the side of the couch, Melanie sprang up, sifting through the discarded clothes on the ground until she pulled out her phone and dialled.

"Lanie, it's okay. I'm good. Believe me."

Ignoring him as she waited for the phone to connect, Melanie pulled on his tee and covered her luscious curves. Ricky groaned, lying back down and covering his eyes with his arm. With his eyes closed, he heard the conversation and swore.

"I need you to answer my question. Just my question. No comments or quips or I will lose my shit."

Melanie paused, and the person on the phone answered as she hissed out, "What do you give someone for blood loss?"

A bark of laughter sounded down the phone, and Ricky opened his eyes again, pulling himself up and watched Melanie pace the living room.

"Lanie…" he sighed but she snarled to quieten him.

"Answer the goddamn question, Donnie." Melanie's voice broke as Ricky reached up and pressed his fingers to the still open wound.

When Donnie heard the tone, he answered quickly because Melanie was out of the room before he could take another breath and strode back in carrying a pint glass of orange juice and a plate of biscuits.

"Drink," she ordered, shoving the glass at him. Ricky drained the juice in one go and grinned as Melanie shoved the cookies in his direction. "Eat."

"I'd rather eat you."

Melanie's nostrils flared, her hand trembling. "No. This...this is never happening again. I nearly killed you."

"No, you didn't. And hell yes, this is happening again. Fuck, Lanie. That was something else."

Ricky lifted his fingers from his neck, watching her eyes darken as she tracked the trail of blood that was seeping from where her pretty fangs had pierced his skin.

"Lanie, you need to close the wound."

"I can't."

"Yes, you can. Just lick over it, and that will stop the bleeding."

"I might hurt you," Melanie hissed, hesitant.

"It will hurt more if I bleed out."

Melanie wrestled with her demons for a minute more, her eyes never straying from his neck. Fists clenched to her side, she walked cautiously over to him, crouched down and leaned in. Ricky heard her sharp intake of breath, as if she were inhaling his scent, and then her tongue was stroking up his neck, and his body hardened again.

Ricky had never felt like this before. Damn, the sex had been unbelievable, and he knew it was because it had been with Melanie. She got him hard from running her tongue up his throat.

He moaned her name as she swirled her tongue over the puncture wounds, sealing them with her saliva. She pulled back, tears in her eyes.

Ricky never wanted to put that look on her face, where she was terrified of hurting him and withdrawing into herself. He could see it happening before his eyes. Not wasting another second, he dragged her down to him, capturing her mouth and kissed the hell out of her.

He was the one to pull back, teasing her and tempting her.

She glared at him, scowling, her fingers on her lips as she shook her head.

"Just so we are on the same page, babe."

"Page, we're not even in the same library!"

Ricky grinned and reached out to cup her cheek. "If you have a thing about libraries, I'm down with that."

Melanie's eyes widened even more, blinking as she said, "I didn't say anything."

Ricky frowned. "Sure, you did. You said we're not even in the same library."

"Ricky, I never said it *aloud*. I said it in my head."

Ricky smirked and let a barrage of images flow through his mind, let feelings wash over him until he heard Melanie gasp.

"Seems like drinking each other's blood came with added benefits."

"That's not a benefit!" Melanie exclaimed, squealing as Ricky hoisted her up and into his arms. "I don't want to know what you're thinking!"

Ricky moved slightly, pressing his length against her. "What am I thinking now?"

"We can't."

Ricky leaned in and pressed an open mouth kiss to the curve of her neck. Melanie leaned into him, the only encouragement that he needed. Wrapping his arms around her, Ricky got to his feet, and Melanie instantly locked her legs around his waist, her arms going around his neck. He walked until her back hit the wall, and as she slid her body down, he thrust forward, filling her in one stroke. She leaned her head back against the wall.

"Hold on to me, Lanie. Don't let me go."

He didn't wait for her response, his hips moving, slowly, teasing her until she breathed his name and he lost control, his balls tightening, his body trembling, sweat glistening on his skin as he slammed into her, once, twice, three times. Her body eagerly clenched around his cock until she was mewling, and when she came, burying her face in his neck, Ricky followed after her, his legs buckling. He would not drop her; he would not let her go. Never.

Melanie shivered in his arms, but Ricky knew it was not because she was cold. Hands still wrapped around each other, he walked them to the bedroom, laying the woman he loved down on his bed and sliding in beside her. Lying on his back, he swept her to him, so she had little choice but to cast a leg over him and snuggle into his chest.

They reclined in silence for a couple of heartbeats, neither of them seemingly able to find the ability to speak. His heart began to stop its racing, his body calming with the fucking bliss of finally having Melanie. He wished he could convey exactly how he was feeling, what she meant to him, but he was struggling to find the right words.

"You don't have to say anything."

Running his fingers through her hair, he said, "Stop reading my mind."

"Then stop thinking so loud. I want to sleep."

Ricky chuckled and reached down to pull a blanket over them. There were hours before dawn, but they were both exhausted. Ricky grinned to himself. If he woke her early enough, he could feed his addiction, this growing need in the pit of his stomach that was only for her.

He'd gotten high, felt the euphoria of it. But, the high of drugs and alcohol did not compare to the high he felt when Melanie was in his arms.

"Ricky..." Melanie sighed, and his grin deepened but he said nothing.

A few minutes later, his vampire girl was fast asleep, curled up against him. For the first time in a long time, Ricky felt a contented happiness wash over him, and he realized that he finally had everything he ever wanted in life.

"I love you," he muttered sleepily as he succumbed to tiredness, knowing Melanie had not heard his declaration, as all kinds of realizations had come to him moments before he was asleep.

Some hours later, Ricky was woken by a vampire with her mouth wrapped around his dick, giving him the best wakeup call in the world. After, they showered together, and he got to return the favour. Ricky helped her dress, feathering kisses along her shoulders and face, laughing when Melanie swatted him away.

He didn't tease her when she drank two bottles of blood. She was obviously afraid of drinking from him again, but that was a conversation that they would have another day, when DeShane was in custody and he and Melanie could decide which path their future would take.

There was something he needed to do first.

While Melanie was in the other room, and their new mind reading ability was muted by distance, he picked up his phone. Ricky shot off a text and waited a few minutes. Erika flashed in, took one look at his neck and grinned. "Maybe I should have a word with your girlfriend about hiding where she's snacked off ya."

"Don't bother. I'm fucking proud to bare her mark. Can you take me to Caitlyn's? Come back and get me in an hour? And keep Melanie distracted?"

Erika eyed him curiously, but said nothing as she nodded. Holding out her hand, Ricky slipped his into hers, winked as Melanie walked into the room, and suddenly, he was standing in Caitlyn's kitchen.

Erika let go of his hand, vanishing as Caitlyn strode into the kitchen, wiping sleep from her eyes. She didn't seem surprised to see him, but then again, to him, Caitlyn seemed celestial, like she saw everything.

Clearing his throat, Ricky shoved his hands into his pockets. "May I speak with you? And Donnie."

SHORTCUT TO THE GRAVE

Now Caitlyn studied him curiously, especially given his polite tone. She inclined her head, called out for Donnie and motioned for Ricky to sit. Donnie came in silently, a nearly impossible feat for a man of his bulk and stature. Ricky waited, suddenly nervous as he cracked his knuckles.

Donnie was the first to break the silence, pointing to his neck as he queried, "You good?"

"Never better, bud. Never fucking better. She over reacted; we sorted it out."

Donnie chuckled, holding up his hand. "I don't want to know anymore."

"Good, because what happens with me and Lanie is no one's business but ours."

Caitlyn had been suspiciously quiet since they say down, his gunmetal grey eyes not missing a beat. The wisdom held within them only outdone by the sadness that still tinged the edges of her soul. Ricky wasn't sure how he knew this, why he could see that in her, but he pushed it down as he steeled his resolve.

"I've not been a good person," Ricky began, shaking his head when Donnie made to argue. "I let my own shortfalls impact my life, and thought the good that I did with P.I.T. would outweigh the bad. It came to bite me in the ass."

Ricky paused, scratching the stubble on his face as Caitlyn bowed her head, waiting for him to continue. He set his elbows down on the table and dug his fingernails into his palms.

"I love her. I think I've always loved her from the very first moment that I saw her. I was so closed off to the possibility that I, we, almost lost her." Lifting his eyes, he stared into Caitlyn's. "I never thanked you for changing her. I forced you to do what you never wanted to do again, and I want to apologize for that."

"You do not need to apologize, Ricky," Caitlyn said softly, her accent thickening with emotion as Donnie reached out and took his mate's hand in his.

"I do," Ricky said firmly. "I asked you to save her because I was being selfish. I didn't consider your feelings; only my own. So first I wanted to apologize and thank you."

Caitlyn leaned forward, made to reach out to him, but snatched her hand back. "You mated with her?"

"I'm sorry, what?" Ricky stumbled over his words, not knowing what Caitlyn was talking about.

"Did you drink her blood at any stage ...uh...before or after she drank from you?" Donnie asked, the vampire obviously embarrassed to have to ask Ricky the question.

Ricky shrugged, colour flushing his cheeks. "Yeah, I mean she was being coy about biting me, and I wanted to show her it wasn't a big deal. I cut her palm and ...yeah well it happened."

"Then the question you have come to ask is irrelevant as you two are already a mated pair. I can smell it on your skin."

Ricky snapped his head up to hold Caitlyn's unwavering gaze. "How the hell were we to know? Don't tell her. I don't want her to think I tricked her. As her sire, Caitlyn, I wanted to ask for your blessing, to mate or marry her."

Caitlyn leaned back in her chair, and Ricky ran a hand over the back of his neck, uncomfortable under her death stare. She folded her arms over one another as she tilted her head and said, "And if I said *non*?"

Ricky pushed up the sleeves of his top and folded his hands together. "I would be disappointed, but I'd still love her and want to be with her. She makes me a better man. When I am with her, the darkness is kept at bay. Melanie is my night and my day. With her and Zach, I have everything I never knew I wanted.

"When I dated Sadie, I did it because I wanted what I never had; a family, a white picket fence and all that. But family isn't perfect. Its messy and complicated. Family is whatever you make it. I feel whole when she smiles at me. I know her heart, and she knows mine. I haven't even thought of being high since

I saw her again. I've found a new addiction, and I don't want to be cured."

The gaping silence that followed made Ricky's heart race with fear that the one person who could influence his Lanie, her sire, the person she respected most in the world would not give her approval. It cut him deep, and Ricky realized that, even after all they had been through, he wanted her approval even more so.

Caitlyn smiled. "I know what it is like to find someone who brings light into your life when darkness is all consuming. When you speak of our Melanie, I can hear how much you love her. I can see it. I knew the day she died that you loved her enough to ask of me something that I swore never to do again. I asked myself, even then, had I not done the same thing to keep Donnie with me, even when I knew nothing more than this gnawing sense that he was meant for me."

Ricky swallowed hard, watching as Donnie grinned. "Plus, she was dazzled by my good looks. I was dying, and she stood there staring at me."

Caitlyn ignored him, her focus on Ricky. "You have my blessing. You never needed my approval for anything, Ricky. You had it. Always."

Ricky swallowed hard, flashing Caitlyn a smile. "I won't force her. She can choose. I hope she chooses me. I come with baggage. She might not want that life."

"She will want you. All of you."

Erika appeared in the kitchen, snapping Ricky back to reality, as she popped her gum and beckoned him forward. He thanked Caitlyn, let Donnie pull him into a hug, and then he was taking Erika's hand and home before he could even blink.

Erika bowed at her waist, a Cheshire cat grin playing on her lips and then she was gone. Melanie had her back to him, facing out the window, her body tense until Ricky ensnared her around the waist.

"Where'd you go?" she asked, and Ricky inhaled, taking in the scent of her apple shampoo as he pressed a kiss to her shoulder.

"Nowhere important." He was careful to keep his thoughts neutral. "Just had something to take care of. You ready to end this?"

Melanie said nothing for a while, and neither did he. He waited until her heard her voice inside his head, asking the question she couldn't force herself to say.

What are we now, Ricky? What are we?

"You are mine, and I am yours," Ricky answered aloud, tightening his hold on her. "We can be whatever we want to be. We make the rules, Lanie. We are happy, and we make each other happy, isn't that all that matters?"

Melanie didn't answer him. She untangled herself from his arms, lifted her hand and cupped his cheek. "It's okay... you don't have to love me. I understand."

Ricky placed a hand over her own, the other tipping her chin so that when she looked in his eyes, she would know exactly how he felt about her. "There's something I need you to know, before we go do what needs to be done." He kissed her once, twice, quick presses of his lips against hers. "I love you. I think I have always loved you. I just forgot how to show it for a while." He kissed her again, rough, possessively.

"You took the air out of my lungs, and finally I can breathe again. I love you, Melanie Newton. And I always will."

Ever sat on the edge of her bed, staring at the floor as if she could wish away the predicament she was in. She knew, deep in her heart, that she was carrying Derek's child, but by the gods, how could she bring a child into this war? She couldn't.

Valkyrie pregnancies did not last as long as human ones, and she would only have a short window to make a decision. *Four months of pregnancy was like eight normal months, a Valkyrie's body so filled with magic that a child would grow even faster inside her.*

She wanted to have Derek's child. She wanted to be a mother.

But if she were slain by Odin, then her child would be slain, too, and then her joy, her hopes and her fears would be for nothing.

Her phone chimed, indicating it was now time to look at the test Erika had brought her. But, after three other tests, she was sure that this one would read as all the rest had.

Pregnant.

Silent tears cascaded down her cheeks, as Erika crouched in front of her, hands over hers in comfort. There was no denying it, and there would be no hiding it much longer because her scent would change, and Derek would know. And he could never know.

"Tell me what you want me to do, Ever. Tell me and I will do it."

Ever brushed the tears from her face and swallowed the sickness of her decision as she said to Erika, "Get me something to terminate the pregnancy. No one can ever know."

CHAPTER THIRTEEN

There had been little more to say after Ricky's declaration. When Melanie made to answer him, telling him that she was also very much in love with him, Ricky kissed her again, and she had lost all train of thought.

Now, they were making their way through the city streets, and Melanie stared out the window, watching the city she had grown up in pass by in a blur.

Ricky's fingers tapped nervously against the steering wheel. She reached out and rested her hand on his thigh, returning the smile that he gave her. It was smile just for her, and it made her all gooey inside.

They reached their destination far too quickly, and she equally wanted to flee and get it over with. She hoped that Greg would not slip free of their grasp. She needed an end to this weight she'd been carrying around for so long.

"Hey, you good?" Ricky asked her, concern written all over his face.

"Ya, just ready for this to be over."

Ricky grinned, leaning over to give her a quick peck on the cheek. "Me too. I swear, once this is over, you and I will be spending a weekend in bed and not moving except for me to eat."

Melanie laughed, rolling her eyes like she always tended to do with him. "Did you forget that you have a small human that might have something to say about that?"

"I'm pretty sure one of his many aunts and uncles would be happy to have him for a few days while I keep you chained to my bed."

Melanie smacked him hard on the shoulder, but she continued to laugh. "I'm not sure chains could hold me."

"Then chain me to the bed, woman, and have your wicked way with me. I'm yours to do as you wish."

Ricky pulled into an empty spot in what seemed like an abandoned carpark, his nose wrinkling as if he could smell the magic that protected the warehouse. Once he shut off the engine, they sat in the car, as if neither of them wanted to leave the cosy bubble surrounding them. Snapping off her seatbelt, Melanie reached out and grazed her fingers over the bumps on Ricky's skin where her fangs had punctured. Ricky shuddered as she danced her fingers against his pulse.

"I could have killed you," Melanie murmured quietly, dread washing over her because she never wanted to hurt him, physically or emotionally. Had Caitlyn been right all along, on those midnight strolls she made Melanie go on. Had she been romanticizing what she was now?

"I've always known what and who you are. Doesn't matter a fucking bit."

Melanie snorted, making to get out of the car. "I'm starting to hate this mind reading thing already."

Ricky followed her out, locking the car. He held out his hand to her, which she took without hesitation. The familiar heat of him, the scent of leather and oil, gave her courage to face what lay ahead. Melanie glanced around the empty carpark.

"You trust me?" he asked, a mischievous smile lightening up his eyes that would give Loki a run for his money.

"Always."

Pulling her to him, he kissed her slowly until she felt her body react to him, as it always did, melting against him as he sidestepped while still kissing her. Melanie felt the chill of magic, and then the sights and sounds and smells of the room assaulted her senses, and she hissed.

Ricky held her to him, allowing her to adjust to the sudden impact, keeping her safe. She knew she would always be safe in his arms. It took a few minutes for her to centre herself, and when she stepped back from Ricky, she rose up on her toes and pressed her lips to his.

"Thanks," she said against the curve of his lips.

"Anytime."

Taking his hand once more, Melanie noted her surroundings. There was a noticeable lack of light, causing the basement floor of the warehouse to appear dark and intimidating. Where she and Ricky stood, only a solitary poker table was in view, down a level and surrounded by suit clad guards. Waitresses in skimpy outfits handed out drinks to those seated at the table, five men with wads of cash stacked in front of them.

"Looks like I forgot my millions, darling," Ricky crooned as Greg lifted his gaze, roaming his eyes over Melanie. She could not hide the disgust from marring her features, her grip on Ricky's hand tightening, but her warlock uttered not a word.

Ricky waited with her until the game finished, and Greg dismissed the other players to the bar for a moment. Greg beckoned them down, and they descended the three steps to the lower level, Ricky's hand drifting to the small of her back, the heat of him like a brand on her skin, burning her through her clothes.

Melanie almost snarled as her former best friend, Jaime Cross, shimmied her way over to Greg, and when he patted his lap, she eagerly perched her skanky ass where she was told. Melanie smirked, wondering how she never saw how perfectly suited they were to one another.

Greg mistook her smirk for jealousy, and he beamed up at her with that charming smile that fooled most people. However, Melanie was no longer fooled by the façade he wore to lure people in. His opinion of her didn't matter anymore.

"Mel, it's good to see you again. Drink?"

Playing the part as much as she could stomach, Melanie clasped Ricky's neck possessively and grinned. "Nah, thanks. I've had my fill for today."

Ricky chuckled, the rumble of sound vibrating through her fingertips. "Honey, I'm not sure I like you boasting about our bedroom antics in front of everyone."

"Then take the smugness out of your tone, babe."

Ricky's laugh deepened as her looked at her, his eyes full of carinal desire and promise.

"Shall we get back to business?" snapped Greg, swatting away Jaime's hand as she moved to comfort him. She scowled, glaring at Melanie. Melanie flashed her fangs, and Jaime froze, dropping her gaze.

Melanie studied Greg as he reached forward and grabbed a bottle of Landshark, offering one to Ricky who declined before he took a swig of his beer. Greg was a creature of habit, and Melanie could read in his stance, the way his eyes never strayed from watching them, the confident way he sat in his seat, that Greg had them figured out.

He knows.

I know. Stay sharp, Lanie.

Melanie couldn't help but stare at Greg, wondering how she had ever loved him. It was easy for her to blame her family, the love she should have received from them sending her into the arms of the first man who showed her affection after such miserable teenage years. It was easy to mistake her need to be loved for being in love. Ricky had shown her just how you should love and be loved in return.

Greg snapped his fingers, and Tadgh walked slowly into the room and down the stairs to stand with them. He sported a rather impressive bruise along the side of his cheek, and Melanie flashed him a toothy grin.

"Kenzie?"

Tadgh didn't answer her, just reached into his pocket and tossed a bag of White Rabbit on to the table. Melanie felt Ricky tense under her grasp as Tadgh stepped back from the table to stand beside Greg.

"I know you are still working for P.I.T. I've always known. Melanie is far too much of an injustice fighter to sink to my level. If you want to persuade me that you are not still Agent Moore and Agent Newton, then you'll indulge in White Rabbit. Or I'll kill you both."

"No," Ricky ground out, and Melanie heard the resolve in his voice as he continued, "The drugs don't work. They never helped. They made things worse, and I nearly lost sight of what was important." He spared her a glance before turning his focus back to Greg.

"Yes, I am still Agent Moore, and I'm here to bring you down. You won't hurt anyone else with your drugs. Not while I have breath in my body."

Greg slid his hand over Jaime's thigh, giving her a squeeze, and then she stood, letting her own magic wash over her. Melanie tried to stand in front of Ricky, save him from being under Jaime's spell.

"Ricky. Sweetheart. Put your hands around Melanie's throat."

Melanie tried to step out of his reach, but Ricky had his hands around her throat, his eyes glazed over, as he gritted his teeth trying to fight against the siren's magic. Melanie rested her hands on his chest, pushing and pushing but to no avail. He couldn't suffocate her, but if Jaime ordered him to burn her to ash, he would do so. It would kill her, and Ricky could never live with what he did.

Melanie thought back to her training with Erika, never considered that she would have to use what she had learned against the man she loved. Using her own strength, Melanie kicked out with her boot, catching Ricky in the shin and used the momentum to lean back, pulling him with her.

Her back hit the ground and Ricky landed on top of her, his hands falling from her throat as he rolled off her and stood, clenching his fists by his side while he fought against the compulsion. Melanie scrambled to her feet.

"Punch her, Ricky."

Melanie side stepped the blow, hooking her leg around the back of Ricky's calf and sweeping it forward so he crashed to the ground, the breath leaving his lungs. She planted a booted foot on his chest and pushed all of her strength into keeping him safely there.

Focusing on Greg, she noticed he was now standing, draining his beer and looking at her with disgust. "What happened to you, Greg? When did you become something that I would scrape off my boot?"

"You always thought you were better than me, Mel. And maybe you were. Doesn't really matter now."

Greg cast a glance at Jaime as he walked past her, Tadgh falling into step with him. Melanie watched him retreat from the room, slipping out the side of the building as the rest of the poker players scattered.

Jaime folded her arms across her chest, pursing her lips. Melanie wasn't sure if she could reach her former friend; Greg's influence would be hard to break through. Jaime had once been as lost as she, and Greg had a way of making you feel found.

"It's not too late, Jaime. Let us go. I can get you a good deal. You don't have to be his pawn."

"He loves me."

Melanie's heart almost broke as she replied, "He doesn't love anyone but himself, Jaime. He never will. Greg only looks out for number one. Even now, he left you here, with me, knowing that I could kill you and not even flinch."

"You always were a heartless, bitch." Jaime said, spitting on the ground as she called her magic forth. Melanie tried to rack her brains, thinking back to when they were younger, for any limitations in Jaime's magic.

Then it hit her. Jaime always had to be in close proximity in order for her magic to hold sway. If this was still the case, all Melanie needed was to get Jaime away from Ricky, no matter what. And stop her from uttering a word.

Melanie moved like lightening, stepping off Ricky and diving forward, her fangs extended, and her body filled with adrenaline. Jaime ordered her to stop, but seemingly her magic only worked on the living. The sudden realization that she was being hunted causing Jaime's scent to fill with fear.

Slowing her pursuit, Melanie stalked after Jaime as she backed up, her feet stumbling over the steps. Jaime landed on her butt, holding out her hands in surrender. Tears welled in the woman's eyes, and Melanie let that halt her. Jaime's expression turned sadistic, and she crooned.

"Ricky, burn the vampire to ash."

Melanie ducked as blue flame flew over her head; Ricky now on his feet. She braced for another hit, but when she cast her gaze over her shoulder, Ricky was turning his magic on himself, fighting as hard as he could to not hurt her.

Without another thought, Melanie yanked Jaime to her feet and placed her hands firmly around her neck. Closing her eyes, Melanie growled and twisted hard; she heard the snap of bone and dropped Jaime's body to the ground. The shock was instant, her body trembling. She'd never killed someone before. She hadn't been sure she had that in her, but she ended Jaime's life without a second thought because Ricky was in danger.

Strong arms wrapped around her as Ricky gathered her in his embrace, and she wept for the life she had taken. He held her as she fell apart, holding her up when she might fall down, his familiar scent tinged with a burnt smell.

When her tears had run dry, Ricky brushed the hair from her face. "I love you."

"I love you too."

Ricky kissed her briefly, and then he let her go, giving her space to stand on her own two feet. "You good to go?"

With a glance down at the lifeless eyes that stared back at her, Melanie lowered herself into a crouch and closed the eyes looking back at her. Getting to her feet again, she nodded.

"Let's go get the bastard. He's ruined enough lives."

They quickly left the way they came, getting in the car as Ricky called in and explained to Derek that they had been made. Now, they needed to head after Greg and Tadgh. Melanie heard Derek explain to Ricky that Kenzie had stormed out when Caitlyn told her Tadgh had been the one to sell Ricky drugs. She had marched right into the morgue and socked him one.

Melanie suppressed a grin when Derek also said that Kenzie had threatened to disembowel Tadgh if he so much as looked in her direction again. Ricky rattled off Greg's number, asking Derek to ping his phone and send a location. They promised to wait for backup, to stay right where they were for the team of arrive, and then they would go together.

Ricky tossed his phone on the dash, his knee bouncing as the same adrenaline that was coursing through his veins, sparking the adrenaline in hers. Ten minutes passed in silence, apart from the occasional swear word that slipped free of Ricky's lips, impatience driving him.

"Ricky," Melanie began when her own phone rang, an

unknown number appearing on the screen. She didn't have to answer it to know who was calling; she felt in in her marrow.

"What?" she snarled, answering the phone.

"She's dead then." It was a statement, not a question, so Melanie didn't answer but rather asked a question of her own.

"Tell me where you are, Greg. We started this, let us finish it. Don't you want it to be me that brings you in?"

Greg sighed with indifference. "So you can kill me like you killed Jaime? When did you become what we once hated? You once told me how much you despised how supernatural creatures lorded their strength over us humans."

"I said I hated how those with power lorded over us. Anyone who uses their power to manipulate others, supernatural or not, those are the people who make me sick."

Greg laughed at her. "And I supposed that is aimed at me. Easy to say over a phone call, Mel."

"Then tell me where you are, and I'll say it to your face."

"Oh, no doubt. I'll see you soon, Mel."

Ricky's phone chimed, and he snatched it up. Fear radiated from him as he stared at the screen, flames of blue streaking up his arms. Melanie reached out and took the phone from him. She clicked on the link in the message and watched in horror as a video showed Killian and Zach in the front garden of Ricky's mothers house, under the night sky, messing about.

A shimmer of magic and then Zach pounced on Killian, Ricky's brother laughing heartily at his nephew. Melanie heard a voice say, "Targets in sight. Waiting for orders."

"He's just a kid, Greg. You're not such an evil monster to harm a child?"

"Come meet me at the place you died. Come and help me understand you more because the creature you are now means nothing. Come meet me, and I will keep him alive."

The line disconnected. Ricky tried in vain to call his mother and his brother before he managed to get through to Donnie.

He begged his friend to go to his mother's and save his son and brother.

Ricky all but threw the phone onto the dash again, letting out a roar of frustration, the magic rolling off him in waves. Melanie wanted to help him, reassure him that everything would be okay, but she wasn't sure.

Going back to the place she had died wasn't something Melanie had ever wanted to do. Too many nightmares, too many memories of the man who killed her. At least he had granted her a second chance at life. It was a sad testament that she had to die in order to feel alive for the first time.

"We won't let anything happen to him. Take a second to vent, then put your game face on and we go. We finish the job, and we finish it well. I need you with me, Ricky. I need your help to end this."

Her warlock turned his gaze on her, his green eyes streaking blue as he worked through his emotions. The flames rescinded, and Ricky snapped his seatbelt into place. He reversed out of the spot and spun the car around as tires squealed. Melanie rested her palm on his thigh and squeezed.

A wave of murderous intend washed over her, and Melanie knew that she would kill everyone who stood in her way. No one threatened her family and lived.

DANAE SLAMMED a fist on the table, the remaining Valkyrie not so much as flinching as the ruthless warrior growled out her frustration. They had been sequestered to Valhalla for centuries, forced to watch as their queen fought for their survival and this current incarnation of their queen, Ever Chace, refused to even acknowledge their existence.

"We cannot stand idly and allow Odin to strike down our queen again," Danae grunted out, her hand grabbing the hilt of her sword as if she were primed for battle.

"*Ever has chosen her champion and his band of supernaturals over her own kin,*" Rebekah spat out, nothing but venom in her words. "*Why should we even help her?*"

"*You should help her because she is your queen, and you swore an oath to protect her.*"

The remaining four Valkyrie spun round as Erika strode into the cabin, hands on her hips, an air of cockiness following after her.

"*The battle is near. Ever may not have come to call you forth, but I, Erika, general of the armies of Valhalla, daughter of Tyr, and goddess of war, call you now to take your rightful place beside your queen. What say you?*"

Danae was the first to react, unsheathing her sword, the metal scraping as it is pulled free. The Valkyrie who was once Erika's enemy dropped to her knees and offered her sword to Erika. It wasn't long before Rebekah, Marya, and Almira followed suit.

Erika told them to rise, her grin as frightening as her skills as a warrior. "*Then let us go and introduce ourselves to our queen, lest she forget who we are.*"

CHAPTER
FOURTEEN

Ricky had felt fear before. Fear when his father used to go red in the face, his hand lifted as if to strike him. Fear when he applied to be a guard and worried that his Da would somehow stop him from living his dreams. Fear when saw Melanie hanging from the rafters, life draining from her. Fear when he became a slave to drugs that made him a person he didn't like very much.

But he had never felt fear quiet like the bone chilling fear that had rooted in his spine and chilled his skin. His knuckles were white from gripping the steering wheel far too tightly, and Ricky felt Melanie's hand on his leg in comforting solidarity that they would stop DeShane from hurting Zach.

When he got his hands on Greg, Ricky would start at his toes and work his way up, sending shocks of fire through the man's nerve endings until his teeth rattled. Then, Ricky would run his hands over the jerk's flesh as it bubbled and blistered, leaving scars as a reminder that he shouldn't ever threaten those Ricky cared for. Depending on if he was feeling more psychotic than usual, he'd fry the fucking tattoos from the Viking's body so no one would know who he was. If Ricky had his way, Greg

DeShane would have his organs boiled from the inside out and die in excoriating pain.

It was strange that Ricky could feel such unconditional love for his son, from the moment his eyes fell on the little boy standing in his doorway, sadness in his eyes and carrying the weight of the world on his tiny shoulders, Ricky loved him. He loved Zach before he even had concrete evidence that the boy was his, even though, one look and there was no denying that the child was. His love for Zach outweighed the anger he had for Sadie for not telling him she was pregnant, that he'd had a son, and keeping him from Ricky for five years.

He would do anything to keep his boy safe and would kill anyone who dared wish Zach harm. And not a single person could stop Ricky.

Reversing out of the car park as if he was auditioning for a part in *The Fast and the Furious* franchise, the tires screeched as he shifted gears and darted down the narrow city streets, carefully avoiding any late-night revellers or badly parked cars. Not bothering to obey traffic lights, Ricky zipped down a side street, ignoring the angry honks of horns as he steered the car alongside the Mercy hospital on the banks of the River Lee and went up and over the ramp without a second thought.

The bumper of the car scraped over the road, and Melanie clicked with her tongue and teeth. Ricky knew he was driving like a maniac, but he didn't care. His car could be replaced. His son could never be.

"It'll be okay. Greg is a lot of things, but he'd never harm a child."

"No, the bastard would just threaten to blow off his head. Still makes him an asshole."

"Nobody's saying he's not an asshole."

Ricky sighed, not wanting to fight with her about something so trivial. He suspected Melanie was goading him into a fight to take his mind off Zach. She was trying to protect him. Ricky felt a rush of love wash over him.

The junction up ahead looked clear, and Ricky gunned it, pushing his car to the limits as he pressed the pedal to the floor. They had barely made it passed the junction when Ricky saw a blur of movement to his right and slammed on the brakes. The car was already in motion, and Ricky could not avoid the crash no matter how much he pressed on the brake.

He yelled for Melanie to brace for impact, his words cut off as the black van rammed into the side of the car, the world turning on its axis as the force of impact flipped the car, turning once until Ricky's Ford lay on its roof. As the car rolled, Ricky's body was thrown in all directions, the seatbelt cutting into his skin, his organs doing a merry dance inside his body. His head hit the side of car as it ground to a stop, the lights flashing and the horn blaring until Ricky punched the dashboard, and it halted its wailing.

Ricky's ears rang, his body screaming in agony, and the scent of copper filled the air. Ricky ran his eyes over Melanie, but his vampire girl looked unscathed, her side of the car seemingly unaffected. Ricky tried to move, but his body was trapped under the weight of the dash, the side of his car totally ruined. From the burst of agony when he inhaled a breath, he suspected he had broken ribs, or at the very least they were seriously bruised.

Glancing outside, he saw the van reverse as far as the traffic lights before it surged forward again, and this time when the van crashed into the car, they were shunted into the wall, already damaged by the car in the first impact. Ricky's side of the car hung perilously over the edge, the violent currents of the River Lee beneath him.

"Don't move," Ricky managed to groan out, the fucking burn in his chest, the searing pain in his abdomen leading him to belief that he had some serious internal damage. Dangling upside down, Melanie used her vampire strength to try and kick out her door, but it would take more than that to sort out the tangled mess of metal.

Ricky coughed, lifting his hand to his mouth and cringing when he spotted the blood on his palm. Melanie turned her attention to him. Her expression was worried, especially since the van still had not left as if it were making sure that they were dead or seriously injured. Ricky pressed the button on his seat-belt, but the thing was jammed.

"Can you see a phone?" I can't reach mine."

Ricky glanced around, remembering that he had tossed his on the dashboard that was now pinning his legs. Come to think of it, he couldn't feel his legs.

"Ricky!" Melanie exclaimed, obviously hearing the thought in his head. Swallowing down the panic as he began to cough in earnest, he felt his magic reach out, sensed it the moment something triggered within the car and smoke began to rise from the engine. If he was right, they had little time before the fire sparked and car began an inferno.

Melanie needed to get out of the car now.

"Lanie, you ...you go. Get help." Ricky coughed, spitting blood onto the roof of the car in order to try and clear his throat.

"I'm not leaving you." She growled in response, punching against the door until her hands were bloody and raw. Tears of frustration, tears of understanding, fell from those pretty green eyes, and Ricky felt his heart ache as if it was filling up with love before it would no longer feel anything.

Again, Ricky tried to move his lower body, the blood rushing to his head as black spots came into his field of vision. He knew he was concussed by the lurch in his stomach to vomit, but as he tried to gulp in some air, his lungs burned and the bones in his ribs rattled. Each intake of breath was a wheeze, and when he was wracked with another fit of coughing, the amount of blood that he coughed up was anything but normal.

"Lanie," he wheezed out. "Lanie, listen. I'm not getting out of here. You need to think with your head, not your heart." Melanie looked at him with those eyes of hers, and Ricky almost couldn't get the words out.

"Get help. Get to Derek. Save my son. I need to know that you will do that for me. Lanie? *Please.*"

"I can't just leave you here." she cried, and Ricky wanted nothing more than to take her in his arms and comfort her. But there was no time for that.

The smoke thickened, bringing a spark of orange as the car burst into the flames and Melanie screamed. Lifting his hand, Ricky reached out with his magic, used his power to halt the path of flames while Melanie got out of the car. His strength was wavering, teeth gritted against the immense pain all over his body as he growled at Melanie to get the hell out of the car.

Clicking free her seatbelt, Melanie turned as she fell, crouching down as she used her foot to kick backward and try and dislodge the car door that was preventing her escape. The damn thing would not budge.

There was so much that he wanted to say to her. So many messages that he wanted to tell her to pass on; to Derek, to Sarge, to Donnie and to Caitlyn. Words of wisdom for a son who would know more death in a year then a child should know in a lifetime. He'd jinxed himself, writing his will and handing it Donnie. But then again, perhaps he knew in his gut that death was looming over him.

"Hey!"

Ricky snapped his eyes in Melanie's direction. "Don't you dare give up! You hear me. You can't just make me fall in love with you and then fucking leave me."

Ricky barked out a laugh. "As you can see, I'm not going

anywhere, Lanie. The last few days with you, I can't even tell you what it has meant. You need to know that I love you. And I regret nothing."

"Ricky...please...I can't"

I can't do this without you. How am I supposed to live...? Without you?

Asking the question in her mind that she couldn't bear to ask aloud, Ricky couldn't answer her. The strain of keeping the flames at bay, trying to stay conscious and trying to speak caught up with him. His magic wavered, and the flames licked up the side of the car.

Ricky felt the heat of it against his skin, knew that the car would explode sooner rather than later. And still Melanie would not leave him. She was what he had searched for his entire life, his ride or die, the woman who challenged him as much as she encouraged him.

"Kiss me, Lanie. Kiss me and tell me you love me. *Please.*" He wasn't so proud that he would not beg her; if he was going to die, it would die with her taste on his lips, the sound of her love in his ears rather than the ringing that was there now.

His body convulsed as he hacked up more blood. Melanie leaned in, kissing him upside down as she muttered the words he needed to hear against his lips. By gods, he wanted forever with her.

He would only get one chance at this. Ricky would have to time his magic perfectly, because as soon as he released his hold on the flames, he would have mere seconds to use some fancy tricks he had learned in order to ensure that Melanie lived; even if it meant certain death to him.

Reluctantly pulling back from the kiss, Ricky reached out and tucked a hair behind her ear. He winked as he saw the van surge forward again. They were out of time.

Time seemed to slow as Ricky relinquished his hold on the

flames, lifting his palm to place it over the place where Melanie's heart once beat as he screamed. "Vade!"

Magic swirled around his vampire as her eyes widened. And then she was gone, standing on the pavement, her eyes wild, her mouth open as she screamed his name. But all Ricky did was smile.

His Lanie was safe, that was all that mattered. Melanie would make sure Zach was safe.

The van crashed into the car, the roof of the vehicle sliding over the road with a groan as heat encased the car as it exploded, metal scraping as the death-trap rolled off the edge and plunged into the frigid waters of the Lee. The car was the right way around now, yet Ricky was still embedded in the dash, the flames from the explosion bouncing off his skin as if they knew that he could not be felled by flames.

Water began to surge up inch by inch, the flames still searing through the interior as the car floated for a brief few minutes, then it began its slow decent into the waters. Ricky finally managed to yank his seatbelt free, however, his lower half was still trapped. As he tried to pull his legs free, Ricky knew he wasn't getting out of this car alive. That didn't mean he had to go down easy.

The water continued to rise in the car and soon enough, it was submerged. Ricky did not have the strength to stay awake after the injuries he sustained; his organs were failing as he opened his eyes to stare out into the black of the water. His teeth chattered together, and his body began to tremble, either from the shock or from the harsh, bitterly cold waters that were drowning him.

I'll never hear my son call me Dad.

The thought popped into his head as tears welled in his eyes. He'd never see Zach grow into the person he was destined to be. Ricky would never see Zach off to college. He'd never be introduced to his girlfriend...or boyfriend. Ricky would never see him marry or watch Zach with his own children.

Ricky wished he'd had more time, but he knew that Zach would be well looked after. When he approached Fionn, asking for permission and his signature for Caitlyn to become his legal guardian should anything happen to him, Fionn had signed without a second thought because Caitlyn was the only one any of them could think of taking care of Zach. He hoped to tell her, give her the heads up and prepare her. Because she had lost her own children, he wondered if it was cruel to ask her to look after his.

Donnie had assuaged Ricky's fears, telling him that Caitlyn would be honoured for him to think so highly of her that she was chosen to watch over his son.

When Ricky had been in Armagh, after a particularly bad session, he had lost his temper with Zach, because even though the little boy was playing and speaking with him, he refused to call him anything other than 'Ricky'.

After Zach went all furry and stormed off, Ricky sat beside his mother, and she said to give Zach time. He barely knew the man who he was now living with, it would take time for Zach to call him Dad.

However, Ricky didn't have time. He'd never hear the words he longed to hear fall from his son's lips, and it cracked open his heart.

Melanie would never know that he wanted to marry her. She would never know that he was already hers, and she was his. If he had been brave enough to love her, brave enough to take down the bricks encasing his heart one by one, he might have had the chance to ask her to be his bride.

His heart broke, sobs wracking his body, stealing the air from his lungs as Ricky tried to get hold of himself. His fight or flight instinct kicked in, and he struggled, struggled hard against the evitable.

The life he might have had flashed before his eyes as water filled his lungs, covered his nose, and in one final rush, covered him from head to toe. His heart faltered; the organ worked overtime to compensate for his other injuries, but it was not strong enough to combat the inevitable death that was coming to knock on his door.

Ricky did not fear death. He had lived his life on a knife's edge for so long, he could not fear his own demise. He had always fought his way through, each and every step of his life had been a fight of survival. All those times before, it was all about his own selfish self-preservation, nothing mattered but the outcome he wanted for himself.

A memory flashed into his mind, of when Caitlyn had drunk his blood in order to clear his system of any drugs floating in his veins. He'd lost control of his magic and almost died. He remembered not being able to speak, but realizing in the moment that he didn't want to die. He didn't want to die now, knowing what he had to live for.

As his body shut down, his magic began to leak out, his skin bursting into flames, melting the metal on the dash as he braced his hands on it. He should have considered that before, but if he had, Melanie might have not escaped. He was content to know that she was safe.

His team would come for him, claim his body from the river. If they came to him while his magic was volatile, someone was bound to get hurt. Reaching down to his finger, he yanked the ring that helped him control his magic off and tossed it into the water.

There was a moment of sheer peacefulness before his body was on fire, literally, as the flames lashed against his skin, struggling for control in his weakened state. The scent of burning flesh and metal filled the air, the car changing from solid to liquid all around him. His magic was a violent storm of pent up rage, loss, and now, one final attempt at survival.

The car vanished around him, leaving him floating free under the murky waters. His magic was gone, his strength no more. He had nothing left to give but himself, and he gave himself over to death. His eyes fluttered shut, and death came to claim him.

CHAPTER
FIFTEEN

Melanie could do nothing but watch as the car slipped under the water, with Ricky in it, and out of her field of vision, a soft blue flickering under the water before it burst into flames. Melanie shielded her eyes from the glare, dropping her arm once the light flickered and faded.

Oh god, oh god, oh god. What could she do now? Oh god, was he dead?

Her legs moved of their own accord, rushing forward and over to the edge of the water. Without so much as another thought, Melanie leapt over the wall and its railing, dropping into the water with a splash. For a moment, when the shock of the cold hit her, Melanie panicked, trying to breath in the icy current, but then it dawned on her, amidst all the confusion and panic, that she didn't need to breathe.

Opening up her eyes, Melanie felt the sting in in them before she adjusted and swam a little deeper and closer to the wrecked remains of Ricky's car. After a quick glance, she almost cried out in frustration. Her warlock was not to be found. Eyes darting around in the near black, Melanie willed herself to be strong because his life depended on it.

The stupid, reckless, brave idiot had sacrificed himself for her. He gave his life, using the last of his magic to make sure she was safe. He begged her to kiss him, tell him that she loved him, and she did, her own long dead heart breaking.

Melanie swam deeper, praying to whatever god or gods that might be listening to find him and bring him back. There was still time... there had to be still time.

Suddenly, as if someone heard her pleas and prayers, she spotted Ricky floating, his body lingering a few feet away from her. Melanie hauled ass over to him, wrapping him in her arms. His skin was charred from the fire and ice cold to the touch, and Ricky was never cold. He just wasn't.

Dragging him upward, Melanie broke the water's surface in a surge, swimming backwards until her back hit the wall. His weight and height made him awkward to carry. Treading water, she glanced around and spied a ladder. He wasn't in any condition to climb, so she grabbed the closest rung, one arm burning as she held on to Ricky with an iron grasp, and climbed as quickly as possible without losing hold of her precious cargo.

Her wet boot slipped on the last rung of the ladder, her arm reaching up to hold onto the wall, her shoulder popping from its socket and sending a shockwave of agony rippling through her hand. She almost let go, but she was resolved to never let him go.

Gathering all her stubborn resolve, Melanie used her supernatural ability to surge up and over the wall, tumbling onto dry land. Without a second thought, she pushed her arm up and popped her shoulder back into its socket. She rode the wave of sickness that coursed through her body, because she would live though this, Ricky might not.

Dropping to her knees, she knelt over Ricky, feeling for a pulse and checking his breathing. His eyes fluttered open the moment she placed her fingers to his neck, at the exact point where she had bitten him only two days ago. Had it only been two days ago? Right now, it felt like an eon ago.

His gaze was unfocused, and Melanie cupped his face in her hands. "You stay awake, do you hear me? Don't you dare close your eyes! Please, Ricky. Come on, stay with me."

His eyelids closed, and his head lolled to the side, his dark hair clinging to the sides of his face. Melanie shook him, but he did not respond. Leaning in, she did not feel his breath tickle her skin, nor his pulse under her fingers. Hands entwined and pressed over his heart; Melanie began to work to keep it beating.

"You're okay. Breathe. Just breathe. Open your eyes, Ricky. Come on. Come back to me." Melanie began to weep as she continued to press down. "It's okay. It's over now. You're okay. Wake up, please wake up. Don't do this to me. Don't do this to me. I love you so much. Come back, *please*."

She screamed his name, would have given anything to hear him answer her back with a sarcastic comment, his lips curling into a smile that was equal parts seduction and calculating at the same time. But her warlock stayed silent. He needed to breathe; he needed to breathe.

Leaning down, Melanie made to breathe air into his lungs when it dawned on her that she was long since dead, the air non-existent in her lungs and useless to save Ricky's life.

She alone could not save him.

The realization that she was not human enough to save the man she loved staggered her, halting the rhythmic movement of her hands, her ears ringing, tears blurring her vision.

"Hey, lady? You guys okay?"

Melanie snapped her head in the direction of the voice. "Are you alive?"

"What?" he asked confused, his gaze narrowing as his eyes darted to Ricky.

"Are you human?" she growled, starting the man who was wearing what she thought was a security guard's uniform.

"No, Ma'am. Vampire."

Shit...shit.... shit...think, Melanie, think... you need to call someone...

"Phone? You got a phone?" she yelled at him, even though he was standing so close she could smell the alcohol on his breath.

"Yeah here." The man handed her the phone, and Melanie snatched it greedily from him, pressing for emergency services. She popped it on loudspeaker and waited as the operator greeted her, and then the words were tumbling from her mouth.

"This is Agent Melanie Newton from P.I.T. I have an agent down. I repeat. I have an agent down. Get me through to Derek Doyle now!" Melanie snarled.

There was a moment of silence, a click, and then she heard Derek's gruff tone muttering his surname, the sound of sirens in the background.

"Derek. Oh god, please. You need to get here. He's not breathing, and I can't fucking breathe for him. I can't fucking breathe for him!"

"Where are you?" No nonsense from Derek, especially now.

"North Gate bridge. Hurry, Derek. He's dying."

A curse sounded from the phone, but Melanie had little time to worry about Derek's grief, her own threatening to shackle her. She continued to pump her hands over his heart, trying to keep it alive as the sirens she heard on the phone sounded from behind her, and she cried out in relief.

The screech of tyres, the sound of a door opening, and suddenly strong arms were pulling her back, engulfing her even as she fought against them.

"Rest now, *ma petite* vampire. Let Derek try and save your mate."

And that's what he was, her Ricky, her mate. She'd felt it the moment they had drank each other's blood, terrified to tell him because she hadn't known that's how it happened. She always believed, like Donnie and Caitlyn, the words had to be spoken.

Melanie watched as Derek took over and began to breathe

his own breath into Ricky's lungs, his hands on his best friend's chest, beating for him when Ricky could not do it himself.

Melanie sobbed when Derek cursed, roaring at someone to hurry the goddamn ambulance up. Like a wish was granted, the ambulance skidded to a stop as Derek continued to try and keep Ricky alive.

"How long has he been down?"

Derek glanced at Melanie, who stepped out of Caitlyn's arms. "He was in the water for maybe five minutes. He opened his eyes, he looked right at me. He's been unconscious for five, maybe ten, minutes. I don't know. I'm sorry."

The paramedic lifted his gaze to Derek's. "We need to move him."

Melanie could do nothing but stand there and watch as they carefully put Ricky onto a backboard and hoisted him up, Derek and Donnie working together as the paramedic hooked him up to a monitor. The machine showed Ricky's heartrate all over the place.

The medic shouted for the paddles, Melanie winced as he rubbed the defibrillator together and yelled clear, just like they did on TV, and then placed them on Ricky's chest. Nothing.

The medic cursed, saying words like V-Tach, and shocked Ricky twice more. When the machine beeped steadily, Melanie's legs gave out. If not for Caitlyn's arms, Melanie would have crumpled to the ground. She tried to reach out with her mind, but she got no response. Still, she told Ricky he would be okay now.

They hoisted him into the ambulance, Derek telling them to take Ricky to the private facility where they treated supernatural creatures. The man in the ambulance told them to meet him there, even as Derek protested, asking for them to let at least one of them travel with him.

The medic said he didn't have time to argue, slammed the door closed, and sped off. Melanie lunged for the ambulance as it drove out of reach. Another ambulance appeared, the medics jumping out and racing toward the van.

Melanie heard a groan from inside the vehicle. She hadn't even considered to check on the driver, assuming the idiot would have run off if he was able. She brushed off Caitlyn's hands and stalked over to the van. Yanking the door open, she leapt up, ignored the medic as they tried to help their patient and dragged the man out of the van and tossed him to the ground.

Tadgh stared at her, the fear of death in his eyes, and Melanie snarled. Lifting her boot, she placed it on his chest, using her strength to stop him from moving. Tadgh squirmed, but when she snarled, her eyes going red and fangs elongating, he stopped moving.

"Melanie...." Derek said softly as Donnie and Caitlyn came to stand beside him.

"No," Melanie snarled, pressing down harder with her boot. "He hurt my mate. He might have ...killed ...what is mine. It is my right, under vampire law, to avenge Ricky."

"He's not dead yet, Melanie. Tadgh will pay for his crimes. Don't let him do this to you."

Melanie lifted her gaze, ignoring Derek's words of reason, and looked to the one vampire who may agree with her. Caitlyn returned her gaze, answering Melanie's question without her having to ask it.

"You are correct. Under vampire law, you are within your rights to kill him. I will not stop you. But ask yourself, can you kill him in cold blood?"

Derek stepped forward, not afraid as she flashed her fangs at him, and hissed, "We need to get to the hospital. Either kill him or arrest him. In my opinion, death is too easy for him."

Melanie glared down at the man by her feet. The monster in her relished in his terror, and she wondered if this was the way

Donnelly had felt as she was strung up, naked and afraid, while he drove his knife in and out of her flesh.

The world might think that some supernatural creatures were monsters, and some even enjoyed having that reputation, but she would not become a monster because of her grief. She would not let Greg turn her into a monster. She would not be like Stephen Donnelly. She was better than that.

Lifting her foot, Melanie turned her back to Tadgh and heard Derek read him his rights. When she looked back to her team, Tadgh was being taken away by a uniform.

Derek was already moving, striding over to his car, and Donnie slung an arm around her shoulders and steered them over. Melanie was frozen as Donnie helped her into the back of Derek's car. Caitlyn buckled her seatbelt, and then Derek drove, siren's blaring as cars moved out of their way.

I wish he'd known. I wish he'd know that he was my mate.

"He did."

Donnie's voice caused her to glance up. His blue eyes watched her; the vampire had turned in his seat to hold her gaze. "Ricky found out that ye had mated, and he asked us not to tell you because you had to figure it out for yourself. He wanted you to make that decision and not feel compelled by it."

"Stupid, idiotic man." Melanie burst into tears, and Caitlyn pulled her into a hug, rubbing the strands of her wet hair and whispering in French. Melanie allowed herself this crack in her defences, surrounded by people who loved Ricky as much as she did.

"Wait," Melanie began, sitting up and clearing her throat. "Where's Zach? Are he and Killian okay?"

She met Derek's eyes in the rear-view mirror. "It was all for show. Lure you into a trap. Zach was never in danger. When we banged on Ricky's mom's door, Zach and Killian were curled up on the couch watching movies. They were never in danger."

Relief washed over her, her shoulders sagged and her knee bouncing impatiently. She silently begged Derek to drive faster. After an agonizingly long drive, the car pulled into the hospital car park, the very one she had once been kidnapped from. Melanie was up and out of the vehicle before anyone could stop her, pushing through the door of the emergency room until a familiar person stepped in front of her, hands resting on her shoulders.

As Sarge gave her a weak smile, Melanie scented Derek, Caitlyn and Donnie come up beside her. The smells of the hospital overwhelmed her, and her mind fogged. The bear squeezed her shoulders and dragged her attention to him.

"How is he? Where is he?" she asked, her voice quiet, not quite being able to ask Sarge if Ricky was dead.

"He's in surgery. He's in a bad way, but the stubborn SOB is hanging on."

Derek blew out a breath beside her, his voice choked with emotion as he said, "Tell me his injuries."

"Broken ribs, punctured lung, got quite a blow to his noggin, but I'm hoping it will knock some sense into him." Sarge gave a small smile, but it didn't reach his eyes. Melanie felt like there was more that her boss and friend was holding back, so she growled low in her throat.

"Tell us."

Sarge sighed. "His spleen needs to come out, and he's bleeding into his chest. The magic he used to free you both did a lot of internal damage. He has burns on fifty per cent of his body," Sarge swallowed hard, his Adam's apple bobbing as he struggled to find the words. "They think he might have some nerve damage done to his lower extremities. We'll know more if he gets through surgery."

If.

And that was it, right? If. Maybe if she'd have been alive, then she could have saved him. If she could breathe, then she could have willed his lungs to work. Melanie never even contemplated that she would wish to have been human again, but now, as Ricky's life hung in the balance, she would have given anything to keep him alive.

"Stop." Donnie's rough snarl was the only warning she got as the older vampire caught her by the shoulders and gave her a shake. "You stop that, you hear me? If you were alive, then you could not have dragged him from that river. You saved his goddamn life. You stop this fucking pity party, and you fight for your mate. You fight, you hear me!"

Melanie said nothing as Donnie pulled her into a brief hug before storming away from them. Caitlyn followed after him, torn between Melanie and her own mate, only moving away when Melanie nodded her head. Watching as Caitlyn placed her hand on the small of Donnie's back, Melanie ached to be there for her own mate.

"Can I see him?"

Sarge shook his head. "Not yet, my dear. Maybe once he is out of surgery. Make yourself comfortable; we could be in for a long night and day."

Melanie rubbed her hands up her arms, a sudden chill on her skin, her wet clothes clinging to her skin. She let herself be steered towards a metal chair, and Derek removed his jacket and hung it over Melanie's shoulders.

She smiled at him gratefully, accepted his hand in hers as she glanced up at the werewolf. "What do we do now, Derek?"

He stared at the floor, hiding his own emotions, as the wolf had always done, apart from the slight tremble in the hand that was holding hers. They all looked to Derek for the path to follow, and now, more than ever, she needed his guidance as her world slowly fell apart.

"We wait. All we can do now is wait."

Melanie inclined her head, leaning back into the chair, her eyes on the clock that hung just over the receptionist's desk. She watched the minutes go by, tick by tick, each minute like an hour, each hour like a lifetime. She sat in silence, her eyes not wavering from the hands of the clock, as night became dawn too quickly, shutters coming down over the windows to block out the sun. She stayed alert, refusing to drink or change her clothes. She would not move until she knew.

People came and went. Cops came to stand sentry because one of their own was down, and there was nowhere else they would rather be. Donnie, Caitlyn, Derek and Sarge remained stoic by her side. Erika and Ever came by, disappearing after an hour or two, Ever kissing her own mate's cheek before she left with Erika.

Hours passed and still there was no word on her Ricky.

Leaning forward, Melanie rested her chin in her hands, her eyes never once so much as straying from watching the clock.

She would wait…. all she could do now was wait.

CHAPTER SIXTEEN

RICKY

"Wake up, sleepyhead."

Ricky blinked his eyes open and rubbed his brow. His head was pounding as he lifted his gaze, landing on a woman who smiled down at him, her eyes full of adoration, a steaming cup of coffee in her grasp.

"Good morning, honey. You were sleeping like the dead, babe. You still have time, but we have that appointment at ten and then you have classes all afternoon."

Ricky jerked into an upright position and stared at the woman crouching beside his bed, eyes an earthy brown, hair long and loose around her shoulders, and full lips smiling at him. Ricky felt a tug in his heart for reasons he could not figure out.

"Sadie?"

Sadie frowned, brushing her fringe from her eyes as she handed him the mug. Resting the back of her hand on his forehead, Ricky flinched, and her frown deepened.

"Are you feeling okay? You're a little warm."

His head was banging, and he tried to remember yesterday but he couldn't. Lifting the mug to his lips, he took a sip, smiling over at her as he shrugged. "I'm all good. Just a headache. Feels like I hit it or something."

Rising to her full height, Sadie ran a hand over her bulging belly, and Ricky's eyes widened. Setting the mug down, he reached out and placed his palm over Sadie's stomach, a shot of pure joy in his heart as he felt some pressure against his palm.

"Is it mine?" he blurted out, wondering why he would even ask such a question. Of course, the baby was his...why was he being a dickhead?

Sadie laughed, the hearty sound of it carrying across the room. "I would hope so. I can already tell that our little girl is going to be a daddy's girl. Already giving you headaches."

Leaning in, she pressed her lips to his forehead. "Now hurry up and get dressed. Or I might forget that I'm the size of a house and join you back in bed."

Ricky's mouth hung open, and she laughed again, walking slowly out of the bedroom. He was up and out of the bed, his bare feet standing on plush carpet. He remembered picking out the carpet with Sadie from a shop that specialized in shifter home furnishings, the tactile nature of the carpet perfect for cats. She had joked that she was too old to roll around on the carpet, and Ricky had teased her until her cheeks had burned red that he would prove her wrong.

Glancing around the room, he was surprised to see the bedroom he shared with Sadie, but he couldn't understand why he was so surprised. This was his home, wasn't it?

Walking over to the dresser, he opened a drawer and pulled out a pair of black jeans, socks and underwear. He dressed quickly, spending a considerable amount of time searching for a band tee to wear but for the life of him, he couldn't find a single one. Every single drawer contained sweaters and shirts that Ricky was sure he wouldn't be caught dead in. Glancing in the mirror, his hand shot up to run over the nape of his neck, pausing over his pulse before he finally ran his fingers by his ears.

His black hair was clipped short, his face had just a sprinkling of stubble. Ricky wasn't sure he had been so clean shaven in his life. He stared at his reflection and did not recognize the man staring back at him.

"You okay, Dad?"

Ricky whirled around to see a figure leaning in the doorway. Zach noticeably taller, his black hair tied back in a ponytail, his eyes hidden by rimmed glasses that slipped down his nose. He looked at the boy, about ten years old, and wanted to know why he felt as if it was the first time his son had called him Dad.

"Five by five," he said, the phrase tugging on some memory he couldn't quite recall.

Zach rolled his eyes. "Stop trying to be cool, Dad. It doesn't work."

Ricky pulled out the darkest sweater he could find and yanked it on over his head. The knitted material itched, and he wanted to pull it off again as soon as it touched his skin. He felt like he was living someone else's life.

"What time do I have to be at work?" Ricky muttered, but of course Zach's cat ears heard him.

"You have the final scan with mom this morning, and then you have classes this afternoon. Just like every Tuesday. Mom said you weren't feeling well."

Classes? Since when did he go to classes?

Ricky strode over and placed a hand on his son's shoulder. "I'm good, son. I'm good."

A horn honked outside and Zach groaned. "I gotta go to school. We still on for tonight?"

"Tonight?" Ricky asked as Zach sighed.

"You promised to help me with my history assignment. It's due next week, and I have hockey practice the weekend."

"Why the hell would you ask me for help with history?" Ricky blurted out, his headache causing dark spots in his eyes.

The horn sounded again as Zach rolled his eyes. "Stop playing around, Dad. I asked the history teacher to help me. I'll see you tonight."

Zach was gone in a flurry of movement, tossing a black panther backpack over his shoulder as he kissed his mother on the cheek, waved goodbye to Ricky who now stood at the top of the stairs, and then closed the front door behind him.

Taking one step at a time, Ricky tried to clear his mind as he took in his collection of sweaters and Zach telling him he was a history teacher. He wandered into the sprawling kitchen and watched as Sadie cleared up after breakfast.

The kitchen had an open floorplan, leading down into a sitting area that held a table that seated six or eight people. It was meant for dinner parties, but Ricky ran a hand over his chest as he thought. *I'd rather get shot than host a dinner party.*

"Headache still bad, babe?"

Sadie had strolled over to him, leaning into him. Ricky felt his body stiffen. She felt it too, because she tilted her head to peer up at him, tears in her eyes.

"Hey, I'm good. Sorry. Just feeling a little weird today for some reason. We good?"

"I know you've been stressed lately with work. Don't worry. I'm just overly emotional. Happens when you're two weeks out from welcoming this little girl into the world."

Ricky closed his eyes, and when he opened them again, he was seated in a hospital room, holding Sadie's hand, grinning at the screen as he heard a heartbeat. It was a wonderous thing to see, this tiny person he had helped create, heart beating so vividly, it made him squeeze Sadie's hand ever so tightly.

The nurse turned and smiled. "Everything looks on course for the 29th." She printed out a picture and handed it to Ricky, who stared at it in amazement for a few minutes as the women laughed at him. He tucked the photo into his pocket and helped Sadie from the bed.

They walked hand in hand down the corridor, Ricky feeling very uneasy, thinking that he should not be here, holding her hand, feeling this kind of happy.

Ricky. Buddy, can you hear me?

Ricky stumbled over his feet, Sadie catching him before he face-planted. Nausea rolling in his stomach, he felt overly warm, the voice in his head so familiar, yet he couldn't place it.

Closing his eyes, he muttered. "This feels all wrong. What am I doing here?"

"Richard?"

Sadie's voice snapped his eyes open, and he was standing in the middle of the quad of the College of Paranormal Studies, students milling about and passing him by as he stood there gawping. Students greeted him, including a title that Ricky was sure he was dreaming.

"Professor Moore!"

Ricky turned to see a petite blonde woman hurrying toward him, her blue eyes falling on him in relief. She came over to him breathless, but his memory pricked, and he knew this woman was stronger than any of them could have imagined.

Them? Who was them?

"Professor Moore, I need you to take over my four thirty class on introduction to supernatural creatures. I have a meeting that I can't reschedule."

Ricky must have been staring at her in complete shock because the woman laughed, clasping him on the shoulder as she brushed past him. "I know. No one wants to teach the newbies, but I think you can handle them, Ricky."

The woman strode away, and Ricky spun on his heels and collided with another woman, heard the sound of her hiss of pain as she fell to knees. He dropped to his own knees, reached out and helped the woman up, scolding his carelessness as she struggled to stay upright.

"Gods, I'm sorry. I should have been watching where I was going."

"It's okay. I'd joke and say I was visually impaired, but it wouldn't necessarily be a joke."

Ricky chuckled, his breath hitching as eyes of green held his own. He knew this woman. He *knew* her. He remembered the teasing conversations, the feeling in him when he was with her, he knew the press of her lips against his, he knew the feel of her body against his.

"Have we met before? I feel like we've meet before?"

Her red hair glinted in the dying sunlight, a smile curving her lips, and Ricky, damn him, felt the urge to press his lips to hers. He stumbled back, earning a frown from the beautiful woman.

"Nope. Don't think so. I sat in on your magical physics class last semester for fun. But us mere mortals have no place attending magic classes. I'm just here for the techy stuff."

The young woman smiled as she nudged her laptop bag. Ricky returned her smile, and the urge to kiss her and hold her in his arms grew stronger as his headache punched louder in his head.

Ricky, Buddy. Can you hear me?

Brushing the dirt off her knees, she gave him another breath-taking smile. "Well, I gotta go or I'll be late for class."

"Again, I'm so sorry for running into you...Ms...?"

Holding out her hand, Ricky took it, his brain telling him that her hands were normally not as warm as they were now. "Melanie. Just call me Melanie."

Lanie.... she's definitely a Lanie.

Ricky held onto her hand for a moment more, then released it reluctantly. "Well it was nice running into you, Lanie."

The girl blinked at the nickname, then grinned as Ricky felt a small pang of guilt for being flirty when he had a wife and kid at home. He stood as night fall upon them, watching the girl walk away from him and wondering why every instinct in him begged and pleaded with him to go after her.

Mate.

Mate.

Mate.

Ricky, Buddy. Can you hear me?

Ricky scolded himself, thinking of his wife back home, turning to walk in the opposite direction of the girl when a blood curdling scream rendered through the air from the direction Melanie had gone.

Ricky bolted toward the scream that had now gone silent, crossing through the quad, his mind screaming that he was in danger, to call for help, but he could not stop from rushing forward. He rounded a corner, standing in the archway that led to the main building, a cry of anguish in his throat as he spied a mass of flame red hair sprawled against the reddish-brown brickwork on the ground.

It took Ricky a moment to see the pool of blood staining the ground. He screamed for help as he lunged forward, dropping to his knees and taking the bleeding girl in his arms.

A memory washed over him, a nightmare quite like the real life one that he was living now, of him holding Melanie in a similar way, close to death but not entirely so. He smoothed her hair like he did in the memory, promising to look after her but his promises were empty, as empty as the green eyes that looked blankly at him.

He felt the crowd gather around him, but he would not relinquish his hold on the dead girl until a hand fell upon his shoulder, and Ricky dragged his eyes from Melanie and landed on a stern face with eyes of hazel. A sense of unbreakable trust filled him.

"You need to let her go, buddy. We have to pronounce her and try and see if we can catch the monster that did this."

One of the most beautiful women Ricky had ever laid eyes on crouched down in front of him, her face a mask of cold that had him shivering. She didn't so much as look at him when she uttered something beneath her breath in French as Ricky laid Melanie down on the ground. His head ached, and he stumbled.

A strong hand steadied him, Ricky glancing up to thank whoever it was that had held him up.

"Donnie?" Ricky mumbled, his legs trembling as he tried to concentrate and figure out what was going on.

"Do I know you?" Donnie said, the vampire studying him as Ricky stumbled away from them.

"This isn't real. This isn't how it's supposed to be!" he shouted the last part, the pain in his head now almost debilitating. He held his head in his hands and retreated until his back hit the wall, and then he slid down until his ass hit the cold ground. He cradled his head in his hands.

"This didn't happen. We saved her. She didn't die."

Ricky knew he was rambling like an idiot, like someone who was embarking on a psychotic break, but he couldn't stop the words from tumbling from his lips.

"We save her. Caitlyn makes her a vampire. Ever kills Donnelly. Sadie and Cain are dead. Caitlyn and Donnie finally get together. Derek and Ever know that she's a Valkyrie and Odin's trying to kill her! Melanie's a vampire and we …we…"

He could feel everyone's eyes on him and felt warm hands on his shoulders as he peered up to see Sadie standing there with her rounded belly, and Ricky knew he was dreaming.

"Ricky, you are not well. We will take you to the hospital, and we will make it all go away."

Ricky shook his head vigorously, tears now streaming down his face. "There was a crash. I went into the Lee. I don't think I got out. Am I dead?"

Ricky felt arms lift him up, saw the wolf who he knew was his brother, and the vampire who was his best friend standing beside him, holding him up as they all but carried him toward the ambulance. He glanced back, and Melanie's body was gone. It wasn't real. He had to wake up… he had to get back to his mate.

Ricky felt his magic surge deep in his body, and he roared as he shoved the supernaturals away from him, the blue flames engulfing his skin as he tossed the flames to the side and ran. He heard nothing but the sound of his feet against the concrete, the rush of blood in his ears, and he ran and ran until he ground to a halt at the intersection by North Gate Bridge.

There were no screech marks on the road, no crumbled wall where his car had plunged into the bitter water. There was no indication that he and Lanie had been here at all. He felt a gust of wind against the nape of his neck and whirled round; the vampires were standing in front of him, standing not as close as he knew they did now, the obvious tension there for even Ricky's muddled mind to see.

"Guys, this isn't real. Cain is dead. Kenzie killed him. Your niece, Caitlyn. You and Donnie are mated, and you guys are happy. Caitlyn, you smile when you think no one is watching."

"He really is delusional," muttered Caitlyn, a deadpan expression on her face.

Donnie's gaze was narrowed as he observed Ricky, and Ricky wasn't sure any of them would believe him; he wasn't sure he believed it himself.

"Donnie, mate, don't you remember the pub crawls we used to go on? The gigs we played? We went to festivals and couldn't remember what we did for those three days. You've seen inside my head and still kept my secrets. Look into my head now and see I'm telling the truth."

Caitlyn and Donnie vanished, and Sadie stood in front of him, Zach by her side, her hand resting on her stomach. The world around them darkened, the city disappearing as she stepped forward.

"Stay here with us, Ricky. Don't leave us here. Aren't you happy with us?"

Ricky coughed and water filled his lungs as he stumbled back. His family gone in the blink of an eye. Darkness settled in, the road a vastness of nothing, and his headache burned inside his skull. Ricky screamed, but no sound came out.

This wasn't the life for him. He wanted to live. He wanted a future with Melanie.

The water rose up behind him, flooding the streets and rising up to cover his ankles. Ricky tried to move his legs, but they would not move. Suddenly he was on his back, water covering his body. Then, he was floating in an endless black, water in his nose, his mouth, and his lungs. He felt the cold hand of death wrapped around his neck.

He wanted to scream; he wanted to call out. He wanted someone to hear his final pleas as his magic sparked to life inside his veins. His blood boiled, his flesh searing as his headache lifted. For a brief moment before he succumbed to darkness, Ricky smiled.

CHAPTER
SEVENTEEN

EVER

E ver stood on the fringes of the park, Thor beside her, as they waited for evening to draw in and for those playing within the amenity park to go home for the evening. Loki had woven some magic around the park to prevent Odin or Ever from striking out against one another as they sat around the conclave.

Nervous, Ever had to stop her hand from drifting to her stomach every so often, cursing herself for how much she really wanted the child, but knowing that this little ploy of Odin's would not end in any peaceful resolution.

Loki strode up to stand beside them both. He whispered softly, and the park emptied out, those who had been playing making for the safety of their homes, unaware of the threat that was no doubt watching from a safe distance.

Ever felt the prickle of Erika's aura just before she flashed in, and Ever took a step back when she realized Erika was not alone. Danae appeared first, the blonde Valkyrie was almost as tall as Thor with wide shoulders and a wicked looking axe strapped to her chest. Rebekah followed, her wavy mouse brown hair woven across the crown of her head and falling into one long braid down her back.

Almira came next, the quiet Valkyrie was not much for battle, having spent centuries keeping a watch over Fólkvangr. Her eyes held no fear as she regarded Ever, bowing her head slightly in greeting. Little Marya was last to arrive, her red hair so similar to Melanie's that it hurt Ever's heart to think of what her friend was going through right now.

Standing there, facing her remaining sisters, Ever felt a slight burn in her veins, spreading out in her blood and across her back.

One by one, the Valkyrie fisted a hand over their chests and bowed their heads.

"We have come to stand beside you, my Queen," Danae said, her tone unwavering as she lifted her gaze to clash with Ever's.

Folding her arms over her chest, Ever inclined her head. "Thank you. It is long overdue that we stand side by side once again. Let us remind Odin just how powerful we are, standing together as one."

Loki grinned as he lifted his hands, whispering an incantation as he strode forward. The park was covered in a shimmer of waves for a moment and then a dais with a table on top of it replaced the swing set.

Ever heard the cawing of crows and watched as Hugin and Mugin flew into sight, landing on the back of the chair seated at the head of the table. Loki sighed and manifested a second chair on the other end of the table.

"No magic can be used once you and Odin are seated. I cannot stop him from striking out at you. Be on your guard."

"I always am," Ever told Loki, wishing that Derek was by her side, but her mate was torn between her and his best friend. Thor told Derek to stay where he was and that he would watch over Ever as he had done for years. Derek had seemed a little more at ease then, still torn but confident Thor would stand beside her. So, Derek stayed by his friend's bedside, to be there for Melanie who could lose her mate.

Ever knew what that felt like and did not wish it on the vampire.

"Are you ready?" Thor asked her softly.

Ever didn't trust her voice, because she didn't feel ready. But what choice had she left?

Striding forward, she felt Erika move to walk beside her and felt the other Valkyrie at her back forming a protective circle around her. She walked across the park, her heart pounding in her chest, taking the seat that Loki held out for her, leaning back into the seat and resting her hands on the arms of the chair.

Odin appeared in his seat to no fanfare, his appearance changed from what it once had been. He looked older now, his white hair and beard even longer if that was possible. Wrinkles crinkled his eyes, his mouth, and his cheeks, and Ever wondered if this was all a trick to appear older, more vulnerable.

Thor rested his hand on Ever's shoulder, and Odin's eyes watched the movement, a smug smile curving his lips as he tapped his staff twice on the ground. A platoon of Asgardian warriors gathered behind them. Erika swallowed hard at the sight of the god of war at Odin's back, Loki resting a hand on her best friend's shoulder in comfort.

Loki let his eyes roam over the warriors, the power coiled within him leaking from his pores as his clothing changed, his long green cape falling into place, the horned helmet gleaming as it appeared on his head.

"I have not made a promise in over a thousand years, but I am promising you this; if any one of you harm a hair on her head, I will end you all. I will do so smiling, and I will bathe in your blood."

Erika reached up and rested her hand on Loki's. "He says the most romantic things, right?"

A teether of laugher rumbled from Ever's camp, yet the moment she held up her hand, the laughing stopped. She had the attention of her father, the monster who had killed her so many times. Silence stretched out across the table, not a single person uttering a syllable. Ever's patience wore thin, and Odin glanced around as if searching for someone.

"You asked for this meeting, Odin. Will you not get on with it already?"

Hugin cawed at her angrily, and Odin reached up to pet the monstrous bird. "I was awaiting your mother's arrival. How is she after her ...accident?"

Ever blinked in surprise, not knowing what the hell Odin was talking about, which only caused the god's smile to deepen as Danae answered.

"Freya is getting better every day. Already she stands by her own fruition. Severing her spine has only made her more determined to kill you."

Ever's eyes darted to Erika, who shrugged, the Valkyrie not having filled either of them in on Freya's condition.

"Well since the lovely Freya is not making an appearance, shall we continue?"

"Go ahead," Ever replied to her father, wondering if he could change his tune after all these centuries.

"Give me Valhalla. Give me Valhalla, and I shall break the spell. You can go and live a life with your wolf, and I will make Asgard and Valhalla great once again."

Ever snorted, tapping her fingers against the arm of the chair. "And here I was thinking you may have changed your mind. Perhaps you had realized that Valhalla is not the answer to your problems. Even Ragnarök is not the answer to your problems. My answer is no. Valhalla is our home; we will not have you destroy it."

Odin banged his staff on the ground in frustration, the ground trembling beneath their feet but Ever did not so much as flinch. Showing weakness in front of him would not be a wise thing.

"You have not stepped foot in Valhalla for over a century. Yet you still call it home."

"You have not stepped foot in Asgard in over a century. Yet you still call it home. Tell me, Father, when was the last time you sat under Yggdrasil and pondered your life?"

Odin had no response to her words, his cheeks blazing with colour as his eyes grew angry and the skies with it. Lightening flashed, and the ravens cawed on response.

"There are not many days that you have left, Daughter. I can save your friend, the warlock that is dying. I would do so, because you love him, and your mate loves him. All you have to do is hand over the keys to Valhalla."

Ever's heart beat a little faster as she considered it. However, no matter how much she wanted Ricky to be alive and well, she could not be selfish and hand over Valhalla to Odin for the sake of one man. Death was a way of life, and if Ricky did die, then that was the way it was meant to be. They had already messed enough with the path of destiny.

"The life of one man is no more important than the fate of the world. If you unleash Ragnarök upon the world, thousands will die. I cannot weigh one man's life over the lives of thousands of innocent people. You must see reason in that. Or maybe not, considering you are willing to see the world burn in order to bring Frigg back to life."

Odin flinched at Ever's words, his eyes full of hate as he regarded her.

"Then we are finished here,, he spat out, shoving his chair back, turning his back to her, and stepping off the dais. Ever shook her head, wondering why she had wasted such precious time because Odin would never change. He would never give up this foolish quest for power.

She stood next, sighing as she faced Thor. "We tried. He will never change."

Thor's shoulders sagged, and her brother finally understood

SUSAN HARRIS

that there was no way back for Odin. Only death could cure the world of him. The dais disappeared as Odin beat his staff twice, and the Asgardian warriors vanished, with Tyr watching Erika before he went. She slumped in her chair, exhaling a breath as Loki rubbed her shoulders.

"Valhalla will be mine, Ever," Odin's voice dragged her attention back to him, and she watched as Marya, the youngest of the Valkyrie, jumped in front of Ever. She smiled, knowing her sister would have her back, proud of the young teen's desire to protect her queen.

"You may not have set foot in Valhalla in an age, Ever, but I have."

Ever had little opportunity to react, and time seemed to slow as Odin lifted his staff, the end of it sharpened into a spear. He could not hurt her in these grounds, but he could hurt Marya. Ever cried out, moving to stop the young woman and take the blow, when Marya grabbed the staff with a practiced ease, her smile darkening as she whirled around and said, "Hail to the Allfather."

Ever didn't breathe. She didn't so much as move as death came looming in the form of another family member who wanted her dead. Marya drove the staff downward, and Ever closed her eyes, surprisingly calm as she waited for the blow that would end this saga once and for all.

That blow never came.

Thunder rumbled in the air, and screams caused her to fling her eyes open once again. The head of Odin's speared staff was inches from her face, blood staining the metal. Ever caught Thor's body as it crumpled to the ground. She screamed his name, the force of his fall bringing her down with him. She scrambled out from beneath his body, his hammer dropping from his hand as she pulled the staff from his chest and placed her hands over the wound.

"You'll be okay. You'll be okay."

Loki was beside her in an instant, muttering as he waved his hands over Thor, but Ever knew there was nothing that could be done. Thor was dying.

Ever snapped her head in Odin's direction, and Marya darted over to Odin, standing defiantly beside him. He shrugged. "He chose the wrong side."

Odin was gone a second later, talking the betrayer with him, the rest of the Valkyrie standing in shock. No one tried to wrangle Marya from Odin's grasp.

"Ever, I am at peace."

Tears streaked down Ever's face as she cradled Thor in her lap, unable to tell him how much she loved him. How much he meant to her...

Thor reached up and cupped her tear stained cheek. "She will be worthy."

Then his hand fell, his head lolled to the side, and her brother, the god of thunder, the seemingly invincible mountain who was gentle and kind, protecting humans his entire life, faded into death. Thunder rumbled overhead, and then the night was silent once again.

As Ever cried in earnest, Loki brushed Thor's amber hair from his face, closed his eyes and said, "And now, until we meet again, may the blessings of Asgard be showered upon you."

Thor's body shimmered and faded away, leaving Ever kneeling in the dirt, her beloved brother dead because of her. She screamed her grief into the night, lightening crashing into the ground around her, the force of it vibrating along the dirt and into her toes.

No one tried to comfort her, Erika simply resting a hand on her shoulder until Ever felt herself rise, shoving down her grief and her loss and facing those who remained. Every single one of them seemed affected by the loss of Thor.

The time for talking was over. Ever would avenge her brother's death. And then she would go find him in Valhalla and tell him of how she cut off their father's head.

"Um...Ever...what do we do with that?"

Ever glanced down to the spot where Thor had been slain, his faithful hammer laying where he had dropped it. Loki reached down and wrapped his fingers around it, yet Mjölnir would not be swayed.

Loki gave Ever a weak smile. "I guess I am not worthy."

"There is no one who will ever be worthy to wield that hammer but Thor. I mean how the hell could they be. I'll kill Odin for this. I will gut him like a fish!"

Anger radiated through her, that fire in her veins sparking, her palm itchy as she reached out her hand for something to steady her. A collection of shocked gasps caused Ever to look in the direction of where all eyes were focused, and Ever almost lost her control.

Mjölnir was firmly seated in the palm of her hand, blue streaks flowing over the weapon as Ever lifted it into the air, and thunder sounded all around them. Power flooded through her, and Ever smiled, her blue eyes filling with lightning as she regarded the rest of the Valkyrie.

She opened her mouth to speak, yet as she stood there, she felt it again, a weird burning coursing through her veins. Except this time, it was stronger. Pain, red hot and searing across her back, caused her to let go of Mjölnir and drop to her knees, crying out and reaching around to try and stop the fire between her shoulder blades.

Through the haze, Ever heard Erika cry out in pain, then one by one the rest of the Valkyrie dropped to their knees, clawing at their backs as Ever was. In between one breath and the next, the pain was gone, and Ever stumbled to her feet, almost falling over as weight on her back caused her to tilt forward.

Ever lifted her gaze to stare open mouthed at Erika, who was grinning like an idiot. Spanning out from Erika's back were the most beautifully haunting pair of wings. Their feathers were an inky shade of black, so black they were almost blue. Erika moved her shoulders up, once, twice, every movement seemingly easier with each stretch of her muscles.

"Erika, oh my god!" Ever exclaimed, wondering why Loki was grinning at her and not staring at the wonder protruding from his girlfriend's back.

"Ever, look." Loki wiggled his fingers and a mirror was in front of her a second later. The sight caused her to clap a hand over her mouth. Wings like spun gold nestled between her shoulder blades on her back, each feather soft under her fingertips. The mirror vanished, and the rest of the Valkyrie tested their own wings.

Erika beat her wings, once, twice, and she hoovered off the ground and let loose of whoop of joy. Back in Valhalla, before they had agreed to this battle, they had all been awaiting the battle that would mark them as true Valkyrie, the one that would give them their wings and cement that they were great warriors. They practised how to will them forward and will them away.

Ever closed her eyes, ordering the wings away, feeling the burn as they did. Standing in the park, the war almost upon them, Ever held out her hand and grinned as Mjölnir wavered and flew up and into her palm. Missing her glorious wings already, Ever lifted her head.

"The great war is upon us. We have been betrayed by our own family, by our own kin. It is time to gather our forces. It is time to gather our allies and ask them to stand with us. Erika stood in my home and asked the strongest supernatural creatures in Cork if they would stand beside us. Now, you must travel the nine realms and ask those who wish Asgard, Midgard, and any other realm to remain standing against Odin to come join us."

Ever looked at Mjölnir, the gift her brother had given her,

and then she held it high in the sky once again, letting thunder gather overhead, letting Odin know that she was done waiting. She would bring the war to him.

"I ask you now, Valkyrie, to stand beside me and prepare for war. Make sure Freya gets whatever help she needs. The time is now. What say you?"

The Valkyrie said nothing, willing away their own wings, each a unique shade that was attuned to the Valkyrie who wore it. They dropped to their knees and fisted a hand over their hearts, pledging their swords and their lives to Ever.

Erika wiggled her wings, shivering as Loki ran a hand possessively over the feathers. "What do you want us to do first?"

Ever smiled, flashing her teeth as she said, "Find those who could be Valkyrie. Find them and bring them to Valhalla. It's time we opened the doors and welcomed any who wish to join our ranks to do so. Let us see if they are worthy."

Erika nodded to Danae who led the Valkyrie away to embark on their mission. Erika stayed behind, her hand slipping into Loki's. "Hospital first?"

Ever nodded, willing the hammer away for safe keeping, and then she stepped closer to Loki and prayed that Ricky would survive the night for she could not bear another loss.

CHAPTER EIGHTEEN

MELANIE

Melanie snapped back to awareness, shifting in the chair and taking in her surroundings. Somewhere between clock watching and now, she must have drifted off to sleep, her still young vampire body needing to rest. Brushing the hair from her face, she groaned and straightened, glancing around the room.

She was in a hospital room, the smell of disinfectant and bleach so overwhelming she nearly gagged. The beep of machines alerted her to Ricky's presence in the room with her. Lurching forward, she was at the side of the bed a second later, her hand in Ricky's. His skin felt cold against hers as she studied the machines around her.

One monitored his heartbeat, and another pumped air into his lungs through a tube in his mouth. A drip was inserted into the vein in his arm, and Melanie could not stop the tears from slipping from her eyes.

The man she loved was so full of life, of laughter, of love. The man before her was a pale comparison of the one etched on her soul, her entire being. Melanie wasn't sure how she was still standing, the world tilted on its axis as she watched the rise and fall of his chest.

"He's been like that since they brought him back from surgery."

Melanie cast her eyes around to see Donnie sitting in the corner, tiredness darkening his eyes. She assumed he had been watching over Ricky and her as well. Donnie rose, dragging his chair with him, kicking another in her direction so she could sit her weary body down. He sat beside her, saying no more, but Melanie couldn't stand the silence.

"Did you bring me in here?" Her voice was nothing more than a whisper.

"Ya," was all he said. Donnie didn't embellish, and Melanie was glad for it.

"Thank you."

There was a lull of silence as the machine attached to Ricky beeped once, twice, three times before Donnie leaned his head against the bars of Ricky's hospital bed.

"I can't get into his head. I can't see into his mind to make sure he's okay, and it's killing me."

Melanie didn't know how to answer him, so she simply rested her free hand in Donnie's, and they lapsed into a comfortable silence. They sat there for an age before Caitlyn slipped into the room, running her fingers over her mate's head briefly before coming to stand next to the bed. Caitlyn tucked a stray strand of Ricky's hair behind his ear.

"Any change?" she asked Donnie, who shook his head. Suddenly, he leapt to his feet.

"I need some air."

Melanie watched him storm from the room, glanced up at Caitlyn before she said, "Go after him, if you want. I'll be okay."

"He cannot go far; the sun is still up. I told Ricky's mother I would watch over him. I will continue to do so."

All Melanie could do was nod, turning back to look at Ricky as Caitlyn occupied Donnie's vacant seat. Melanie ran her thumb absentmindedly over the palm of Ricky's hand. The steady beep of the machine proved what Melanie already knew; Ricky had a strong heart, and he would pull through.

"Does Zach know?" Melanie asked Caitlyn, worried for the little boy who had lost his mother so suddenly.

"He does not. It was decided to keep it from him until we knew more. Do you know," Caitlyn began, leaning forward to rest her arms on the side of the bed, tilting her face to look toward Ricky as she smiled. "I had not laughed in maybe a century until I met Ricky. Oh, he was terrified of me at first, as were you. But he bought me flowers on my birthday, made a joke about how he spent hours trying to pick out flowers that were as beautiful as I was. I scowled at him, and he grinned at me with that smile of his, saying he did it to piss Donnie off and I laughed. I could not help myself."

"He has a way of making everyone feel at ease."

"Yes, even if he does not realize it."

Melanie allowed herself to look away from Ricky. "He gave you custody of Zach, should anything happen to him."

"I am not worthy of such a gift."

"Yes, yes you are."

Caitlyn let loose a sigh. "It matters little, for Ricky will awaken soon and charm us with that smile of his."

I hope so. Ricky, if you can hear me, please squeeze my hand. Please.

Nothing happened, and Melanie closed her eyes.

A knock sounded on the door, opening slowly as Derek came in. Melanie rose, instantly going into his arms. Sarge followed in after alongside Donnie. Melanie allowed herself to stay in Derek's comforting arms for a second more, stepping out of his embrace as Sarge told them the doctors were ready to speak to them now.

Melanie went back to her chair on shaky legs, sitting down and taking Ricky's hand once again. Donnie, Derek and Sarge leaned against the wall, Caitlyn laid her head down on Ricky's leg. Melanie heard the door open again, the doctor slipping in with a chart, a grim expression on his face.

"Talk to his mate. She needs to hear it."

Melanie sat upright when she realized they were talking about her. The doctor, a man in his fifties, pulled a chair over and, sitting down, opened his chart and began to speak.

"Ricky sustained serious injuries to most of his vital organs. His magic was so powerful, and when he didn't have control over it, he turned it in on himself instead of causing an explosion that might have injured civilians. His organs are failing. The machines are the only things that are keeping him alive. If we take him off the ventilator, Ricky will pass away peacefully."

Melanie looked at the doctor, unsure of what he was saying. She didn't understand. She didn't want to understand. The doctor was wrong. They needed to run more tests. They needed to do something else, instead of sitting there and telling her that her mate was dying.

"Melanie, do you understand what the doctor is telling you?"

Melanie ignored Derek. She turned away from the doctor and focused on Ricky. The doctor was wrong. They had thought she was beyond saving, when Stephen Donnelly had done everything to end her life, but Ricky fought for her to stay alive. She would do the same for him.

Melanie heard Sarge thank the doctor and ask him for some time. They didn't need time. They just needed to be left alone. When the doctor left the room, Melanie rose, walking over to the windows and closing the blinds. Caitlyn had spun round to watch her as she did, her brow furrowed as Melanie calmly faced down every supernatural creature in the room.

"Well, who's going to do it?" Hands on hips, she lifted her brows expectantly, waiting for the rush of volunteers. None came.

The men seemed oblivious to her meaning, but Caitlyn

knew where Melanie was going and stood to face her. "It cannot be done. He is too ill."

"Fuck that. Are you not even going to try? Are you just going to stand there and let him die? He would do anything to save you all… he did so for me and now, now you are happy to stand there and watch him die!" Her voice carried in the small room, and everyone flinched at her words.

Derek's growl only angered her more, and Melanie pointed a finger at him. "Change him. Make him a wolf."

"He doesn't carry the gene."

"I don't care. Just do it."

Most people thought that if you got scratched by a werewolf or bitten that you became one, but they were wrong. The only ones that changed were the ones who carried the gene that initiated the change. If Ricky didn't have the gene, then he wouldn't survive the bite. Derek didn't answer her, so she dismissed him with the wave of her hand.

"Then go, because you are of no use to us."

Melanie ignored Derek's growl, but it was her mate dying in that hospital bed. She would fight every last one of them with blood and sweat to bring him back to her. She strode up to Donnie, whose head had dropped. He could not look at her, so Melanie poked him in the chest, ignoring the rumble as she ordered.

"Then tell me what to do. Tell me how to save him." Melanie demanded, frustrated that none of them were willing to help her, help Ricky.

"There is no saving him. His body is too weak to handle the change. Besides, magical creatures never take the change well from one supe to another," Donnie said quietly.

"Bullshit! Bullshit" Melanie cried pounding her fists against his chest until the vampire she thought of like a brother, grabbed her wrists gently, tears staining his own face. Ignoring his state of grief, Melanie snatched her hands away, turning and indicating to Caitlyn.

"She was a human who was a hunter. She became a vampire and is one of the world's most powerful vampires. So, I say bullshit. Do something to save him or get the fuck out of the room! How can you give up on him? How can you give up on him so easily and leave Zach an orphan?"

Not a single person moved, but they all flinched at the words that she spoke. Going deathly silent, Melanie stood still for a second. Donnie stepped forward, and she moved away from his hands as he made to reach for her.

"Don't you think we would do anything to save him? We would. You love him, Mel, but so does every other person in this room. I can't lie to you. I would gladly take his place, give my life for his, if it meant taking the pain away from you. If it meant giving Zach back his dad, I'd fucking do just about anything. There is fucking nothing we can do."

Melanie tasted the truth in his words, her walls crumbling as she sobbed, screaming at them to leave her alone. She ignored them as they did so reluctantly, the door closing softly behind them as the team left her to mourn her mate.

Pushing down the bars on the side of the bed, Melanie lifted Ricky's arms so that she could curl up beside him, resting her head over the beat of his heart, her leg tangled with his as she wept for a long time, until her tears rang dry, her chest still heaved. She lay there, for an age, begging and pleading with Ricky to wake up and prove them all wrong, yet, her warlock remained unmoving, not a glimmer of hope left inside of Melanie as she tried to come to terms with the fact she had found the love of her life and lost him before they could ever be.

She did not want to live a life without him. She could not see any future. When she tried to see it, all she saw was an endless nothing. She would turn cold like Caitlyn after the loss of her husband and children, spending centuries walled off, never loving again because Ricky was it for her.

She pressed her lips to his chest, and she promised to follow him into death.

"Why are vampires such morbid creatures? I mean, he was going to die anyways, long before you. Why cry tears now?"

Melanie darted upright, snarling at the intruder who was casually leaning against the walls, her features hidden by the shadows. Slipping off the bed, Melanie braced herself for a fight, but a bark of laughter caused her to falter.

"Oh, that's cute. I'm not here to hurt you, vampire. I'm here to help you."

The woman stepped out of the shadows, the lights flickering overhead as Melanie gasped. Half the woman's face was skeletal, the other a vision of beauty. The lights flickered again, and Melanie ran her eyes over the mysterious being.

Sandy brown hair fell down to her shoulders, her face now one in its beauty. The features were familiar, but Melanie could not place them. She wore a pink t-shirt with a koala riding a unicorn, a pair of khaki combats over her legs and boots similar to those that Erika liked to wear. She twirled a hair in her fingers, grinning widely, flashing pearly white teeth.

Melanie could almost smell the power oozing from the women's pores, and she guessed by the similar scent of it, some Norse legend had stumbled upon her and wanted in on her misery.

"Oh stop, I want no such thing. You want to fix him, right? I mean he is handsome and all kinds of yummy. I might just keep him."

Melanie growled possessively as she stepped in front of Ricky, blocking him from the girl's view. She waved dismissively at Melanie, clicking her fingers and popped a lollipop into her mouth.

"What do you want?"

"I'm offering you a chance to save him. I can do it. Well... I think I can, but I might need some help."

"Why would you help me?" Melanie asked. "You don't even know me."

"Oh, but I do, Melanie Newton. She who died and was reborn. She who is the seeker of truths. She who is very much where she needs to be. I can save him, but I ask two things from you."

Waiting, Melanie folded her arms over her chest, and the other girl grinned. "Excellent. So, if you want me to help you change him into a vampire or whatnot, then I need a life for a life. Bring me another person's soul, and I will take that in exchange for Ricky's life. Bring me a tainted soul, they taste better."

Melanie's eyes wandered over the girl who looked like she was ready for a day out with her besties, talking like she was ordering take out and not a goddamn soul. Suspicion flooded Melanie's mind, yet she was willing to do whatever it took to bring Ricky back.

"And the second thing?"

"What second thing?" The woman replied, grinning as if she hoped Melanie would forget.

She hadn't.

"You said two things. I can't do the second without knowing what it is first."

The girl clapped twice in excitement. "A favour. One small favour of my choosing at the time of my choosing. Could be next week. Could be sometime in the next century."

Melanie didn't have to think twice. Holding out her hand, she said, "Agreed."

The woman took it, and they shook hands. Melanie felt a shock of cold at their touch.

"Excellent." The strange woman clapped her hands again, and a small ancient looking dagger appeared. She handed the weapon to Melanie. "Stab whichever poor bastard you want through the heart and bring the dagger to me. Then, I'll fix your heartthrob."

Melanie turned away from the woman, hoping she was doing the right thing in trusting this stranger. Pressing her lips to Ricky's cheek, she ran her fingers through his hair. "I'll be back. The next time I put my lips on yours, you'll be kissing me back. I promise you."

Turning back to her unlikely ally, Melanie wondered how in the hell she could track down Greg. He was a rotten soul and responsible for Ricky's condition, and he would be the one to fix him with his death. Ricky would come back to her, and everything would be okay.

It had to be.

Putting the dagger into the clip at her belt, Melanie wondered how she could get passed the entourage standing guard outside and make it back. Night would be looming soon, and then she would go.

Melanie stole a glance at the woman who watched her with an eager curiosity.

"Why are you helping me?" Melanie queried, shifting on her feet slightly.

"Call me a romantic. I mean, Earth has so many rom coms. I absolutely adore the Hallmark channel. Don't you?"

"It might take me time to track down the soul. How will I find him?"

"Oh, dearie, I can help you with that."

The woman closed her eyes, lifted her hands up and then faced them downward. Melanie stepped back as the ground swirled, a pitch-black pit opening up for a brief moment before the woman clapped her hands shut, and the ground was normal once again.

"Greg DeShane is currently hiding out at a place I think you are familiar with. I believe you once lived there with him."

Melanie growled, eager to get this over with. Quietly walking to the door, she inched it open slightly, peaking outside to see that darkness had fallen. Her eyes fell on the faces of her friends who sat outside, their own grief kicking her in the stomach.

She would fix it... she would fix it.

But she had to get passed them first.

"Oh, I can help you with that, too!" the woman squealed excitedly. Melanie was sure that this... whoever she was, said 'oh' a lot.

The woman clapped her hands together again, and the hospital wall opened up with some sort of portal. Melanie had watched enough sci-fi movies to know that most of the time, portals could get you killed, but she had nothing left to lose.

Walking up to the portal, Melanie cast her attention back to the grinning girl who was hopping from one foot to another with great enthusiasm. Melanie stepped up to the portal and paused. "Thank you for helping me, um... I'm sorry, but I didn't catch your name."

The woman tossed her hair off her shoulder, her grin deepening as she replied, "In this time, people call me Helen. But all my friends call me Hel. You can always call me Hel, Melanie. We are going to be good friends, you and I."

GREG SAT *in the fireside chair as the wall in his old apartment opened, and death stepped out to face him. She was paler than when he last saw her, and he wondered if her warlock had died. Greg didn't dare ask as she pulled a dagger from her waist. Her eyes, red from crying, were fixed on his. Fangs that now marked her as the predator flashed as her lips curled up in disgust at the sight of him.*

The hole in his wall closed, and Melanie stepped forward.

"Come to kill me, Mel?"

"Something like that." She snarled, twisting the dagger in her wrist, and Greg held out his hands.

"Take your best shot. Show me the monster you have become. Tell me first, though, did he die in your arms?"

"He's not dead yet."

"Pity."

Greg stood, watching as Melanie's hand began to tremble. "You could have been so much more, Mel. You and I could have changed the world."

"You didn't want to change the world, Greg. You wanted to inflict pain on the supernatural community."

Melanie held out the dagger and stalked toward him, the tip of it pressing against his chest through his t-shirt.

"Do it, Mel. Do it!"

The moment he shouted the last part, Melanie drove the dagger into his heart. Greg felt a wave of torturous pain before she yanked the dagger out. He fell to the ground, and the last thing he saw before he died was the love of his life walking away.

CHAPTER NINETEEN

MELANIE

The blade began to glow the moment she yanked it free of Greg's chest, and it hadn't stopped its illumination. Melanie stood in the carpark and wondered how in the hell she was gonna stride into the hospital and sneak past the gathered crowd with the magical weapon beaming like a beacon in the loop of her belt.

And that was before the vampires and wolf smelled the blood staining the metal.

Running her hands up and down her arms, Melanie took a step forward. A figure stepped out of the shadows and raised a brow at her.

"And how did you manage to sneak out without the parentals noticing?"

Kenzie flicked her hair off her shoulders and grinned. The blood-kissed human niece of Caitlyn had become such a fast friend of Melanie's that she knew it was useless to even try hiding it.

"I killed Greg."

Kenzie did not so much as flinch. The former assassin of the first vampire, Cain, shrugged. "I hope you made it hurt."

The blade glowed even brighter, causing Kenzie to motion to it and say, "Do I want to know?"

"If it works, I'll tell you all about it. If it doesn't, then it won't matter much."

"Need me to cause a distraction?"

Melanie gave Kenzie a small smile. "Please."

She didn't say another word, simply inclined her head and headed inside to where the rest of the team waited. Cautiously, Melanie slunk up to the doors and slipped inside, as Kenzie began to raise her voice.

"I want five minutes alone with that rat bastard! Give me five minutes, and he'll be singing soprano with his goddamn testicles kicked north."

In any other circumstance, Melanie would find it absolutely hilarious, the sight of Kenzie squaring up to Derek who was trying his best to calm her down. But Derek thought that Ricky was dying, the complete and utter devastation of grief he wore was mirrored on the faces of Donnie and Caitlyn as they tried to quiet Kenzie.

True to her word, Kenzie managed to drag attention to her. With the team's backs to Melanie, she snuck in the hospital and dodged forward, her hand on the handle of the door to Ricky's room. Pausing, she spared a glance behind her, and eyes of gunmetal grey clashed with hers. Caitlyn gave her a weak smile before she turned away as if she had seen not a thing.

Once inside the hospital room, Melanie's eyes immediately went to where Ricky lay, tubes still in his mouth and monitors still continuously beeping. Some part of her had expected to walk in and see him sitting up, grinning at her with a smile that made her weak in the knees. But her Ricky was as still as he had been.

Hel, on the other hand, was seated beside him, her hand resting on the edge of the bed as she smiled up at Melanie.

Noticing the glow from Melanie's belt, she jumped up and clasped her hands in glee. She strode over to Melanie, her features flickering as she came closer. Melanie took a step back on instinct.

"Oh, you did it! We can save him now. There's just one more thing …I need you to give up your abilities."

"I'm sorry, what?"

Hel batted her eyelashes in innocence, a small smirk curving her lips. "You need to give up your truth-seeking abilities. Doesn't work on me, but it will be a powerful bargaining tool."

Melanie would give anything to save Ricky's life, yet if she gave up her lie detector ability, would she be any asset to the team? Sure, she was a vampire, but every single person on the team had a little extra to give. This wasn't the agreement they had shaken on, and Melanie wasn't about to roll over and hand her power over to Hel.

"That was not the deal," Melanie growled, pulling the dagger from her belt and pointing it at Hel. "The deal we shook on was for me to bring you a soul. I've done that. It's rotten to the core. And a favour. Unless the favour is that you want my power, then you can't change the deal after it has been shook upon."

Hel glared at her for a moment, then a grin spread across her face. "Good girl! I knew you were smart. Now, give me the dagger, and we can get started."

Melanie handed over the dagger hilt first. The moment Hel wrapped her fingers around it, she sighed, her eyes fluttering closed. The dagger glowed even brighter, and Melanie had to shield her eyes from the brightness, trying to keep a watchful eye on Hel. The girl shuddered, her features darkening as the glow seemed to crawl over her skin and seep into her pores. The blade stopped glowing as Hel popped open her eyes again. Licking her lips, she made the dagger vanish into thin air.

"Yummy."

"That's just creepy."

Hel grinned, her lips curling as she muttered something

SHORTCUT TO THE GRAVE

Melanie couldn't understand, and an audible pop sounded in the air as Loki, Ever's brother and Erika's boyfriend, appeared in the room. Standing tall and lean, Loki gave the impression that he was harmless, but Melanie knew that inside the Norse god of mischief, there was a power that could flatten the world. Dressed in jeans and a round neck jumper, Loki looked wrecked, his cheeks tear stained, and his eyes filled with sadness.

"What happened?" Melanie asked softly.

"Thor is dead. Odin killed him," Loki replied after he cleared his throat. His eyes wandered from Melanie to Hel, who wiggled her fingers at him. He narrowed his gaze as they settled on Melanie who tried very hard not to squirm under the intensity of his stare.

"Tell me, little vampire, how is it that you have made friends with my daughter? She has not deemed it necessary to be in my company for more than a century, and now she calls me to her, as your paramour lies dying."

What in the name of god? Loki's daughter?

"Hi, Daddy."

The girl walked over and threw her arms around Loki, the man stiffening before returning Hel's embrace. She was not too up on Norse mythology, but Ricky would know, would have made some Marvel reference, and they would have laughed. Glancing over at the still body in the bed, Melanie felt a pain in her chest. She walked back over and sat on the chair next to the bed.

Eyes still on the embracing pair, Melanie saw Loki step out of the hug, give Hel a small smile and ask, "Why have you summoned me, Hel? Why have you come here?"

"I made a deal to give Ricky back his life. I need your help to do it. Don't worry, Melanie killed someone, and I ate his soul, so the balance is still righted. I am sorry about Uncle Thor. He was always kind to me, even when others were not."

Loki glanced over at Melanie, then his eyes fell on Ricky. An unreadable expression fell over his features as he muttered, "There has been enough death today. There must be balance."

Inclining his head toward his daughter, Loki folded his arms across his chest. "What do I need to do?"

Hel clapped her hands together, squealing loudly and excitedly as if she were going on an adventure rather than saving a life. "Oh, excellent. Melanie, has Ricky drank some of your blood?"

Pushing aside her embarrassment, Melanie nodded. Hel grabbed Loki by the arm and led him over to the bed. Hel placed two fingers on Ricky's forehead, bowed her own head, and said, "Yes, yes… he's still in there."

Hope ignited inside of Melanie, silent tears slipping down her cheeks as she covered her mouth to stop herself from letting loose a sob. Loki placed a hand on her shoulder, gave it a little squeeze as Hel began to slowly pull the tube from his throat. The machines shrieked, and Melanie reached over and switched it off so as not to alert anyone to what was going on.

Hel beckoned Loki forward, her eyes landing on Melanie. "I take it you want a vampire, not a ghost, or a ghoul, or anything that might be less solid?"

"I don't care what he is once he's here with me."

Hel nodded her head, turning her attention to Loki. "Daddy, I need some of your blood. Immortal blood to help with the transition. We can avoid all that horrid three days in the dirt crap and wake him up here and now. My blood won't do, it is chilled too much by death. But you seem full of life right now. I'll have to meet your little Valkyrie."

Loki said nothing in reply, but he held out his wrist. Melanie watched as Loki motioned with his other hand and a sharp gash appeared, blood and magic dripping from the wound. Hel grabbed his arm, held the blood-stained wrist over Ricky's mouth and pressed the wound to his lips. She gently worked his throat as Loki stood completely unaffected, as if he were having his nails done rather than giving some of his life force to Ricky.

Loki felt Melanie's eyes on him, cast his gaze in her direction. She looked into the god's eyes and saw a galaxy of stars. There was a wisdom hidden behind those eyes that caused her to shudder and drag her gaze from his. Melanie had seen the universe in his eyes, and it was terrifyingly beautiful.

Loki removed his wrist and waved his fingers, the blood and cut disappearing, replaced by smooth skin once again. He narrowed his gaze and let his fingers wander down to the tattoo on Ricky's arm.

"I never even asked him what it meant. It seemed like something I should have asked," Melanie mumbled as Hel held her hands over Ricky's body.

"*Non Desistas, Non Exieris,*" Loki said, his accent dropping to sound exotic, and his tone was admirable. "It means 'Never give up, never surrender' It's Latin. I believe it is appropriate for your warlock."

Melanie gave Loki a small smile as Hel sighed in annoyance. They turned their attention back to the young woman, although Melanie was beginning to think that Hel was, pardon the pun, a hell of a lot older than she appeared.

"Now comes the tricky part. Things could get weird."

Melanie darted to her feet. "What do you mean? Hel, what are you about to do?"

The lights flickered in the room, and Hel's face morphed into the skeletal features that only seemed to alarm Melanie. The young woman grinned with teeth that were not of this world. "I'm about to raise the dead."

Melanie watched helplessly as Hel held her hands over Ricky's chest, gritted her teeth, and mumbled words Melanie did not know. Magic began to suffocate the air, flowing from Hel's palms into Ricky. The heart monitor beeped twice and then began to race, a shrill sound bouncing around the room.

Ricky's body jerked, his eyes springing open. Black coated his eyes, and his back bowed again. Melanie tried not to scream.

The monitor flatlined, and Melanie yelled at Hel to stop hurting him. Hel ignored her as the door to the hospital room crashed open, and the team burst into the room. Donnie surged forward, a snarl on his lips and a growl in his throat, but Loki held up a hand and froze him in place.

"Interfere and Ricky will most certainly die. The transfer is almost complete. Let my daughter save his life."

"Oh, for the love of Tom Hardy, can you be quiet, please? Trying to raise the dead here!"

Hel placed one hand over Ricky's chest, and the other snatched Melanie's hand. Melanie felt a tingling in her palm, and it began to creep over her skin and crawl inside her. Pain filled her chest, and Melanie rubbed the spot where she felt the ache. For a moment, a very brief moment, she thought she felt her heart beat.

Ricky's body jack-knifed off the bed again. This time when his eyes opened, the green was back. He sucked in a gulp of air, and Hel pursed her lips, puzzled as the monitor attached to Ricky's heart started to beat again.

"Oh, whoops," Hel said as she backed away from Ricky, glancing at Melanie with a sheepish grin. She waved her hand and opened the wall up like she had done once before, stepping back into the void as Melanie called her name. The girl ignored her, vanishing into the void, and the wall closed up behind her.

Silence fell over the room.

"Whoops? Whoops? What the bloody hell is going on?"

Donnie's voice broken through the awkward silence that had fallen, seemingly rousing Ricky from his slumber as he croaked, "Lanie…Lanie…"

Melanie ignored everyone else and clasped his face in her hands. "I'm here. I'm here."

Ricky grabbed his head. "Hurts." He groaned, and Melanie peered over her shoulder.

"He needs blood. Someone, get him some blood!"

Kenzie came forward, pulling up her sleeve as the only human in the room, but Caitlyn stepped forward, halting Kenzie from going any closer. "Melanie, his heart is beating. He is not a vampire."

Melanie shook her head from side to side. "Hel said she would make him a vampire. Not a ghost or a ghoul; a vampire. He needs blood. The monitor is wrong."

Suddenly Melanie was on the ground, Ricky shoved her away from him as he leaned over the side of the bed. "Hurts so bad."

Donnie reached out a hand to help Melanie up, wringing a growl from Ricky as he slipped off the bed on shaky legs and yanked the heart monitor pads from his chest. "Mine," he growled.

Caitlyn rolled her eyes. "Well, he certainly sounds like a newly mated vampire."

Loki causally leaned against the wall. "I think he is something more than a mere vampire, my lady."

Derek snarled in Loki's direction. "What do you mean?"

Loki grinned, drinking in the mischief as his eyes twinkled. "You'll see."

Ricky lurched forward, and Derek got in his way. Ricky caught him and threw him against the wall with a strength that should not have been possible for the warlock or a brand-new baby vampire. Donnie stood in front of Melanie, blocking her from Ricky, which only seemed to anger him more.

Ricky's lips curled into a snarl, but when he stepped forward, he grabbed his head again and let loose a scream of pain. "Hurts. Need...need...I'm...I'm..."

Concern on his face, Donnie stepped up to Ricky as his voice trailed off, and Melanie stepped forward. She tried to go around Donnie, but Caitlyn held her back. Kenzie stood far too close to Ricky with that scythe of hers.

Donnie rested his hands on Ricky's shoulders and coaxed with a calm voice, "What hurts, buddy? Tell me, and we can help you."

Ricky swayed under Donnie's grasp, and Donnie blinked, his eyes glassing over.

"I'm...I'm..." Ricky said again, trying to pull out of Donnie's grasp, but the vampire held firm.

"You're what, Ricky?"

A slow smile twisted Ricky's lips, and he lifted his gaze. Melanie could only describe it as a look of lust in her mate's eyes, but this time, that gaze was not directed at her; it was directed at Donnie. Ricky reached up with his hand and curled his fingers around Donnie's throat.

"Hungry."

No one had the chance to react as Ricky dragged Donnie down and crushed his lips to Donnie's. Donnie's knees buckled, sending them both crashing to the ground. Ricky held Donnie upright as he slipped his other hand around Donnie's neck to hold him in place.

Caitlyn snarled, and Melanie could only watch in horror as Donnie's skin paled and cracked as Ricky's eyes glowed green. Caitlyn screamed at Ricky to stop, but he paid her no heed. Donnie's eyes rolled back in his head. Melanie surged forward, her hand on Ricky's shoulder as she screamed loud in her head.

Ricky! You are going to kill him. Donnie... your best friend.

And thank the gods he heard her, stumbling back and letting go of Donnie. Holding his head in his hands, Ricky scurried back until his back connected with the wall. His body trembled, his hands shaking as he groaned. Caitlyn went to Donnie, and Kenzie lifted her scythe, ready to do what was necessary without so much as a word. Melanie held up her hand as she dropped down in front of Ricky, pausing only when he begged for her to stay away from him.

She looked over her shoulder at Loki who was watching with an amused curiosity.

"What the hell is wrong with him?"

"Nothing," Loki said, his lips twitching as if he were trying not to laugh.

"Your daughter promised to make him a vampire."

"And she did. He is now both warlock and vampire. But he feeds on supernatural energy not blood."

Melanie heard Caitlyn curse in French; she was letting Donnie drink hungrily from her wrist. His colour began to return, and Melanie sighed in relief. Loki rubbed his hands together, crouched in front of Ricky, and spared Melanie a glance as he asked, "May I?"

Returning his look with a puzzled one of her own, Melanie nodded. Ricky lifted his head to peer hungrily at Loki. His lips parted, but Loki chuckled, "Much as I would like to, I have a Valkyrie who would not approve and neither would your mate. It is given freely, so unfortunately, no kissing."

Loki reached out and placed his palm over Ricky chest. He jerked. Melanie felt the exchange of energy as if it were coursing through her, and his eyes closing sleepily after a mere few beats of his heart, his head lolling to the side as he fell into slumber.

Loki lifted his hand, standing without so much as a waver, smiling when Melanie arched her brow. "I have an abundance of energy." He winked. "Just ask Erika."

With a grin, Loki vanished, leaving them standing in the room, and Melanie took stock of those remaining. Kenzie was sheathing her scythe; Donnie was able to sit up and stare at his best friend as Caitlyn ran her fingers over his scalp. Derek stalked forward, hooked Ricky under the arms, and hoisted him up to lie him down on the hospital bed.

Caitlyn lifted her grey eyes to meet Melanie's, an amused expression on her face as she said, "You, young lady, have a lot of explaining to do."

Melanie giggled, covering her mouth to stop herself, but her laughter echoed through the room as she began to cry, unable to stop the tears from falling.

Yeah, she had some explaining to do.

CHAPTER TWENTY

RICKY

R icky came to awareness feeling two things: One, he had glutted himself on too much food, and two, he had an extremely gorgeous vampire curled up next to him. Glancing down, he ran his fingers through Melanie's hair, the fiery strands like silk against the pads of his fingers. His heart felt like it would burst by simply holding her, he loved her so much that he had no control when it came to her.

The last thing he remembered was opening his eyes and Melanie kneeling over him, water dripping from her skin, tears in her eyes. Ricky knew that he had died then, and he was content to know that she was safe. By some miracle, Ricky was living and breathing, holding his woman in his arms.

"There was no miracle, mate. Just sheer stubbornness from your mate who refused to let you die."

Ricky lifted his head to see Donnie sitting in the corner, tiredness all over his face. His buddy looked like he had been on a bender for a week. What the hell had happened while Ricky was out?

"If I'm being brutally honest, Donnie, you look like shit."

Donnie flashed him a toothy grin. "Well that's what happens when your best friend tries to suck the life outta ya."

"Who? Me?"

Blurry memories flashed in Ricky's head made him inhale sharply even as Donnie replied, "Well, it's not every day you get kissed by your best friend."

Ricky stared at him horrified, even as the vampire grinned. "I should be flattered, really. Caitlyn explained why you chose me. You were starving and went for the strongest energy in the room."

"So, you're telling me that I almost killed you because I was hungry, and you're over there, grinning like an idiot because you were the biggest, baddest food source in the room?"

"Pretty much."

"I think I'm gonna be sick." Ricky groaned, rubbing his temple, careful not to disturb Melanie who still slept soundly, her head resting on his chest.

"How am I alive?"

The door to the room opened softly, Caitlyn slipping inside and closing it again behind her. Ignoring Donnie, she walked up to Ricky, who froze, and kissed him on the forehead as she said, "You foolish, self-sacrificing idiot. I am glad that you are well."

"Me too. But how am I alive?"

Caitlyn glanced down at Melanie. "That is her story to tell. I hope you will not make a habit of kissing my mate?" A smile lit up Caitlyn's entire face.

"To be fair, Cait, it was one hell of a kiss." Donnie teased as she walked over and perched on his lap. She leaned in and muttered something in his ear, and he chuckled, a private joke among lovers that Ricky looked away from.

When he peered down at Melanie, her haunting green eyes were open, watching him with a sheen of tears. Ricky brushed away the teardrops with his thumbs, flashing her a grin as he simply said, "Hey."

"Hey yourself."

Melanie burst into tears, and he pulled her into his arms,

marvelling at the strength in his body. He spied Caitlyn and Donnie leaving the hospital room discreetly and knew that they would watch over them while they spoke. But Ricky waited until Melanie was ready to talk, leaving her to cry until she had no more tears left.

She lifted her face from his chest, brushing her hair back as she gave him a weak smile. "I must look a mess."

"I think you look beautiful."

Melanie rolled her eyes, and he chuckled, quickly pressing his lips to hers and pulling back before he was tempted to take things further.

"Ready to tell me what happened?"

Melanie blew out a redundant breath. "Where do I start?"

"Maybe you'd like to explain how I ended up making out with Donnie."

"Now that was kinda hot," Melanie said, her tone teasing as Ricky laughed, shaking his head. "The doctors said your magic had fried your organs, that you were dying. Then this woman appeared and offered to help. I...I..."

Ricky reached out, cupping Melanie's cheek. "Go on, babe."

Leaning into his touch, Melanie chewed in her lip before she continued, "I killed Greg and gave her his soul. I promised her a favour in the future, and she promised to make you a vampire. But Loki said something happened, and now, you are a vampire, but you feed on energy rather than blood."

Ricky widened his mouth in search of fangs, and was a little disappointed not to find any. He felt his heart beat in his chest, felt the heat of the blood in his veins, and knew that he was alive. What kind of vampire has a heart that beats?

Reading his mind, Melanie traced her fingers over his chest, and he all but purred at the touch. "Caitlyn said that whatever magic Hel worked went wonky because you are a warlock, and you became a psychic vampire; that means you feed on supernatural energy to stay alive."

SUSAN HARRIS

Ricky grinned, swallowing down the ice-cold fear that he was just like the incubus who had raped and killed all those women out of mad hunger. "So, like an incubus?"

Knowing him all too well, Melanie shook her head. "Nope. Apparently kissing Donnie was the fasted way to feed, and you were starving. You will learn to control it. Loki gave you some of his energy so you should be full until we can figure it out. Derek and Caitlyn have spent the day trying to get all the information they can on how to help you."

Ricky wiggled his eyebrows. "Please don't tell me I made out with Loki and was not conscious enough to remember it. And did you say Hel? As in Hel, goddess of death? You make the most interesting friend, my mate."

Melanie's eyes widened. "You know. You remember."

Statements rather than questions.

Ricky nodded. "I went to Caitlyn and Donnie's that day when I disappeared with Erika. Caitlyn told me. I didn't know how it happened, but do you regret it?"

"Absolutely not. I knew the moment it happened but didn't understand it until they told me I was your mate. It was always you. It will always be you."

"Lanie," Ricky sighed softly, pressing his lips to hers, gently at first, then Melanie shifted, her body on his, and their kisses become more urgent, more desperate, teeth and tongue and necessity for what death might have taken from them.

Before things could become more interesting, a knock sounded on the door. Melanie groaned, slipping off his body, but still curling up next to him. Ricky slung a protective arm around her shoulder, linking their hands together as his mother stepped into the room cradling Zach in her arms.

His mom looked shattered, her eyes filling with moisture as soon as she saw him sitting up in the bed. She stepped forward, pausing when he flinched. Zach scrambled out of her arms and made for the bed when Ricky froze, terrified that his new vampire self would hurt the child.

Melanie caught Zach and pulled him into a hug to give Ricky time to compose himself. Suddenly, Ricky remembered the dream he had while unconscious. He felt the ache in his chest, knowing what might have been, the image of Melanie dead in his arms and the sound of his son's voice calling him.

"Dad, Dad…"

It took Ricky a minute to realize that a small boy with eyes of emerald green was looking right at him, and the words that were falling from his lips caused Ricky's heart to hitch.

"Dad? Are you okay? Grandma said that you fell down and found it hard to get up."

Ricky couldn't speak; Zach was here, and he was calling him Dad. It was what he had wanted for so long, and now that the kid was saying the words, Ricky was just sitting there with his mouth hanging open. He cursed as tears began to well in his own eyes.

"That's right, son," Ricky said and cleared his throat to try and get rid of some of the thick emotion. "But I'm okay now thanks to Melanie. She saved my life."

His mam came over and hugged Melanie while reaching her hand backward and nudging a small square box into his hand. Zach launched himself at Ricky, wrapping his arms around his neck. Ricky returned the embrace, breathing in the scent of his son and knowing that he would never share what he had experienced while unconscious with anyone. That was never the life that was meant for him.

He was exactly where he wanted to be.

"Now, Zach. Let your dad rest some more, and we can come back later if you want."

Zach gave Ricky one last squeeze and then was crawling back into his grandmother's arms. "Bye, Dad. Bye, Melanie. See you later!"

Ricky dragged his eyes from the door as they left to see Melanie grinning at him.

"He called you Dad."

"Fucking yeah, he did."

Ricky cupped Melanie's cheek. "I love you. I heard you, you know."

Melanie stared back at him confused. "Heard me when?"

"When you couldn't find anyone to help me breathe. You begged me to open my eyes and to just breathe. You told me you loved me, and I heard you."

"How do you remember that? You were unconscious at the time."

Ricky thought back to the moment before he succumbed to the dark, hearing her tell Derek that he was dying, and she couldn't breathe for him. But she had. A long time ago, when he came across a young tech girl sitting at his desk, Ricky had felt the first crack in his defences, and Melanie had breathed life into him once again.

"You save my life. Again and again. Whether it was the day we met, the day we first kissed or what you did to bring me back from the brink of death. I thought I knew what my life was supposed to be. And then you crashed into it, kicking down the door to my heart, and I was stupid to realize that there would be no one else for me."

"Ricky..."

Ricky held a finger to her lips. "No, let me get this out. I should have said it long ago. When you were alive."

Melanie said nothing, letting him say the words he wanted to say to her, from when they were standing in that carpark before she had taken a shortcut to the grave. His world had been upended over and over again, but Melanie, his mate, his love had always been there to keep him upright.

"The night you were kidnapped, I bottled it. I stormed out after you to tell you why I was being a dick and that I was hopelessly, maddingly in love with you. When Donnelly took you, I thought my chance was over, and then you came back to me."

"Because of you," Melanie whispered, her smile sending a pulse of love right to his goddamn heart.

"No more dying on each other. Promise me."

"No more dying on each other. Pinkie swear."

Ricky felt the weight of the box in his hand as he straightened in the bed. Ushering Melanie off the bed, Ricky slid off the side on wobbly knees, not because he was feeling unwell, but because he was about to open up his heart to the one person with the ability to rip it from his chest and feast on it.

Melanie watched him, confusion all over her beautiful face as Ricky said, "We are mated as vampires are. But, technically, I'm not your average vampire." With his free hand, Ricky clicked his fingers, a short burst of blue flame surging forward. He felt in absolute control of his magic. There was no hunger from drugs, no uncertainty left in him as to who he was. "And it seems like I am not your average warlock anymore either."

Dropping down to one knee, Ricky reached for Melanie's hand as she clutched it to her chest.

"What are you doing?"

"Take my hand."

"Why?"

Ricky grinned at Melanie as she seemed to realize what he intended to do. "Because I'm trying to ask you to marry me, so take my goddamn hand!"

Melanie laughed. Rolling her eyes, she extended her delicate hand for him to lightly take hold of. Twisting his other hand, Ricky popped open the box with a sparkling diamond ring inside, his grandmother's engagement ring, and he silently thanked his mother.

"Melanie Newton, I love you with everything that I am. Would you make me the happiest man in the world and agree to be my wife?"

Melanie nodded as he slipped the ring onto her finger before dragging him up and into a kiss so full of love and passion it stole his breath.

"I'll take that as a yes then."

He kissed her again and hugged her to him, only breaking apart when rapturous applause sounded in the room. Ricky turned them so that he could see the faces of his family, the ones who had stood by his side through all the fucked-up shit in his life. They were still standing strong. Ricky accepted the pats on the back and the delighted congratulations.

Donnie tossed him some tracksuit pants and Ricky pulled them on, joking about everyone having seen his bare ass now so they definitely must be family. Melanie shook her head as Caitlyn admired her ring, but his vampire girl only had eyes for him.

"So, when's the big day?"

Ricky flashed Melanie a grin. "What day is today?"

When Donnie told him it was only Tuesday, Ricky's grin deepened as he arched a brow at Melanie. "How you fixed for Friday, babe?"

Melanie matched his grin with one of her own as she retorted, "I'll have to check my diary."

Caitlyn scowled at them and shook her head vigorously. "*Non*, we cannot arrange a wedding in three days. We must find a celebrant. We most order flowers and cake and find her a dress."

Ricky strode over to Melanie and pressed his lips to her cheek as he looked at Caitlyn. "I think we know a few Norse gods who could officiate. And we don't need a big wedding as long as we are surrounded by family to share in the night. Plus, Melanie could wear jeans and a t-shirt, and I would still marry her."

Caitlyn looked horrified at the thought, and they all laughed, their laughter halting when Ever walked into the room.

Everyone fell silent as Derek took her in his arms, and she patted his back absentmindedly.

Ricky felt something, a pull, a new energy in the room. His new powers kicked into gear, and he stepped away from Melanie just in case he hurt her. Right at that moment, he could sense the strength of energy in every single person in the room but Ever. She was something else.

Her energy tasted like her own, like sunshine, but there was another energy carefully sheltered in hers that to Ricky tasted like sunshine and wolf.

A realization washed over him as Ever walked up to him, his eyes widening as hers begged him to be quiet. "I believe congratulations are in order."

Before Ricky could utter a word, Melanie tucked herself against Ricky and gave Ever a small smile. "I'm sorry about your brother."

"Thank you. Thor died a warrior's death. His sacrifice will not be in vein."

Ricky couldn't help but notice the ice-cold tone in Ever's voice as if she had shut down her emotions in order to deal with the pain of losing her brother. Ricky knew what it was like to try and numb out the pain, and the consequences that came with it. He opened his mouth to speak, to say something hopefully profound and comforting, but Ever turned away to speak with Derek.

Feeling a hand in his, Ricky glanced down at his soon to be wife, pulled her in close and kissed her until there was no one in the room but the two of them. It was Melanie who broke the kiss, laughing as Kenzie teased them for having too many PDA's, and Melanie slapped her friend.

Kenzie steered Melanie away just as Caitlyn came to stand beside him. "I am very happy for you both."

Ricky glanced at Donnie, who had slipped his arm around Melanie's shoulder. "Who would have thought that the two of us, who had both closed off our hearts, would be happily mated now?"

Caitlyn chuckled, a husky sound that dragged another smile to Ricky's lips. "It is because we managed to find the two people who refused to let us stay closed off. We have been given a gift, you and I; we must not squander it."

Caitlyn was quiet for a few minutes, and then she whispered under her breath. "You would have given me your son?"

Her voice held an emotion that Ricky couldn't quite translate, but he nodded his head and peered over at Caitlyn. "There is no other person in this world I would trust more with my kid. I have seen how you have cared and looked after Lanie and Kenzie. Shit, you've looked after me more than I let my own mam for years. You may have been robbed of the chance to be the mother that you were meant to be, Caitlyn, but you are still a mother. My son would have been in good hands."

Caitlyn said nothing more, patted his cheek and strode over to Donnie, who inclined his head, hearing every word that had fallen from Ricky's lips. Melanie came back over to him and pressed her lips to his as Ricky joked, "You know, I'm kinda upset I don't have fangs."

"Me too." Melanie grinned up at him as he chuckled, and he was the one to roll his eyes this time.

"I can't wait to call you wife, Lanie."

Melanie made to reply, but he kissed her again, not caring who saw them, as the final piece of the puzzle that was his life fell into place. Ricky finally found his happiness in his vampire girl's arms.

CHAPTER
TWENTY-ONE

MELANIE

Melanie could barely stand the happiness. It was threatening to overwhelm her as she took a moment to herself, sneaking a peak over her shoulder at her new husband and mate as he laughed happily at something Derek said to him.

Husband. Mate.

The words still seemed foreign to her, even after they had exchanged vows in front of a Norse god, under the most romantic sky that twinkled with stars, surrounded by their family and friends. Melanie had never dreamt of a fairy-tale end for her, but as she watched Ricky, dressed in a slick black suit, his hair gelled back and a thin line of stubble roughing his features, she couldn't help but pinch herself just to make sure it was real.

Caitlyn had been the one to walk her down the small makeshift aisle in the spawning backyard of Caitlyn's home. She had not hesitated to say yes when Melanie asked her if they could have the wedding at the first place she had ever felt at home. Caitlyn said that happy memories needed to happen here, so that they could all remember this home fondly.

Caitlyn presented Melanie with a dress bag, and she unzipped it to find a simple yet beautiful Shakespearean style dress in a rich cream. When she gasped, Caitlyn had smiled and said, "This was my wedding dress when I married my Bass. Should Jessamine had lived and married, she would have worn it on her wedding day. It is only fitting that my other daughter wears it on hers."

Melanie hadn't known what to say, the gesture so utterly life altering. Her birth parents hadn't cared about her when she was alive, and hadn't cared when she died. She had gained so much when Caitlyn had made her a vampire, and Caitlyn's words etched deep in Melanie's soul. She embraced her sire and thanked her for the gesture. Caitlyn merely smiled, helping Melanie into the dress and pinning it, moulding it to Melanie's skin before taking it off carefully. Caitlyn had worked through the night to take in and shorten the gown.

Ricky asked Loki to officiate, and the god was surprised yet delighted to do so. Donnie, Derek and little Zach stood beside Ricky, while Caitlyn and Kenzie stood for Melanie. The women had worked hard to decorate the garden with lanterns to light the way. It was simple and exactly what Melanie had wanted.

When she had asked Ricky if he wanted all the trimmings that came with a wedding, Ricky had thought hard and long about it, revealing another part of himself as he said, "Sadie wanted a big wedding. She was the one who planned the entire thing, apart from the music, and I hated every second of it. But I thought I loved her, and it made her happy. Cost a fortune for a day that never happened. I meant it when I said I'd marry you in jeans and a tee. I don't need a lavish wedding, Lanie. I have everything I need right here, right now."

They exchanged vows promising to never give up on one another, to never go to bed angry, to be truthful and honest, to make each other laugh and to challenge each other. It was the private vows that they made in each other's minds, ones that neither of them would repeat to another soul, that made Melanie's toes curl.

When Loki had declared them husband and wife, Ricky had dipped her low, like in some romantic movie about the guy who gets the girl, and kissed her. The kiss held a promise of passion to come, not only for the night but for the rest of their lives.

Then they had danced under the moonlight, confetti thrown over them before speeches were made. From Donnie telling jokes and Derek telling them that Ricky was a better man for knowing Melanie, to Caitlyn welcoming Ricky to their family as a vampire, even if he was not a real vampire.

Every single one of their friends was extremely happy for them, and the joy on each of their faces made Melanie's unbeating heart ache, if that was even possible. She had even spotted Hel standing off to the side, lifting her glass of pink champagne in a toast before she disappeared, leaving Melanie to wonder when Hel would come to claim her favour.

It had taken them a few days to understand the extent of what Hel had done to Ricky, tests that had her heart in her mouth as they tried to see how durable he now was. Ricky moved with the speed of a vampire and had the strength of one with none of the side effects like an aversion to the sun or the thirst for blood. But Ricky found that when his energy was depleted, his own energy lust, as he called it, kicked in. Then, he was like a vampire who hadn't fed.

Ricky was a quick study, learning when his energy stock began to lessen and how to take from those around him without affecting the individuals. Everyone was surprised at how seriously Ricky had taken learning about his new powers, the focus Ricky had. Melanie knew that her mate had not wanted to hurt any of his family or friends.

She felt a little tug on the end of her dress and peered down to grin at the small boy standing next to her. Zach really was Ricky's image, from the shoulder length black hair to the green of his eyes. The way the little cat was studying her now made Melanie crouch down to face him.

"Hey, Zach."

"Are you going to be my new mom?" the little cat asked her, his face serious.

The question hit Melanie like a punch in the gut. He was technically her stepson, but Melanie was not sure how to approach this. Ricky ignored her fears by telling her she would know what to say when the time was right. Melanie was afraid of not only hurting Zach, but tainting any memories that Zach had of his mom.

Melanie smiled at the little boy as she said, "No honey, I'm not. There is not a single person in this universe that will ever replace your mom. But I think you and I will be very good friends."

"Will you be upset if I don't call you mom?"

"Never. Melanie is just fine by me."

"Okay, Lanie."

Melanie couldn't help but laugh. Her words seemed to appease the boy. He nodded and ran off to Caitlyn where he waited until she opened her arms to crawl up into them. The look of pure peace on Caitlyn's face was a sight Melanie would never forget. Ricky's son was just as much of a charmer as his dad was.

Melanie turned her attention back out into the night, smiling as she did. A part of her remained sombre, despite the fact that she felt so full of happiness she could burst. Ricky had joked to her last night, before they separated at Caitlyn's request, that they had half-assed it by having two funerals and a wedding. Melanie had known that Ricky was masking his grief for his father, having just stood beside his mother and brother to say goodbye to a man who had not understood her Ricky, someone who missed out on the amazing man he had grown to be.

Standing beside him, Melanie had begun to think about the lives she had taken out of necessity. Jaime had died by her hands, the sharp twist of her neck breaking was a sound that haunted Melanie still, even if she did not regret taking her former friend's life. Ricky might have killed her; she might have killed him. With Greg, Melanie found that she had no remorse in her for his death. Even though her hands had shaken as she plunged the blade into his chest, Melanie was more upset that it was nothing to her to kill him to save Ricky.

And she'd do it again, kill, if it meant keeping her family safe.

Soon after Ricky's dad's memorial, they had been welcomed into Ever's home while she raised a glass to her brother, Thor, who died to save her life. It wore heavy on Ever, who didn't seem herself. She avoided Melanie and Ricky for the most part as she huddled in the corner with Erika. Both women wore serious expressions.

An arm wrapped around her waist; hot lips pressed against the curve of her neck. Melanie leaned into Ricky's touch as he whispered words he had said once, but now, now they meant so much more. "Do you have any idea what I want to do to you?"

Melanie rolled her eyes, turning to face her husband, a slow, sly smile tugging at her lips as she wrapped her arms around his neck. "I have a pretty good idea."

Ricky kissed her slowly, deliberately, Melanie felt the smile on his lips as he claimed her, running his tongue over her fangs that had extended the moment he had pressed a kiss to her neck. Melting in his arms, she felt the pull of his magic, felt him pull back and grin sheepishly at her.

"Sorry. I can't seem to think when you kiss me."

Melanie smacked him on the shoulder, earning a bigger grin as Ricky pecked her on the lips before he asked, "Hey, you know I can never lie to you. What's up babe? What's got you hiding out here and neglecting your husband? Are you feeling a bit overwhelmed?"

"Aren't you? I mean, you were dead on Monday. Today's Friday, and I'm now married to you."

Melanie reached down and twisted the band on Ricky's finger as he frowned.

"Just a little. But things worked out the way they were meant to. You regretting things already?"

Melanie smacked him on the shoulder. "No, you idiot. I could never regret us."

"Good because I'm never letting you go. You and I, we are in this forever."

"Forever sounds good to me."

Ricky leaned in, and Melanie inhaled his scent, leather and oil and everything Ricky. He held her, not bothering with words, as they both took a moment of blissful peace before they had to return to their guests.

"Would you have ever imagined," Melanie began to say, running her fingers through Ricky's hair, "that you and I would be here now when we first met?"

"No," Ricky said, his eyes twinkling with mischief. "This is better than I could ever have imagined. I have a wife who is fucking smart and funny and beautiful. I have a son that I adore and who adores you...although...being a vampire helps you... me, I'm not a real vampire according to Zach. We have a job that has given us a family and a purpose. Life is pretty fucking good if you ask me.""And the future?" Melanie asked, wondering if after all the trials and tribulations the team had been through, would they all survive what Odin had to bring. If he could strike down his favoured son without so much as a flicker of regret, what chance did they have?

"The future can wait until tomorrow. For now, let's just live a little."

He kissed her once more before dragging her from the quietness of the night and into Caitlyn's front room. Melanie couldn't help but watch Caitlyn, perched in Donnie's lap, resting her head on his shoulder as he spoke to Derek, a small black panther curled up asleep in her lap. Donnie had a hand clasped possessively on Caitlyn's thigh, but she no longer seemed to mind it as much.

Erika sat cross legged on the ground, her back against the long lean legs of Loki, his hand cupping her neck. Even Derek, who was engaged in a conversation with Donnie, held Ever's hand, the Valkyrie queen staring off into space, or rather at the hammer that rested on the ground in front of them.

The only one missing from the room was Sarge, who claimed that he had had enough for one night, grumbling about it being a young person's world as his Anna escorted him from the room. Melanie had embraced the bear, thanking him for his part in her story. Her boss told her that he had known how special she was, and he hoped never to have her in cuffs at his station again. Sarge had shaken Ricky's hand then, telling her husband that he had done good. Ricky hugged the man before Anna ushered him out.

Ricky sank down onto the armchair left free, pulling Melanie into his lap, taking the glass of whisky that Donnie handed to him. Ricky sipped on the whiskey with restraint, and Melanie wondered if he was worried that his addiction would resurface, upending this peace of tranquillity that was now in every fibre of Ricky's being.

I'm good, babe. Stop worrying.

Taking his advice, Melanie grinned, squeezing his hand as her warlock stared over at the hammer by Ever's feet and grinned as the words tumbled from his mouth. "Why has no one tried to lift it yet? I mean, if this isn't Avengers' gold for a re-enactment, then what is?"

Donnie and Derek burst into fits of laughter. Derek reached into his pocket, withdrew a twenty euro note and handed it to Donnie. Ricky growled at his best friends, causing them to laugh even more. He grumbled to himself and flipped them off, but Melanie knew he wasn't even pissed off at all.

Melanie watched as the hammer began to shake, just a little tremble that no one seemed to notice but her…and Ever.

The clear night sky was interrupted by a rumble of thunder in the distance, Ever's eyes widening as a cracking boom rang out, impossible in a night that had been forecasted to be clear skies. The sky darkened, turning to charcoal before their eyes. The sound of rolling thunder brought Ever to her feet as her eyes widened, an o forming on her lips. She took a step forward.

"Ever," Erika began, scrambling to her feet. "It's not him, we saw him die."

"Does a god truly ever die?" Ever asked, her eyes stuck on the grey skies as another boom of thunder rolled in, closer this time, the untamed power reverberated and echoed across the green landscape. Lightening crackled, striking the ground outside, the scent of scorched earth hitting Melanie's nose. The thunder rolled for another beat of a drum before the skies cracked open, as if the heavens had opened above them. The entire team raced out into the night, but Melanie could not take her eyes off Thor's hammer.

With one final crack of lightening, a figure dropped from the skies and crouched down, a long red cloak flapping in the wind around the stranger. Head bent down, the figure lifted a hand, and a whistle of sound rang as the hammer sailed through the air, bypassing Ever and landing firmly in the grasp of the kneeling stranger.

Melanie hurried to Ricky's side as Ever uttered Thor's name, but anyone who looked at the figure would know that this person who was worthy to wield Mjolnir was not Ever's brother.

With hair of dark chestnut brown streaked with blonde through the ends, the figure rose up. Melanie gasped to see a teenager staring back at them. Her eyes were an unusual shade, almost amber much like Derek's when he was in wolf form. She was stunningly beautiful, with full lips, high cheekbones and skin that was tanned but not overly so. Grinning down at the hammer in her hands with a wolfish grin, the woman began to stride toward them, the metal of her armour glinting in the moonlight. Derek growled, Donnie pushed Caitlyn inside to guard Zach, and Melanie herself had to duck under Ricky's arm to catch another glimpse of the girl.

But the girl was not afraid. She rolled her shoulders back, squared her resolve and stared down some of the most powerful supernatural creatures alive today. Melanie could see recognition in her eyes, as if she knew who they were.

A smirk played over her lips. Ever stared open mouthed as the girl stopped, tossed Mjolnir into the air and caught it again. Her amber eyes scanned down the path, stopped when they landed on Melanie, and she grinned, continuing perusal until her eyes clashed with Ever's.

"There is a war coming. The fate of the world has fallen to all of you. But the future is changeable, free will leading to paths that alter the course of destiny and how the future unfolds." Her gaze wandered over the assembled crowd once more, and she began to address them one by one.

"The vampire queen and her consort. The god of mischief and his goddess of war. The seeker of truth and her not-so-vampire husband. All with parts to play."

Her eyes fell on Ever once again, and the girl swept her arms out in a mock bow. "The Valkyrie princess who has not yet claimed her crown. And her champion, the alpha wolf who has a collection of non-wolves in his pack. Can you withstand the impending storm? Are you ready to save the world?"

"Who are you?" Derek demanded, taking a step toward her. Her gaze snapped to him, and the amber flared in her eyes, brighter than before. Power leaked from the young girl's body, and Derek halted when a roar of thunder rolled overhead again. The girl's smirk deepened.

Bowing low once again, the girl straightened, her chest

puffed out in pride as she said, "My name is Ashlyn Kyria Doyle, and someone is about to fuck up the future."

Her gaze drifted from Derek's to Ever's, and Ashlyn ignored Derek when he stumbled a little at her declaration. The Valkyrie queen's hand rested firmly on her stomach, and she blew out a breath. "She will be worthy."

The girl smirked, tossing the hammer into the air once again. She inclined her head to Ever and said, "Hey, Mom."

THE KNOCK CAME AGAIN at his door, and Sarge pulled on his shirt and descended the stairs to see who the hell was beating down his door. First, it was god knows what time in the morning. Second, they rarely got visitors at their secluded cabin by Farran woods. He reached for the handle as the knock sounded again, and he yanked the door open while the person was mid knock.

"What the hell has got you knocking on my door at this god forsaken hour?"

The man gave Sarge a chilling smile. It was one he had seen many a time while sitting across from the very worst of the monsters within the supernatural community. The man in his doorway had the same cold eyes as some of the worst killers Sarge had witnessed in his years on the Paranormal Investigations Team. He knew he was in trouble when the man smiled another sadistic smile, and Sarge didn't have his gun on him.

"Thomas Delaney?"

"Who's asking?"

"That doesn't matter. What matters is the message you're gonna help me deliver."

The man's accent was pure Cork, but Sarge had never laid eyes on him before, never seen the man with freckles on his face and typical Irish ginger hair. Sarge held his ground, thankful that his Anna had been called into work and was not here. Tom Delaney had never backed down from a fight, and he never would.

When the man realized Sarge would not go down easy, excitement filled his features. Sarge asked him who the message was for.

"Derek Doyle."

He pushed his way inside Sarge's home, shoving the older man back. The man grinned, flashing as he swept his hand out and flames blocked Sarge's retreat. Smoke filled his lungs with a rapid pace that wasn't possible... or wasn't naturally possible.

"Derek will kill you," Sarge growled, coughing as the man spread his hands once again, and the walls became nothing more than orange flames around.

"I'm counting on it."

The stranger leaned forward, placed a hand around Sarge's throat, burning his airways and halting his breath. Before the man let Tom Delaney go, the bear was already dead. The man whistled as he left the burning cottage, pulling a phone from his pocket. "It's done."

"Excellent. Keep up the good work. Derek Doyle's world is amount to crumble down to ash."

Disconnecting the call, Sarge's murderer stayed to watch the flames a little longer, his smile never fading under the wail of sirens sounded in the distance. Satisfied with his work, he waited until the sirens drew closer, and then he vanished into the night much like he had arrived.

Silent, deadly, and filled with hatred for Derek Doyle.

ALSO BY SUSAN HARRIS

ALSO BY SUSAN HARRIS

THE EVER CHACE CHRONICLES

Skin & Bones, book 1

Collateral Damage, book 2

Smoke & Mirrors, book 3

Night of the Hunter, book 4

Never Back Down, book 5

Shortcut to the Grave, book 6

Arsonist's Lullaby, book 7

Of Gods And Monsters, book 8

DEFY THE STARS

A Tale of Two Houses, book 1

Until Death Do Us Part, book 2

In Defiance of the Stars, book 3

Shattered Memories

THE SANGUINE CROWN

Chaos Theory, book 1

Butterfly Effect, book 2

Wicked Game, book 3

Burn Notice, book 4

Fight Song, book 5 (coming January 2022)

CHARACTER PLAYLIST

MELANIE:

11 Minutes (with Halsey feat. Travis Barker)—YUNGBLUD
Get Down On Your Knees And Tell Me You Love Me—All Time Low
Thing Called Love—NF
Promises (with Sam Smith)—Calvin Harris
Baby—Bishop Briggs
Eastside (with Halsey & Khalid)—Acoustic—benny blanco
Smoke—PVRIS
This Isn't Everything You Are—Snow Patrol
Chasing Cars—Snow Patrol
Lost Without You—Freya Ridings
Bloodletting (The Vampire Song)—Concrete Blonde
F.W.T.B.—grandson Remix—YONAKA
Wish You Were Somebody—YONAKA
I Was Made For Loving You—Tori Kelly
I Wanna Know (feat. Bea Miller)—NOTD
mother tongue—Bring Me The Horizon
Nothing Breaks Like a Heart (feat. Miley Cyrus)—Mark Ronson
Monster—Acoustic—Walking On Cars
Give My All to You—HENRY
What Is Love—Jaymes Young

All of the Love in the World—Lily Kershaw
Bad Company—YONAKA
You Mean The World To Me—Freya Ridings
Breathe (feat. Jem Cooke)—CamelPhat Just Chill Mix
—CamelPhat
Walk Me Home—P!nk
Racing Cars—Ruti
Not Ready to Say Goodbye—Leah Nobel
The Champion—Carrie Underwood
Carrion Flowers—Chelsea Wolfe
Can We Pretend (feat. Cash Cash)—P!nk
Never Let Go—LYRA
I Knew You Were Trouble.—Taylor Swift
Assassin—Au/Ra

RICKY:

11 Minutes (with Halsey feat. Travis Barker)—YUNGBLUD
Before I Cave In—Too Close To Touch
Habits—Marmozets
Let's Make Out—Dream Wife
I Fall Apart—Post Malone
Alone In A Room—Asking Alexandria
Concrete—Tom Odell
Burn—Too Close To Touch
Pray For Me (with Kendrick Lamar)—The Weeknd
Sober—Tom Grennan
Everybody Loves Me—OneRepublic
The Drugs Don't Work—The Verve
Over My Head (Cable Car)—The Fray
Sober—Demi Lovato
Figure It Out—Royal Blood
Here Without You—3 Doors Down
All I Think About Is You—Ansel Elgort

I'm Not A Vampire—Falling In Reverse
Natural—Imagine Dragons
Pressure—Muse
Swan Song (From the Motion Picture "Alita: Battle Angel")
—Dua Lipa
Moderation—Florence + The Machine
7 Minutes—Dean Lewis
Lost—Dermot Kennedy
Erased—Koethe
One Drink—Picture This
Demons (Philosophical Sessions)—Jacob Lee
Coldest Water—Walking On Cars
Falling—LYRA
That Sound—Sam Fender
Therapy Session—NF
Therapy—All Time Low
Down Down Down—Charlie Simpson

THE VIKING:

Done His Dance—Bugzy Malone
Heartless—Recorded At RAK Studios, London - Dermot
Kennedy
Better Now—Post Malone
MANTRA—Bring Me The Horizon
Chaos And Earthquakes—Nonpoint
Coldhearted—Bryce Fox
Deeper Underground—Jamiroquai
Thnks fr th Mmrs—Fall Out Boy
Believer (feat. Lil Wayne)—Imagine Dragons
My Love—Raven & Kreyn Remix—Breathe Carolina
Nihilist blues (feat. Grimes)—Bring Me The Horizon
On The Luna—Foals
Killshot—Eminem

Out Of Love—Devault Remix—Alessia Cara
I'm Not Alone—CamelPhat Remix—Calvin Harris
Survival—Eminem
Bad Man (feat. Robin Thicke, Joe Perry & Travis Barker)
—Pitbull
Someone You Loved—Lewis Capaldi
ME! (feat. Brendon Urie of Panic! At The Disco)—Taylor Swift
The Night King (From Game Of Thrones: Season 8) [Music
from the HBO Series]—Ramin Djawadi

Ever:

Disappear (Feat. Lynn Gunn)—Tonight Alive
Run—Snow Patrol
alive—iiola
It's Time For War—LL Cool J
bury a friend—Billie Eilish
it's not u it's me—Bea Miller
Don't Worry Bout Me—Zara Larsson
Don't Pretend—Khalid
Life On Earth—Snow Patrol
Power is Power—SZA

ACKNOWLEDGEMENTS

Rebecca, Courtney & Marya,
Thank you for your never-ending faith in me.
The success we have achieved in the last 6 months
has been down to hard work, perseverance, dedication
and maybe a little magic.Sláinte

Marya,
I absolutely adore this cover for Shortcut to the Grave as I do
with all of my covers!

Melanie Newton,
You already got a dedication, but since you're so awesome,
you also get a thank you in here as well!

Jamie,
My trusty beta reader!
Thanks for all that you do x

My Parents,
Who have been with me on this crazy rollercoaster that is
writing with me,
Thank you for your support and unwavering love.
I guess you guys are kinda okay!

LJ and Taylor,
To Infinity and beyond x

My circle is small, but you guys are the best in the world.

Special thanks to Jaime,
Sorry for making you a bitch in the book, but hey, you did have
Greg!

Cheers Greg, for being this book's big bad, even if you're not the
guy who gets the girl.
PSA, Greg's actually awesome and nothing like his character in
the book!

Helen, who I based a certain character on without telling her!
Loves ya x

To the Readers,
Whether you've been on this crazy journey since day one,
or have recently become part of our extended family at P.I.T,
thank you for all your support!
Words will never describe how much it all means to me.

ABOUT THE AUTHOR

Susan Harris is a writer from Cork, Ireland and when she's not torturing her readers with heart-wrenching plot twists or killer cliffhangers, she's probably getting some new book related ink, binging her latest TV or music obsession, or with her nose in a book.

Susan LOVES connecting with her fans!
www.susanharrisauthor.com

Thank you for reading *Shortcut to the Grave*; I hope you enjoyed my book!

Want to be the first to know when I release new books? Here are some ways to stay updated:

- Sign up for my email list so you can find out about new releases.
- Like my Facebook page.
- Visit my website: www.SusanHarrisAuthor.com/
- Connect with me on Spotify

If you loved *Shortcut to the Grave*, please tell your friends about my book and consider leaving a review. Reviews are like potato chips; you can't ever have enough of them; thanks for reading my book!" ~Susan Harris